THE UNION

THE MADION WAR TRILOGY

S. Usher Evans

Sun's Golden Ray Publishing

Contents

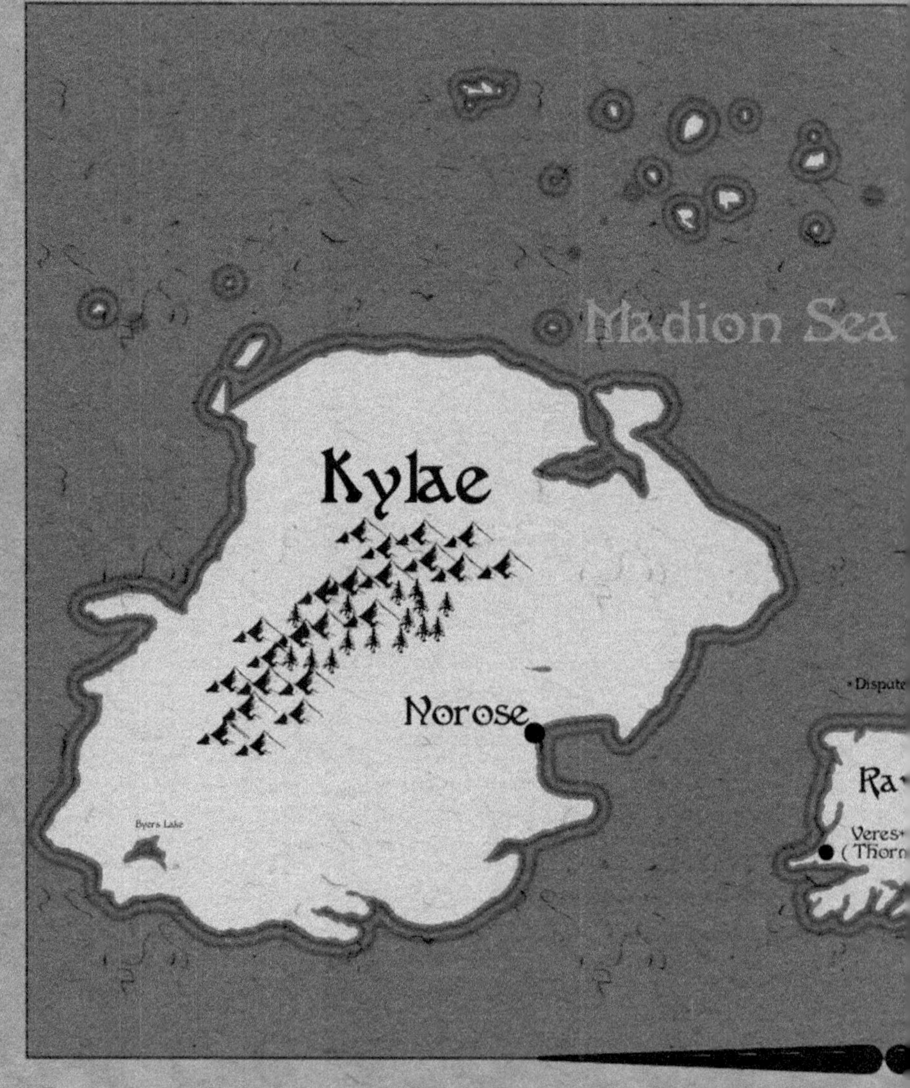

Madion Sea
Kylae
Norose
Byers Lake
Dispute
Ra·
Veres·
(Thorn

Herin
Jervan
Baro
Torpor River
Lakner

PART I

ONE

Galian

The mid-afternoon doldrums usually hit around three or four. Summer in Norose was stifling, as the winds off the Madion Sea stopped, and the hot, moist air hung between the tall buildings. Although the hospital was cool to keep away infection, it didn't keep away the malaise.

To boot, it was a slow day. We hadn't had many scheduled surgeries, and except for a few cases of heat exhaustion, there'd only been a couple of admittances since my shift had started that morning. Dr. Maitland, only two weeks returned from his sabbatical to the country of Herin, had sent home a quarter of the staff, and was considering sending another few if things didn't pick up.

He'd offered me the afternoon off, but I couldn't take it. Even Maitland didn't know that my purpose at the Kylaen Royal Hospital was twofold. To the world, I was Dr. Galian Helmuth, resident. But I was also a courier on behalf of my mother, Queen Korina.

For the past six months, the messages had been mostly

innocuous. Mom was having me receive responses to questions she sent through other channels. Usually, the most I had to remember was "yes" or "no." Sometimes, I didn't even know the question I had the answer for. Mom said it made things safer, just in case I were found out or my contact was a spy.

But I wasn't completely blind to what we were doing. I knew my mother had her hands in several things—most importantly, fomenting rebellion in the island country of Rave, but also in trying to placate several competing interests in Kylae. Our barethium stores had begun to run low, thanks to my efforts—I'd closed the death camp that processed it. But the businessmen who dealt in the material were growing restless.

Although I might've chalked their pain up to "well, that's business," these same businessmen had targeted me in an assassination attempt that had killed my best friend, Dave Martin. It pleased me that while we were helping to find them a new revenue stream, we were also gathering evidence to bring formal charges against them. My father would never go after the miners—they employed a third of our population. So Mom was working to build a case so strong my father would have no choice but to allow a formal trial to go forward.

I glanced at the time—nearly four. The first time I'd received a message for my mother, I'd been a nervous wreck and had driven the nurses crazy. But now, I was an old pro and I had a process. Five minutes before the meeting time, I'd roll over to the nurse's station and start a conversation with Nurse Rima, the charge nurse. I'd ask her about her two grandkids, and she'd go on and on about them. Eventually, I'd casually ask if we'd had any new cases, and then make my move.

"Nurse Rima," I said, handing the gray-haired woman a cup of coffee. "Slow today, isn't it?"

"How many times have I told you not to say that?" she said, taking the coffee and adding two packets of sugar to it. "It's a jinx. Next thing you know, there'll be a tidal wave or something like that."

I smiled and apologized. Kylaens were now paranoid about tidal waves, thanks to one hitting the port city of Duran to the north. My father's scientists had said it was due to an underground earthquake, but I knew better. It had been caused by a massive warhead sent by the Ravens, which I'd helped put into the water. But my father, unwilling to broadcast that the Ravens had escalated the war, had kept that under wraps. I told my mother that the barethium processors should invest in life jackets, as those had become almost fashionable in Norose.

I coaxed Rima to talk about her grandchildren. Teddy had a recital and Jonas was nearly walking, and both of them had been over recently for an afternoon. I feigned great interest, even as my gaze darted to the clock. In about forty-five seconds, I'd begin to steer the conversation back to—

"Dr. Helmuth, your car is ready."

I blinked, too focused on Rima to process immediately what the person had said, at first. I turned to my right and found a blonde, brown-eyed sergeant standing in the hall. Her hands were clasped behind her back, her yellow hair pulled into a military bun. The dress uniform of Kylae's military was immaculate, the same one that my guards wore when ferrying me to and from the hospital.

"Dr. Helmuth?" she repeated, with a nervous glance at the nurse eyeing her suspiciously.

I leaned against the counter, sharing a smile with Rima. "I'm sorry, there must be a mix-up. I don't get off for another three hours."

She took a hesitant step forward. "Your mother has summoned

you."

"Tell her to wait," I said with a small shrug. "I can't just leave."

The ghost of a scowl appeared on her face, and it was all I could do not to smirk. Rima was still surveying the sergeant as if she were an unknown agent, but then turned to me. "Doctor, I think we've got it covered here. If your mother needs you—"

"Oh, Mom always needs something," I said with a laugh. "But if you think you guys will be fine without me..."

"I am sure of it."

I paused. "Let me go check with Dr. Maitland first. I'll see you later, Nurse Rima."

"Always a pleasure, Doctor."

I pushed myself off the counter and started down the hall. The hurried clacking of boots followed me and I could practically feel her irritation at me. "Dr. Helmuth—"

"Sire or Prince Galian, if you please," I said, glancing behind me. "We must stand on ceremony, after all."

That earned me a true scowl. "We're on a bit of a time crunch here."

"This will only take a second," I said, holding open the door to the doctor's lounge.

Dr. Maitland sat at one of the tables, a steaming mug of coffee in his hand and the newspaper splayed out in front of him. He glanced at me, then the sergeant still glowering at me, and a smile appeared on his face.

"Dr. Maitland, it appears I have a royal summons," I said. "My mother needs me."

Maitland shrugged and winked at the soldier. "Who am I to overrule the queen of Kylae?" He pushed himself to stand and gathered the paper and coffee. "Does Rima have your files?"

"Yes," I said with a nod. "Just keep an eye on Mr. Bernard for me. I don't like the look of his blood pressure."

"Will do," Maitland said, patting me on the shoulder. "Give my regards to your mother for me." He closed the door behind him, and the soldier let out an impatient growl.

"If you don't—"

I crossed the room in three steps, pushed her against the wall, and covered her mouth with mine.

She leaned into it for a moment, then shoved me away roughly. *"What the hell do you think you're doing?"*

The pale makeup had smudged, revealing darker brown skin underneath, and several black strands of hair had fallen from beneath the wig. Even when she was made up to look like a Kylaen, I would've known my Theo anywhere. If not from the sound of her voice, then the adorable way her nose crinkled when she was angry with me. Based on the number of lines on her nose, she was livid.

"Sire or Prince Galian?" she huffed.

"All the guards use my title," I said, but I couldn't keep the smile off my face. I'd honestly just wanted to see her reaction.

"And parading me around the hospital? We could've been *seen*! That nurse was giving me the side-eye—"

"Rima gives everyone the side-eye," I said, running my hands along her curves. My fingertips slipped underneath the uniform and found warm, soft skin. "Hi, by the way. I missed you."

She relaxed, but only a little. "I missed you too, *amichai*. But Kader is waiting. We need to get back to the castle and debrief your mother."

"You were gone a long time," I said, ignoring her warnings. "I was worried."

"You needn't have," Theo said, but her face softened a bit. "Kader knows what he's doing."

"But *I'm* not there, and I don't like it..."

She sighed deeply, and I could tell by the way she pressed her lips together she was holding in a comment. Perhaps about my usefulness while sneaking around an enemy country. So, I saved her the trouble of responding and kissed her again. This time, she leaned into it, giving me entry into her mouth. I crushed her against the wall, making sure she knew *just* how worried I was, and wondering if I should lock the door.

When a soft moan escaped her lips, she must've remembered where we were, because she pushed me back. "We can't. Someone could see us."

"Then why'd you come to the hospital to get me?" I asked with a smirk. "You can't possibly expect me to keep my hands to myself."

She opened and closed her mouth, and I could almost see her face growing redder under the makeup. "I...that's..."

"Admit it, you wanted to see me all doctorly," I said, pressing my hips against hers. "It turns you on—"

She glared at me. "Pompous princeling."

"You fell in love with me," I said with a shrug.

"Be that as it may," she said, glancing behind me. "We need to go. People are already curious about why I'm here."

"I'm having a consultation with a patient," I grinned, reaching for her again. "C'mon, let me give you a physical. *Ooh*, even better, I can give you a GYN exam—"

She slapped my groping hands away, but I knew she was on the verge of letting me take her then and there against the wall. Her visits to Kylae were few and far between, lasting only hours before she and Kader left again. We hadn't made love once, not since our stolen night in Jervan before this whole mess began. If I'd been miserable when she was an ocean away, these brief interludes were torturing me. I just wanted an hour alone with her when she wasn't rushing off to the next mission.

"*Amichai*, we have to go," she said softly.

I sighed, knowing she was right. "Fine."

THEO

Galian led me through the maze of hallways in the hospital, his shoulders relaxed and his smile wide. I kept my eyes on the ground, knowing I couldn't keep my lovesick smile to myself for much longer.

Two nurses paused as we passed them, and I hoped he hadn't smudged the makeup too much. In order to move invisibly within the Kylaen royal staff, I needed to appear Kylaen. There wasn't even a dark-skinned maid at the castle, so I'd stick out like a sore thumb. And since the King of Kylae believed Galian and I had fought, broken up, and I'd left to seek refuge in Herin, it was even more important I not be recognized.

It had been stupid and reckless to fetch him myself, as Kader had pointed out very astutely when we'd argued about it. With the media's obsession with him, there was always the danger of an errant photo or some crazed royal watcher writing a story about the blonde sergeant seen with the prince. And if my face appeared on *any* Kylaen media, everything would be over.

But the brief moment of intimacy had been worth the risk. I could still taste him, still feel the ghost of his fingertips on my skin, the pressure of his body against mine. It wasn't enough—it never was. But after six months of spinning my wheels, I would take even a small moment of bliss.

We found Kader parked at the back entrance of the hospital. I felt his gaze on my lips where Galian had smudged the makeup, and he said all he needed to with that one look. I held the door open for Galian and slipped into the front seat.

"Aw," Galian said from the back. "It's one thing to go off on dangerous missions, but now you're opening doors for me?"

I sat down in the passenger's seat and buckled in without lifting my gaze.

"You two are supposed to be in hiding," Kader said, as the car lurched into motion. As expected, he shot a warning glare at me and my smudges. "You don't know how relentless they'll be if they think he's got a girlfriend."

"Oh, but I *do* know," Galian replied, leaning forward to rest his head on the divider between us. He slithered his hand to the back of my neck, pressing small circles into the tense cords he found. "Nobody saw us."

"Nobody that you saw."

"I missed you, too, Kader," Galian said.

Kader grunted in acknowledgement, and I smirked at their tense relationship. I'd known men like Elijah Kader my entire life, tough, mission-focused, and rarely displaying emotion. Despite Galian's insistence that Kader didn't like him, I could tell Kader was fond of his former charge. But I could never convince Galian of that.

"So I take it you two are the message that was getting delivered to me today? Mom could've just told me."

"This was an unplanned visit," Kader said, turning the wheel as we came to an intersection. "Our last meeting ended up wanting twice the amount, which cleaned us out."

I felt Galian's gaze draw to me. "Well, we have plenty of money."

I didn't doubt that, but it always felt like defeat when we had to return from Rave. It was such an ordeal to get there—driving for hours at night, flying in cargo planes to Herin and Jervan, then the constant pressure of keeping one step ahead of the Raven military. When we left Kylaen airspace, I remained hopeful it would be for the last time, and we could come back with something substantial. So far, we hadn't.

Then again, all I'd seen in the past six months was the inside of safe houses.

Neither Kylae nor Rave acknowledged the existence of the super weapon that had nearly decimated Norose, and there hadn't been any mention that Bayard had stuffed *me* inside it. As far as the Raven media knew, I'd just disappeared, and they'd moved on to a new golden child, a fifteen-year-old pilot who'd been the only survivor of some great battle in the south, cultivated, I was sure, by Emilie Mondra.

Galian's thumb had located a tight spot between my neck and shoulder. "What else is new?" he asked.

"We'll debrief you when we get there," Kader replied.

The massage stopped. "So you guys aren't staying very long?"

"No," I said. We never did.

I stared out the window at the city of Norose. Compared to Veres, it was modern and sleek, filled with skyscrapers taller than I'd ever thought possible. They were laced with barethium, a mineral ore that strengthens metals. The smelting process released a highly toxic gas, which had been the reason the work prison in the north of the city had been so deadly. Now that Mael was closed, Kylae's barethium reserves were running low, another complication to peace. Since I'd been in Kylae, I'd seen news reports that Kylaen ministers wanted to reopen the barethium mines at Mael, but there had, luckily, been no movement toward that.

We stopped at an intersection and my gaze fell on a couple holding hands. They stood in front of a chocolate shop, the man pulling his lover closer and kissing her on the cheek as she pointed at the candy. With a shared, adoring look, they entered the shop.

When the queen of Kylae had first asked me to be her liaison, I'd been optimistic that I could find my way to the Raven rebels within a few months, and then Galian and I could be together. I'd promised him I would only try this for six months, and we'd passed that milestone a few weeks ago. Every time I thought about giving up, we'd make another inch of progress, and hope would suck me back in.

"Hey." Galian's voice brought me back to the car. "You okay?"

I released the tension between my brows. "Yeah, just thinking."

His palm rested against my cheek and I leaned into it. Unlike before, when I had been all alone in Veres and making stupid decisions by myself, now I had support. And knowing I could lean on Galian, if only for brief moments, was heartening.

"You two'd better stop that," Kader said, nodding to the looming Kernaghan castle ahead of us. Or, more specifically, the media that seemed to always be camped out there. I'd had a taste of it in Rave, but in Norose, they were relentless.

I pulled the lip of my sergeant's cap down further and stared at my lap as the flashes started. Galian disappeared from between the seats, as did the pressure of his hand against my neck, and I heard him sigh in frustration. The car moved slowly though the photographers, until we'd entered the main campus of the castle. Kader drove around to the western side, typical for Galian, as his private quarters were there. But it was also where Korina staffed her own people, who would be less likely to ask questions of Kader and me.

Kader was quicker than I, and opened Galian's door before I could. His look was clear—no more risk-taking until we reached the safety of Korina's private study. I kept my head down as a junior non-commissioned officer would, and followed Galian and Kader inside the castle.

TWO

GALIAN

The moment Kader shut the door to my mother's study, I wrapped my fingers around Theo's, as it was all the physical contact I was going to get. There would be no privacy for us—not with my brother Rhys and Sayuri Johar waiting for us already. Johar was one of Kader's old Special Operations buddies, and in his absence, she'd been assigned to ferry me to and from work and around town. Cut from the same tall, muscular, angry mold as Kader, Johar didn't seem to think more of me than Kader.

Rhys offered a bright smile to Theo, who returned it a bit sheepishly. I'd never known her to be shy of anything, but she'd also spilled her guts to him when she thought she was about to die in a Raven bomb. She wouldn't even tell *me* what she'd told him, and Rhys was happy enough to dangle that bit of information over me every chance he got.

Instead of joining him and Johar, I led Theo over to one of the antique couches and plopped down, pulling her close to me. She pressed her head into the crook of my neck and I squirmed at the feel of the thick cream on her skin.

"So how long are you actually here?" I asked.

"We're going back to Kader's tonight then grabbing a flight," she whispered, looking very pained to admit as much. "Just need more...money."

"Why does it bother you so much to ask for it?"

She pushed herself out of my arms and frowned. "Because it seems like all we do is give it away and hope they'll reward us for it someday. Meanwhile, life is going on and..."

She didn't say it, but I knew she was worried about keeping our relationship on hold. We both agreed she'd only attempt this new strategy for six months and then we'd be together, but that milestone had come and gone. She hadn't mentioned it, and neither had I, as I'd known that she couldn't walk away, if there was even the ghost of a chance at peace. That was who she was, and I loved her for it, even if it killed me to say goodbye to her.

"I mean, it's not *that* exciting back here either," I said, hamming it up a bit to make her smile. "Now that Maitland is back, I'm working just day shifts, but at the end of the day, I'm smelly and tired. I wouldn't even be awake enough to go down on you—

"*Amichai!*" She gasped, glancing around at the others in the room. If they'd heard my suggestive comment, they had the good grace to ignore it. Theo elbowed me roughly. "Asshole."

"I'm just trying to tell you that you aren't missing much."

"I'm missing you."

I had no good response to that, especially as her eyes grew sad. Her wig had gone askew, so I pulled it off, her black hair seeming darker against her made-up skin. It was balled into a bun, which hung sadly against the back of her head. I wanted to run my hands through her hair, but resisted the urge.

"I'm frustrated, *amichai*. All I do is sit in basements while Kader goes out to do all the work. Why am I even going over there if I'm not doing anything?"

I debated whether reminding her that staying was an option, but my mother strode into the room, a tense but pleasant look on her face. She paused by Kader, taking his hand and murmuring to him, most likely conveying her relief that he'd come back unharmed, then turned to Theo and me. Theo stiffened under her gaze, but my mother's look was all warmth and love for the two of us.

"Welcome back, Theo," she said, sitting daintily on the chair across from us. Kader, Johar, and Rhys joined us, with Rhys taking the spot next to Theo, and Johar and Kader standing behind us, mirrored looks of stoicism on their faces.

"I know we have lots to discuss," Mom started, glancing around. "But I'd like to hear from Rhys first. What news from Duran?"

"It's a mess," Rhys said. "Where do you want me to start? Father won't send aid, Collins won't meet with me, and meanwhile, our people are still living in squalor."

Mom's mouth twitched, but she remained passive. "Start with your father, please."

"Here's the facts as we know them: the city of Duran is still recovering from the tidal wave, but Father's decided they've had enough aid. This is, in case you missed it, thanks to Collins reaching out to Jervan to renegotiate their trade agreement, which was expressly against His Majesty's wishes to restrict all contact with the Herinese and Jervanians, who caused the damned tidal wave in the first place. And so Father's cut off aid to rebuild Duran."

This was all old news to me, but Theo's shocked face told me none of this news had made its way to Rave yet. "And why do the people in Duran suffer because of what Collins did?" she asked.

"Because Collins' company invested heavily in the city," Mom replied. "Most who live there work for him, and most of the aid would go toward helping Collins rebuild the infrastructure that was destroyed in the wave."

Theo nodded and looked a little uncomfortable. "And why do we care about Collins?"

"Because Silas Collins was *also* in negotiations with the barethium processors," Rhys said. "Our plan was to spur their mutual investment in each other, and move the Kylaen economy away from needing barethium and more into shipbuilding. Now, Collins won't even take my calls, let alone meet with anyone we want him to."

"And without Collins, the miners are becoming anxious. We're getting word the barethium miners are putting pressure on Grieg to reopen Mael," Johar said.

Theo sat up straight, her wild eyes landing on me for reassurance. "He wouldn't, would he?"

"Given enough pressure from the right people, he might," Mom said heavily. "But we're not going to let that happen, Theo."

Theo sat back, but didn't look placated.

"So, let's think about this for a moment," Mom said, placing her hands on her knees. "We need to talk to Silas Collins, but our usual lines of communication are down, correct?"

"Correct," Rhys replied.

My mother's gaze floated toward me, and a smile crept up on her face. "Then we'll try a new line. Gally, darling, you've got a preexisting relationship with Collins' vice president of operations, don't you?"

THEO

Galian made a noise, and his face flamed bright red. "Mom, you can't be serious."

"Galian, we have no visibility into the operations in Duran, and right now, Olivia is our only—"

"Olivia?" I said, sitting up. There was only one Olivia I knew of, and based on the way Galian wouldn't meet my gaze, I had a pretty good idea who they were talking about.

"Just hear me out," Korina said, with a half-smile to me. "As far as either Silas or Olivia are concerned, you are uninvolved in all politics and political dealings, correct?"

Galian waited a long time to respond. "Correct."

"And so, if you were to, say, call up Olivia and ask her on a date—"

"*Mother.*" Galian's arm tightened around me protectively. "Theo is *right here.*"

"I'm asking you to take her on a few more dates, son," Korina said with a heavy roll of her eyes. "You don't have to sleep with every girl you take to dinner."

Kader snorted behind me, and, despite all the pressure and my nerves, I found Galian's indignation, as well as his assumption that every date had to end in sex, a little...funny. But I kept my face stoic for his sake, because he looked most uncomfortable.

"Galian, this is very important," Korina said. "We need Silas to meet with the barethium miners. We were nearing an agreement before the tidal wave, and if we don't act quickly, all that work will be undone. Make no mistake, they *will* force your father to reopen Mael. Right now, our only way into Collins shipbuilding is through Olivia."

Galian looked at me, his eyes pleading with me to say something in his defense, but Korina was right. I squeezed his hand. "*Amichai*, it's all right. I know it doesn't mean anything."

"Besides, you're going to have your work cut out for you. If Silas won't even take your call, Rhys, they must be very upset, indeed," Korina replied. "It will take all of your...*charm* to win her over."

"Especially considering how our last date ended..." Galian muttered under his breath. There was a story I desperately wanted to know, but I wouldn't ask him in front of an audience.

"That's settled then," Korina said brightly. "Gally, we'll need you to work quickly, so please give Olivia a call tonight."

"But Theo..."

"Is leaving tonight," Kader interjected, and my heart broke a little at the reminder. "So tonight will be fine."

Galian slumped, so I leaned over and whispered, "Just pretend she's one of those girls in Jervan."

A chuckle rumbled in his chest, and he tightened his hold around me.

"Now, that's settled. Theo, Eli, how are things across the sea?"

Just like that, I was on the spot and my face warmed considerably. Korina made me incredibly nervous—not only was she the queen of Kylae, but, as Galian's mother, I really wanted to impress her. And what I had to say wasn't very impressive.

"It took us a few weeks to get in touch with the right person,"

Kader said, saving me from having to tell the tale. "There's a bakery Anson's using to funnel some of his money, but we couldn't figure out which one. It took nearly ten thousand crowns just to get the name."

Korina nodded. "So you need more?"

I winced and stared at my hands.

"It would appear so. We told the baker we'd be back within the week with the full amount to arrange a meeting. Twenty-five thousand crowns."

I swallowed my discomfort. Although I believed Korina was on the right side of things, knowing that I was giving Kylaen money to the Raven rebels still sat uncomfortably in my stomach. It wasn't so much the source of the money, but that we were giving it under false pretenses. After what had happened to me in Malaske, I was still a little gun shy.

"What will meeting with this baker do? Will it guarantee an audience with Anson?"

I tightened my grip on the folds of my pants as Kader replied, "Doubtful. The baker is simply a front, perhaps fourth tier in the organization. Our hope is that we can secure a meeting with someone on the third level."

Anson was the elusive leader of the rebels. He was once a highly decorated general, responsible for three bases on the northern coast of the country. But he'd had a falling out with Bayard when the conscription age had been lowered from fifteen to twelve, and he'd been fomenting rebellion in the slums of Veres for almost a decade. His military background made him a cunning strategist, and even though he didn't have Emilie's money or resources, he was winning the spin war against her. He had a penchant for poetry, and was known for his heavy use of symbolism to convey messages to the people.

His strategy also consisted of having a web of low-level operatives doing his dirty work. It wasn't unheard of for someone two or three levels into the organization never to have even laid eyes on their leader. That, of course, made arranging a meeting with him even trickier.

"Theo, is there a problem?" Korina asked.

I glanced up, unsure why I had drawn her attention. "N-no. Sorry."

She offered me a kind smile, but there was a little scrutiny in her gaze. "Johar, how are we progressing on the assassination attempt investigation?"

I relaxed against Galian, glad the attention was off me and my extreme lack of progress. But he didn't relax with me. His attention was on Johar, who was spearheading the investigation into who'd tried to assassinate Galian last year, killing his guard, Dave Martin, instead.

Johar had even less to discuss than we did, mentioning that she couldn't investigate fully while still guarding Galian.

"I know," Korina said with a small grimace. "Is there anyone else you'd trust to protect him?"

Kader exchanged a look with Johar, and shook his head. "No."

Johar tightened her smile and nodded. "I'll just have to try harder, Your Majesty."

"Very well," Korina said with a nod.

"Can I help?" Galian asked. "Please?"

"You are," Johar said, patting him on the shoulder.

Galian grumbled about being a messenger boy, shaking his head. Martin's death had been personal for him, and I knew he didn't like being kept out of the action. I couldn't help but feel the same way.

"Thank you all for your hard work," Korina said after a

moment. "I'm very happy with our progress to date. Please be careful out there." Her gaze landed on me. "Theo, could I have a word before you leave?"

I swallowed and nodded before I could stop myself. I'd had a few private conversations with the queen, and they'd always left me second-guessing every word I'd said.

Beside me, Galian grunted angrily. "Mom, she's leaving *tonight*, can't you—"

"Oh, darling, this'll only take a second," Korina said, standing and waiting for me.

I popped upright and glanced back at Galian with an "I'm sorry" look on my face. Then I followed Korina to the window overlooking a lush green garden, filled with the fruits and vegetables of the mid-summer season.

"I'm sorry if I made you uncomfortable asking Galian to meet with Olivia," she said in a hushed voice.

"Oh, no!" I shook my head and glanced at Galian on the other side of the room. "No, that's not..."

She took my hands in hers. "You can tell me what's bothering you."

I stared at the veins in her hand, instead of looking at her. "I just don't... I'm not sure why I keep going over there."

"Why's that?"

"I haven't met with anyone," I said, trying not to look at Kader. "All I do is wait around for Kader to come back. And then, when we run out of money, we come back here for hours just to do it all over again."

"Surely Kader has told you why?" Korina said. "In efforts like this, where meetings can happen at the drop of a hat, we need to keep you close—"

"I know," I said, my gaze drifting over to Galian. "And I know I wouldn't be much happier here either." If there was any hope of me ever meeting with Anson, my relationship with Galian needed to remain a secret. "I just feel like the rebels are giving us the runaround."

"Oh, but, my dear, they are," Korina said with a small chuckle. "That's part of the game. The rebels won't give their trust freely. It takes time and persistence to make headway."

She released my hands and followed my gaze over to Galian, who stood in the corner.

"I know it must be very difficult to be away from your *amichai* for so long. I want you to know how much I appreciate what you've given up, and what you're doing for both our countries." She placed a hand on my cheek and tilted her head. "And if you ever wish to stop, all you have to do is give the word."

"It's not that I want to stop," I said, ignoring the way my heart ached.

"Soon, the rebels will break, and you'll be able to meet with them. And on that day, you'll be grateful for all the work Kader has put in to get you there."

I nodded, but only because I didn't want to keep arguing.

"I know you only have a few moments, so I won't keep you." She released my hands and found Rhys, looping her arm through his and exiting out the door.

Kader and Johar lingered against the door, and Kader held up his hand to indicate I had five minutes to say goodbye to the love of my life.

Again.

"So," I said quietly, unable to look at him.

He snorted. "So. This is it, huh?"

"For now."

He placed his hands against my made-up cheeks and lifted my gaze to his. "I want you to tell me that you're okay."

I opened my mouth to respond, but the words died in my throat. Instead, I said, "Don't ask me to lie to you, *amichai*."

"Then don't go," he said.

"I have to." I swallowed. "Your mother is right. Maybe this will be the time I'll get to meet with someone."

"Now you're starting to sound like me," he said with a small chuckle. "My naive princeling attitude must've rubbed off on you."

I tried to smile, but I couldn't. Not when Kader appeared in the door with a warning glance. I dropped my gaze from Galian, afraid I would start crying and lose my nerve. It would've been easier if I'd just left without saying goodbye, but our mission wasn't without risk, and I didn't want his last memory of me to be cowardice.

"Be careful," he said, rubbing his thumb against my cheek. "I love you, ay-me-key."

I fought to keep a smile off my face. "*Amichai*."

"Ay—"

I shook my head. "Ah."

"Aah—"

I reached up and smushed his cheeks together until he made the right sound. "Ah."

"Ah."

"Me—"

"Sergeant, time to go," Kader grunted from the doorway.

I released Galian's cheeks, but he grasped my hands, gently kissing my fingertips. "Be careful. I mean it."

"I will."

"I'll see you when—"

"*Sergeant.*"

I stepped back from Galian then, in one move, pressed my lips to his and scurried away to join Kader.

Our transport wouldn't leave until three in the morning, so we returned to Kader's apartment to wait it out. I knew part of Kader's urgency to leave the castle was so we wouldn't be seen, but part of it was because he also wanted to spend as much time as possible with his wife.

"Eli!" Rosie was waiting for us in the doorway, and rushed into Kader's arms as soon as we were off the lift.

I kept my head down as they exchanged sweet nothings in the hallway, entering the apartment and making a beeline for the shower to wash off the pale makeup. At least in the shower, I could drown out the reminder that *Kader* got to spend time with his love.

I didn't completely mean that. I would be forever grateful to Rosie for the first night I'd spent in Norose. I was still reeling from the bomb and air rescue then getting my *amichai* back only to walk away from him, so my first moment of peace unleashed a torrent of hysterics. But Rosie had held me as kindly as a mother would have, then fed me until I couldn't fit anything else into my stomach and led me to a warm bed. Every time we'd returned from Rave, she'd been welcoming and caring for me, even as her gaze drifted to her husband. So I kept myself scarce, out of respect for her.

I was thankful for the warm water of the shower, as I'd been taking alley-way rinses for the past four weeks. The pale makeup ran down my arms and circled the drain, although I'd be reapplying it as soon as we reached the Kylaen airfield in a few hours. I turned off the water and wrapped the towel around myself, staring at my bloodshot eyes and wishing I was going to bed with my *amichai*. When I walked out of the bathroom, the apartment was empty. This wasn't unusual; Kader and Rosie would often go out for long strolls, though I never asked where they went. It was another reminder that Kader could walk the streets without worrying he'd blow the mission. I, on the other hand, was trapped in the apartment until he returned.

I returned to the small guest room and dressed for whatever short period I'd have to sleep. I'd arrived in Kylae with nothing but the clothes on my back, but thanks to Rosie, I had more shirts and pants than I knew what to do with. Most of them had to stay in Kylae, as they were very plainly of higher quality than anything we had in Rave, but I did bring the silky underwear and comfortable bras with me. Rosie had even added a few skimpier items, which only sent my mood into a tailspin. She was hopeful I'd be able to use them one day, but...

I slid on the pajamas that were folded on the bed and wrapped my hair in the towel, as I crossed the room to open the blinds. From here, I could see most of the city that had been my enemy for almost my entire life. Six months of working for Korina, and I still couldn't believe the strange turn my life had taken. My gaze fell on the turrets of Kernaghan castle, the only part of the monstrosity visible between all the skyscrapers. Nights like tonight, when I was in the same city as my *amichai* but I couldn't be with him were the worst—

Brriiiing.

The phone ring jolted me from my thoughts. Stepping out of the bedroom, I found the source on the living room table. I hesitated, unsure if I should answer it or not, but who would be calling at this hour of the night?

"Hello?"

"Hey, beautiful."

My heart lifted to the sky and I couldn't help but smile. "You shouldn't have called."

"I didn't get a chance to tell you how much I love you."

"This line isn't secure."

"Then I won't say anything I don't mean. I love you."

I closed my eyes and let the words strengthen me. "I love you too, *amichai.*"

"Do you see the moon right now?"

I glanced through the open window at the bright white orb in the sky. "Yeah."

"I'll be looking at it every night until you get back."

My chest seized, and tears gathered in my eyes.

"Sleep well. See you when you get back. I love you."

"You've said that a few times."

"I want you to remember it." A pause. *"Goodnight."*

"Night," I whispered, the click on the line signaling he'd hung up the phone.

I wiped my cheeks and put the receiver back on its holder. My gaze drifted back to the moon, and the corners of my mouth lifted as I pictured Galian standing in his room, staring at it the same way I was. Breathing in deeply, I exhaled some of my sadness and frustration. Knowing he was there, knowing he loved and cared for me so much, made my heart swell.

The door clicked open, and Rosie and Kader returned, the former with teary eyes and the latter with solemn resignation. He nodded at me and I turned to retrieve my already-packed bag. It was time to return to Rave.

THREE

GALIAN

No matter how many times Theo came and went, it never got any easier to let her go. Knowing she was returning to danger and I couldn't protect her from any of it gnawed at my gut. Logically, I knew Kader was the best man for the job, and he'd take care of her better than I ever could, but I still felt like the useless princeling.

I also knew he'd have my head if Theo told him about my impromptu goodnight call. There was no guarantee that my father's spies weren't listening in, but the risk had been worth it. She'd looked entirely too miserable when she'd left.

But now it was morning, and as I stared into the black abyss of my coffee cup, I considered my own assignment in her absence. I could scarcely believe my mother actually wanted me to pursue Olivia again, and doing so while Theo was in mortal peril made my stomach squirm with disgust.

So when I finished my coffee, I decided I would seek out my mother and decline the task. I found her in her sunroom, discussing her schedule with Filippa, her personal assistant.

"Oh, and Prince Galian," Filippa said, "I've received another request from Gaetna Zygmont. She's dying to speak with you."

"About what?" I said.

"It's been almost a year since you disappeared," Filippa said. "She'd like to get your story on your time on the island."

I shared a look with my mother, and thankfully, she intervened. "I'm sorry, Filippa. Please give Ms. Zygmont the same answer as last year. We aren't interested in talking about it."

Filippa made a note of it, and I heaved a sigh of relief. Zygmont was the newly-promoted lead anchor on one of the Kylaen media stations, and she'd started pestering for an interview the moment she settled into her new role. She was ballsier than most of the media, who bowed to whatever edict my father passed out. But things had become a little less strict in Kylae now that Mael had been closed.

"Filippa, before I forget, I need you to run over to Rhys' office," Mom said. "He's still working on that speech draft and I'd like to see it before he gives it."

"Shall I go now?" Filippa offered.

"Darling, would you mind very much?" My mother forced a pained expression onto her face, but if Filippa thought it was real, she was dumber than I thought. We were playing a very silly game. Filippa worked for my father, and my mother knew it. Filippa also knew that my mother knew who she worked for. But nobody was willing to blink and just be honest. So they pretended this was normal.

"Of course not, Your Majesty," Filippa said, gathering the papers in her folder. "Is there anything else you need while I'm over there?"

My mother thought for a moment. "No, dear. But when you

get back, I need your help deciding on an outfit for the tea with Lady Gren."

Filippa nodded and scurried out the door, closing it behind her.

I flopped down into the seat she'd vacated and shook my head. "So you're letting her pick out your outfits? Aren't you afraid she's going to poison you?"

"Darling, she's just a spy, not an assassin," Mom chided gently. "And it's her favorite part of the job."

"Dressing you?"

"Have you called Olivia yet?"

Damn. "No, Mom—"

"Galian, we don't have a lot of time to waste here," Mom said, picking up the carafe of coffee and pouring herself more.

"Mom, did you ever hear how terrible our one date went?" I asked. "She...well... It wasn't good."

"How so?"

I swallowed. There wasn't much I was embarrassed to tell her about, but this was pretty close to it. "It just was."

"So bad that you don't think she'll even take your call?"

"I mean..." I rubbed the back of my neck. "I kissed her then told her I didn't really like her."

Mom sighed loudly. "Then I suppose you'll just have to make up a believable story about why you were acting so strangely. You could blame your stint on the island. The stress of the hospital and your late nights. Or perhaps even say you've had a change of heart."

"Mom, this feels wrong." Not a few hours before, I'd had Theo curled up under my arm on this very spot. Now she was...who knew where. "How can you expect me to go out with another woman while Theo's risking her life in Rave?"

"Because Theo knows, as I'm sure you do, that this is important. If we don't convince Silas—"

"I know, I know."

She paused and tapped her finger against her chin. "Why don't you just get to know Olivia as a friend, hm? That way you can spend time with her without feeling like you're betraying Theo."

"Just one problem with *that*," I said. "She and I have...literally *nothing* in common. Before I...well, kissed her, she was talking about the Raven people like they were barbarians—"

Mom's brows rose in surprise, a playful smile on her face. "And you still kissed her?"

"*Mom*," I said through clenched teeth. "You were the one who told me to give her a chance!"

She chuckled, and held her hands up in surrender. "Fair enough. Well, son, I suggest you figure out some other topics of conversation. I doubt very much she'll want to be your friend if you constantly argue about the plight of Theo's people. Luckily for us, there are a thousand other subjects to choose from."

I groaned. "I really don't want to do this. Can't I do something else?"

Mom was silent for a moment. "Galian, right now, Theo and Kader are risking their lives trying to make headway with the Raven rebels, and *you* are complaining because I've asked you to take a beautiful woman on a date?" She raised an eyebrow in my direction and dared me to contradict her.

Finally, I heaved out a sigh and stood. "Fine. I'll call her right now."

"Good boy." I didn't get too far before she added, "For what it's worth, I do understand that what I'm asking you to do is difficult, but please keep things in perspective."

At that moment, Filippa reappeared with a folder, and our conversation was over.

THEO

The travel route from Norose to Veres was circuitous, spanning all four Madion nations. Even though there was a diplomatic freeze between Herin and Kylae, the agreement to transfer airplane parts weekly was still in effect. Kader had explained it wasn't about the parts, but about keeping the routes open for Grieg's operatives to move between the three countries undetected. As Korina's assets, we simply took advantage of the situation.

Because there would be questions about why Kylae would allow a dark-skinned soldier in their ranks, I'd reapplied the pale makeup over any visible skin and added the wig when we arrived at the military hanger. As usual, Kader had proffered a forged signature from the king approving our passage, and on we went.

The midnight flight to Herin was serene, and sometimes, when the skies were clear, I watched the moon reflecting on the water and looked for our island, though I could never see anything but darkness beneath us. I wondered if seeing it would grant me any peace; it seemed the only place that truly felt like home anymore.

Once we landed in Herin, it was a six-hour drive in total darkness, through dangerous mountains and barely-paved roads, until we crossed the border into Jervan. Before we reached the military base, we usually stopped at an abandoned house where I showered off the greasy makeup, and Kader and I both changed into Raven military uniforms.

That was when it became tricky. With pale skin and blonde hair, I was virtually unrecognizable. But in my own skin, the risk was higher, especially as we were boarding a Raven military plane. It had been six months since my face was splashed across Raven papers, but it only took one officer with a good memory to out me.

So Kader taught me the art of blending into the surroundings. He would take the attention away from me as I shuffled to the back of the plane. This trip would be transferring old Jervanian airplane parts to Rave, most of which, I could tell, had outlived their usefulness. It was no wonder so many planes failed if we were getting end-of-life equipment from other countries. But I kept my comments to myself and pretended I was part of the Raven crew helping load them onto the plane.

When the dark blue ocean became bright green land, a storm of unease broke in the pit of my stomach. Returning to Rave was always bittersweet. For the first time in my life, the sight of our phoenix flag made me uneasy, like I didn't belong. As far as the Raven government and the rebels were concerned, I didn't. Neither side wanted to ally themselves with me, and it left me feeling adrift.

Keeping my eyes down, I disembarked behind Kader and the pilot, careful not to make eye contact with any of the ground crew. But I saw them all the same—their burns and missing limbs, their invisible scars hiding beneath the surface. I'd seen them when I'd been traveling from base to base for Bayard: those who were too injured to fly, but too poor to pay their way out of military service. They spent the remainder of their twenty-year conscriptions working in military bases. In some ways, they were the lucky ones. Even broken, they'd still survived.

Then again, based on the number of Ravens in Veres who'd never seen a day of military service, perhaps they weren't very lucky at all.

Seeing the realities of the war always reminded me of why I put my life and love on hold. Bayard didn't care for the vast majority of his people, and I knew someone like Anson would. I just hoped that we could expedite the process of deposing one leader for another soon.

I kept my eyes on Kader's bald head as he laughed and joked with the pilot we'd arrived with. Kader was a chameleon—he was Kylaen in Kylae and a light-skinned Raven in Rave. He was gruff and impersonal and then could light the room with his humor and affability. I think the only person who really knew the man was his wife.

But his abilities worked in our favor, as he bade farewell to the pilot and led me to the military car waiting for us. In the backseat, we found a duffel bag of clothes, food, and Raven crowns, as usual. The items had been left by his contact at this base—who he or she was, I'd no idea. Kader had said it was better that way, and I was inclined to believe him. I didn't want to know who amongst my people was actively working with the enemy.

Well, besides me.

I never breathed easy until we were driving a military car off the base, and even that was only a few hours of respite. But while it lasted, I rolled down the window and let the sweet smell of Raven summer wash over me. It drew me back to my childhood, playing fighter pilots in a field of yellow flowers near the orphanage, and to the beautiful countryside just outside Vinolas, where I'd go lie on my days off.

A cold dread slipped into my stomach as thoughts of Vinolas quickly shifted to ones of Lanis. He'd been complicit in helping me escape from Rave, and I was sure he'd been arrested. His fate, however, was unknown to me. With Vinolas to the north, and most of our activities in Veres, it had been difficult to find information about him.

"Kader?" I asked, speaking for the first time in what felt like days.

He grunted in response, not taking his eyes off the dirt road.

"Do you think we could look into Lanis this trip?" I asked.

He rubbed his chin, as he always did when he was about to give me an unpleasant answer. "I'm concerned that this baker is going to demand an exorbitant price from us. Finding information about Lanis requires money we may not have to spare."

So he was giving me a choice. Take some of our money to find Lanis and risk not having enough to appease the baker, or sacrifice my oldest friend and mentor.

"How sure are you that this baker isn't just screwing with us?" I asked.

"Gibbs has been watching him for a few weeks," Kader said, referring to the faceless member of a team that I'd never met. "She's seen a couple of rebel leaders going in often enough that we think it's the real deal. The only question is, have we brought enough crowns to buy a meeting?"

I stared at the yellow fields. "Can't we just, you know, beat him up?"

Kader chuckled, a deep, velvet sound that always put me at ease. "That's awful barbaric of you, Theo."

"So's extortion."

"Fair enough, fair enough." He passed an appreciative look over to me. "In my experience, you catch more flies with honey than vinegar. We could threaten him, but my guess is the information he gives us would be less valuable than if he were our ally. If he's who we think he is—"

"Anson's primary money man."

"—then getting him to believe us is a big step."

I just wished our steps could be a little bigger, but I kept that thought to myself.

We waited on the outskirts of the city until past midnight before driving in. Even under cover of darkness, I lay flat in the backseat until we arrived at our destination. As with the mysterious duffel bag, I had no idea how Kader arranged our safe houses. The past few trips, we'd been staying in abandoned shops and storefronts in the slums, which meant less pressure from the Raven security forces, but a lot more uncomfortable days of sweltering without relief. I could only imagine where we'd be staying this time.

He parked the car in a dark alley and beckoned me to come with him. Wordlessly, we navigated through the dark city, careful to keep our heads down when we saw people and keeping to the shadows when we didn't.

Just when I thought we'd walked to the edge of the country, we turned a corner onto a posh neighborhood. The wealth in Rave was concentrated in a few areas—the apartments where the Raven government had put me up, and a cluster in the north end of the city, where we were. Tall trees rustled in the summer breeze, covered in bright white flowers that smelled of citrus. Kader led me behind the houses, where each house boasted a separate garage and stone-covered yard. I'd thought I was no longer surprised by the disparity between the rich and poor in Rave, but as Kader picked the lock on the backdoor of the row house, I still shook my head at the finery.

We entered a stuffy house, bathed in darkness, and Kader made no move to turn on the lights. Using the limited moonlight, he crossed the white kitchen to another door. This one, he opened silently and beckoned me to go forward into the darkness below. Groping along the wall, I walked down seven steps until my feet hit dirt.

Light flooded over me, and I blinked, my eyes adjusting to the root cellar I stood in. Kader shut the door behind us and joined me in the small, cramped space. It wasn't hot, but it wasn't cool either, and I dreaded spending the next few weeks trapped in there.

"Are you sure it's smart for us to be here?" I asked, picking up an empty crate that had once held potatoes or some other root vegetable. "This place is probably crawling with high-ranking government officials."

"Not at this time of year," Kader said with a wry smile. "You didn't work with Bayard long enough, but when the summer months come, the offices empty out and the rich vacate to the northern coast. I doubt even a quarter of these houses are populated right now."

I nodded, but outrage settled in my stomach. Like so many others, these particular Ravens had skipped conscription and all the setbacks that came with it. They had been free to become educated, to amass wealth that allowed them to create a life where they could summer in the north. Meanwhile, the country burned.

"No thank you?" Kader asked. He'd cracked open a can of chicken and crackers and had set them out for the both of us. I murmured my thanks for the food, but his smile remained. "I meant, for finding you a house instead of a basement."

I looked around. "We're still in a basement."

"When it gets light out," he said, shoving a cracker into his mouth, "you can explore the upstairs. Be careful to stay away from the windows and come back downstairs after dark. But Gibbs tells me there's a nice library to keep you occupied."

"Occupied..." I said with a frown. "So you don't think I'll meet anyone on this trip?"

He shook his head. "Soon, Theo. Maybe this trip, even. If the baker is who he says he is. I'm meeting with Gibbs tomorrow to check in on her surveillance and, if possible, try to arrange a meeting with the baker. I'm sure we have enough crowns to satisfy him now."

I winced. "Will we ever tell Anson that the money is coming from...Kylae?"

Kader quirked a brow. "And how well do you think that will go, Theo?"

I didn't even bother to blush; the heat in the basement was already doing it for me. "Not immediately, but...someday. When they've overthrown Bayard."

"One day, perhaps," Kader said. "Right now, we need to convince them you're on their side. They still think you're a plant from Bayard."

"Would be nice if Bayard would put a warrant out for my arrest and make things easier," I said, rolling my own bed out and lying down on top of it.

"That's not in his best interest," Kader replied, closing his eyes. "You were a symbol of Raven resilience, especially after that speech you gave. For them to declare you a traitor, it would take a lot of effort to spin it right, and they probably don't think it's worth it. As far as they're concerned, you're one person, and they don't see you as a threat."

Considering I'd spent the past four months trapped in

basements, twiddling my thumbs and keeping quiet while Kader did all the work, I couldn't help but think they might be right.

FOUR

GALIAN

"Ms. Collins' office, Dixon speaking."

"Er...hi," I said lamely. "I was looking for Olivia?"

After my conversation with my mother, I'd marched back to my room, found Olivia's number in a box of things I'd taken from my old apartment with Martin...then went to work. But I felt the weight of my mother's words throughout the shift, and by the end of it, promised myself I'd call her first thing in the morning.

"Yes, you've got the right office. How may I assist you?"

"Um...I'd like to talk to Olivia—Ms. Collins."

"For what purpose?"

I stammered for a moment before remembering who I was. "This is Prince Galian Helmuth, and you'll put me through to Olivia this instant."

Click.

"Did...did he just hang up on me?" I said, staring at the phone. I'd never been hung up on in my entire life.

I dialed the number again, but her assistant didn't pick up. Either he hadn't recognized my voice, or he'd been given orders not to pass on my call to Olivia.

"Shit."

I considered my options. Give up and tell my mother I'd tried and failed, which wasn't actually an option at all. Or go to Olivia's offices myself and have to eat crow in front of her.

Delaying the inevitable, I went back to the box where I'd found her number. It had been stuck in the corner of my closet, hidden from view, presumably by some well-meaning servant who'd thought it would be better for my shocked state of mind after Martin died. I didn't even know who'd packed the box, but I figured it must've been Rosie or Kader.

The very first item in the box was a photo of Theo that I'd cut out of a magazine. It had been the only thing I had to remind me of her when I wasn't sure I'd ever see her again. As much as I wanted to put it next to my bed again, it would've been better if I kept it in the box. Not as if my father cared about my love life, but he was under the assumption that Theo and I were no longer on speaking terms and she was somewhere in Herin.

Digging further into the assortment of personal items, I found a black box I hadn't seen before with a few medals. I'd been given a few during my brief military service, but these weren't mine. Neither were the other items in the box—a pair of shoes a size too big, his favorite bottle opener, a couple of old books. And a note:

Dave would have wanted you to have these - H. Martin

H. Martin. Based on the handwriting, probably his mother. I'd met Martin's parents briefly at his funeral, but I'd been so preoccupied with the happenings at the castle, I hadn't checked in on them. I hadn't even gone out to Martin's grave—nor my other brother, who was buried in the same cemetery. I saw death all the time at the hospital, but losing someone I knew made it much more real.

But I could do more for my friend than leave his personal effects in a box on the floor. Carrying the box to the other side of the room, I cleared a spot on the mostly-decorative bookshelf. Then, taking my time, I assembled a small homage to Martin, arranging the books, shoes, and medals in such a way that would honor him admirably.

I stepped back to admire my work and wondered what he might've said. Knowing Martin, he probably would've laughed at me and called me a sap.

And, a guilty voice reminded me, *perhaps ask why you haven't been helping find his killers.*

I turned away from my little shrine and crossed the room to the open windows. My rooms faced west, overlooking the city and the Madion Sea beyond. The barethium-laced skyscrapers reached toward the sky like spindly fingers, and if I squinted, I saw the construction of two more.

I rubbed my face and wallowed in my indecision. I wanted to help bring Martin's killers to justice, but I'd been relegated to this idiotic task of convincing Olivia to spend time with me.

Well, perhaps the sooner I got Olivia out of the way, the sooner I could do something more substantial. So, with a final nod to the memorial on the bookshelf, I spun on my heel and walked out of the bedroom.

My mother, brother, and I lived on the eastern wing of the castle, on the second floor. But down a back stairwell was the section of the castle dedicated to the business of keeping us safe, healthy, and happy. Filled with state-of-the-art Kylaen technology, it allowed my mother's private security to keep tabs on us through video and audio surveillance. On one of the twenty monitors that lined the back wall, my mother sat in her parlor with Filippa. The screen was tinted green and a bright red box stood out on Filippa's hip.

"What's that?" I asked the guard monitoring the feed. His name was Snyder, and he was one of the older guards. But even at sixty, he was still bigger and beefier than I was.

"Voice recorder," he replied. "She wears one every time she meets with your mother."

"Ah," I said with an understanding nod. My rooms were also visible on four screens, and I cringed at the thought of someone watching me put together the shrine for Martin. But none of the cameras were pointed at the inside of my bedroom; instead, they were posted outside the exterior windows.

"What are you doing here, Highness?" Johar walked out of a back office, clearly upset to see me standing there.

"I need a ride."

Her upper lip twitched. "Right this second?"

"I mean..." I glanced around. "Unless you want to tell my mom why I haven't gotten Olivia to talk to me?"

"Are the phones broken?"

"She hung up on me." I half-smiled. "Guess my charm doesn't work over the phone."

Johar grunted, and muttered some colorful curses. "Fine. But make it quick, I have somewhere to be later."

I followed her through a steel door into the underground parking garage. Normally, the cars were brought around to us in the upper level, but Johar, unlike Kader, cared more for getting the job done than keeping up appearances. There'd been a distinct lack of decorum since Kader had been reassigned.

We walked in silence, as usual, until we got to the car. I sat in the front seat, as I'd always done, and she glowered at me.

"Sit in the back."

"No, I like being able to talk with you."

"The glass is more reinforced in the back, and it's safer."

"Kader let me sit in the front."

"Kader's not here. In the back."

With a heavy roll of my eyes that I made sure she saw, I opened the car door and crawled into the backseat. "Fine, Mom. I'm in the back. Happy?"

She said nothing and turned on the car, putting it into drive and leaving the castle behind.

"So can we talk here?" I asked.

"No."

"No, we can't, or no, you don't want to?"

"Both."

I never thought I'd miss Kader. "Look, I'm not the one doling out shitty assignments, so if you're gonna be pissed off at someone, be pissed off at my mother, not me."

The car came to a stop at the front gates of the castle, and Johar let out a long sigh. "I apologize for being short with you. The investigation hasn't been very successful, and frankly, it's been difficult to locate a paper trail that could directly tie anyone to the attempt. They've been extra careful to cover their tracks. They must think their usual methods of sweeping things under the rug won't fly anymore."

"Because Grieg is losing power?"

Johar nodded, and caught my gaze in the rearview mirror. "Been reading the news lately?"

I probably should've been, being a prince and all. "No."

"There have been more unflattering stories than ever. Zygmont's been particularly harsh. Opinion pieces about Mael and closing it, about not sending aid to Duran. Five years ago, those stories would've been quashed before they'd even gone to print. Now..."

Somehow, the thought of my father losing control over the country seemed a bit scarier than him controlling it. We wanted him out of power, but complete anarchy wasn't the solution either. "So that's making the barethium miners jittery?"

"They've thrown in their lot with your father, and that's becoming a political liability. A few of the more progressive ministers have even talked about doing away with the monarchy altogether and there've been no repercussions."

"Probably because there's nowhere to imprison them," I said, watching the people on the street. "At least, nowhere like Mael."

"Fear is a powerful motivator."

I thought about what the country might be like if there were no monarchy, if we were a true democracy like the other three countries (well, Rave's democracy was a bit of a joke). There probably wouldn't be much of a difference in my own life, unless the revolt turned regicidal. I'd just continue working at the hospital, and Theo'd be by my side.

Theo...

"Have you heard from them?"

Johar again met my gaze in the rearview mirror. "Just the usual. Everything's fine right now."

I would've pressed further, but we'd arrived in front of a sleek building with *Collins Shipbuilding Industries* etched into the glass. Luckily, there were only a few photographers, although once word spread that I was visiting my "girlfriend," more would surely arrive. Johar helped me out of the car and walked me to the front door, where she bade me farewell and good luck.

"Thanks," I said with a grimace. "I have a feeling I'm going to need it."

The benefit to being one of the most well-known people in the country was that I didn't have to sign in at the security desk, and I was immediately whisked to the executive elevator and offered a bottle of water by a flushed-looking security guard who wouldn't quite look me in the face.

The lift doors opened directly into a long hallway, and the man held his cap between his hands and bowed. "Sire, I've got to get back downstairs, but Ms. Collins' office is at the end of the hall."

"Thank you," I glanced at the security guard's name tag, "Chuck, for helping me."

"My pleasure. Just let ol' Chuck know if you need anything, anything at all." Chuck bowed four more times before the elevator doors closed.

I chuckled at his nerves then considered my own as I walked the length of the hall. I had no idea what I was going to say to Olivia, nor any idea how to convince her to give me another chance. I found her office easily enough—two glass doors opened into a large receiving area with windows that overlooked the blue sea.

In front of another pair of glass doors leading, I assumed, to Olivia's actual office, sat a man engrossed in papers at his desk. He glanced up once then twice, then finally stood with a look of shock, awe, and, if I were to guess, a little regret.

"Y-your Highness," he stammered, banging his knee on his desk as he scrambled out from behind it. "What are you... I..."

I waved my hand to silence him. "Don't worry about it. I'm sure you get prank calls all the time from guys pretending to be me."

He coughed into his hand and blushed ferociously. "Unfortunately, Ms. Collins is very busy today. M-might I have you come back at a later hour?"

Despite myself, I raised my eyebrows in surprise. Not that I really cared, but I *was* the prince. Perhaps my father's dwindling power was affecting the Collins' shipbuilding offices as well.

"I mean, not to say that... It's just she..." Then again, with the way Dixon sputtered and blushed even harder, perhaps he was simply stepping out of line.

"G-Galian?" Olivia had heard the commotion through the glass doors of her office.

If I hadn't already been in love with another woman, the sight of her would've taken my breath. Her long legs were shapely in a pair of tall black heels, her skirt was ironed and pristine, and the cream-colored silk top showed off her muscular arms. The corners of her mouth had turned up in a curious smile, accentuated by velvet red lips and flawless skin.

"Your High—"

"No need for that," I said, stuffing my hands in my pants. "Can we talk?"

"Sure," she said, stepping back and allowing me entry. "Dixon, please hold all my calls."

Olivia's office overlooked the Madion Sea, which was a gorgeous aquamarine under the hot summer sun. I looked down the side of the building, marveling at how the barethium allowed Kylae's architects to build bigger and bigger buildings. Now that we were without it, I supposed Kylaen engineers would have to devise some other way. The Herinese did it admirably, though they refused to share their technology.

"I take it this isn't a social visit?" Olivia asked, perching delicately behind her desk.

"Hm?" I said, looking back at her. "Of course it's social. What else would it be?"

"Considering how poorly our last meeting went," she said with a smile. "And considering that your brother's been trying to set up a meeting with my father for two months."

I reacted quickly, pushing my brow up in confusion. "Is he? Why?"

"Come now, Galian, I'm sure you're aware of what's going on in Duran."

"There was a tidal wave a few months ago," I said with a shrug then added, "It's been difficult to keep up with current events when I'm working twelve-hour shifts."

"I see," Olivia said, glancing down at the papers in front of her. "So you're telling me this *is* a social visit?"

Guess it was time to spit out the line I'd been rehearsing. "I've been an ass, Olivia. I'm sorry for that. To be honest, it's taken me too long to come over here and tell you to your face because I'm also a bit of a coward."

She sat back in her chair and nodded. "And for what are you apologizing?"

"Take your pick." I sat down on a black leather chair across from her. "The horrible way our date ended, not calling you for six months, the date in general—"

"I was under the impression you didn't like me very much, and I took it as that," Olivia said. "We do share very different opinions on a lot of subjects. I doubt that a relationship between us would work very well."

The memory of her talking about Rave as a petulant child rose up, and I swatted it away. "I'm not saying this to excuse my behavior, but I'd...been working a lot of really odd shifts, and I think I went a little crazy for a while. But now that Maitland is back, it's day shifts. So I'm at least a little more lucid."

She nodded but said nothing.

"And..." I clicked my tongue against my teeth. "To be frank, I still hadn't really processed what'd happened on that island. But I've been seeing someone who's helping me come to terms with it."

"Good," Olivia said, and nothing else.

Good wasn't the kind of response I wanted from her, especially delivered in such a frosty tone. She neither forgave nor liked me, but with my mother in my ear, I knew I couldn't give up that easily. I'd at least made it in the front door, which was more than could be said for Rhys and her father.

"So...was there anything else you needed?" she asked.

I could see the excuse on the tip of her tongue, ready to fly when I asked her out for coffee. I knew this game well enough. She was angry at me, so she'd let me squirm and dangle on the line. Then, when I was nearly ready to give up, she'd acquiesce and tell me she'd give me one more chance.

Olivia had all the power, and in true executive fashion, she wasn't going to give it up without a fight.

"Nope," I said, standing and enjoying the look of shock on her face. "I just wanted to do the right thing and apologize in person. I'm sorry I barged in unannounced, too." I glanced at the glass doors and offered her my most charming smile. "Apparently, your assistant thought I was a prank caller."

Her mouth twitched enough to let me know she'd been aware of my call. "I'll be sure to remind him of good phone etiquette."

"It's very nice to see you, Olivia. Please stay in touch."

She didn't answer either way.

FIVE

THEO

We'd been at this house for over a week and a half, and I was starting to feel the restless malaise that came from sitting still for too long. Even with the whole house to explore, the walls pressed in around me. I'd found the promised library on the second floor and lazily browsed through the titles. There were books on Raven history and lore, a few fiction novels, but mostly, military strategy and law. The house belonged to a general, perhaps. Reading his books was better than twiddling my thumbs for hours on end, but not by much.

To make matters worse, Kader's reports had become repetitive —still watching the baker, not wanting to make a move yet, unsure if he was who he said—and I was beginning to dread the sunsets that would bring him back to the basement.

Finally, he arrived with something new.

"Gibbs saw two men leaving his bakery after midnight last night. She was able to confirm they worked for Anson," he said. "So we paid him a visit this afternoon."

"What did he say?"

"He wasn't surprised that you wanted to meet with Anson, which means our messages have been getting through their system," Kader said. "But he won't talk to me about your plans. He said he wants to put eyes on you and hear it from your own mouth."

I couldn't help myself—I smiled. So my voice *still* had weight, after all this time.

"But I turned him down," Kader said, averting his gaze.

"You...you did?" I said. "Why?"

"It's a risk to bring you out into the open, and Odolf wants to meet you in the middle of the day."

"Why can't we just meet him at night?"

"Because he's testing us. Testing you. Seeing how badly you want to meet with Anson." He rubbed his chin. "I'm willing to call his bluff. The only person I want you to meet with is Anson."

I couldn't believe what I was hearing. "Why the hell am I here if I'm not going to do anything?"

"Do you wish to return to Kylae?" Kader asked coolly.

"No. Yes. I don't know." I stood and began pacing.

"If you go back to Kylae and wait, and there's a small window to meet with someone here—"

"I *know*."

"Not to mention you couldn't be with Galian. Not if you wanted to meet with the rebels—"

"I *know*, Kader. But I just feel trapped. We've been here for two weeks and we've done nothing. We've done nothing for six months. You dragged me across all four Madion nations just to let me swelter in an empty house and amuse myself by reading."

"You could swelter on top of a roof, but it would be less

comfortable than the library."

I made a noise and balled my fists, needing release, but not knowing where to find it.

"I know you miss Galian—"

"Galian is the *last* thing I'm worried about right now," I said, and I hated that it was true. I missed my *amichai*, especially after reading that sappy romance novel I'd found in one of the bedrooms, but this anxiety was based in something else.

"I can see it on your face, of course you're worried about Galian," Kader said. "There's no shame in missing him."

"It's *not* about that," I insisted. "For seven years, I did what I thought was the right thing. I gave up my childhood. I followed Bayard blindly. I lied to children and told them their sacrifices weren't in vain. And what did that get me? Thrown into a bomb and accused of treason. Now, I'm following another person blindly, and it's like I'm back in Emilie's office, folding my hands and waiting for the opportunity to make a difference while—"

"Tell me how you ended up on that island."

I blinked at him. "What?"

He sat against the back wall, his expression unreadable and eyes fixed on me. "Tell me how a pilot who'd survived seven years in the Raven air forces crashed her plane on a remote island."

I clenched my jaw. "You know how."

"How'd you know that the pilot you were flying after was the princeling?" He stretched his hands behind his head and stared at me.

I sighed impatiently. "Radio dispatch said they'd heard his voice. There was a plane flying strangely. I took a chance."

"You took a chance," Kader repeated. "Knowing with no certainty that the plane you were flying after was the princeling, you risked your own life and plane."

"What's your point?"

"Why would you risk it on a hunch?'

I paused for a moment before responding. "I thought if I shot down the princeling, I might've gotten a promotion and maybe a reassignment out of harm's way."

"So you were desperate."

"No *shit* I was desperate."

"And you're desperate now, which is making you antsy." To my wordless glare, he chuckled. "Desperation makes smart people do stupid things, whether it's desperation to get out of a forward operating base, or desperation to be useful. What I don't need is a desperate partner who's willing to screw up six months of hard work because she doesn't trust me."

The word 'partner' took the anger from my chest. I'd long considered myself a chore to Kader, but that he considered me his equal was a bit of a shock. "I trust you."

"Do you? Because you just compared me to the person who put you in a bomb."

I slumped onto one of the makeshift seats. "I'm sorry. I just...I feel like there's so much bottled up, and if I don't *do* something—"

"So do something. Talk."

"Talk? Talk to whom?"

"To me, for starters." His face softened. "You aren't the only one who worries about the direction of the mission."

I compared Kader's stoicism to the emotional hurricane roiling inside me. "You don't look affected."

"I worry about Korina's plan. I know her heart is in the right place, and she's a brilliant strategist, but there are so many spinning wheels in Norose. The missions we do are so delicate, so dependent on what happens over there, that we could do all this work and nothing could come of it." He paused, and considered his words for a moment. "But we do it, because it's better than waiting for someone else to do something. At the end of the day, at least we can say we tried to make this world a better place."

I nodded and exhaled the weight off my chest. I hadn't even realized how much I needed to hear his words until he'd said them.

A wry smile curled his lips as he added, "And I hope you'd know I wouldn't be giving up my time with Rosie just to take you down a path I didn't believe in."

I hadn't considered that either.

"Like I said, desperation makes smart people do stupid things. This won't last forever, Theo. Just be a little more patient, and trust that I'm doing all I can so we can both get back to our lives."

"I do trust you," I said. "But...I'm not a child, Kader. I can handle this. I want to meet with the baker. I want to be useful."

He was silent for a while, and I was almost convinced he was going to deny my request, but he grunted and shook his head. "Fine. Let me watch him a bit more, make sure there's nothing untoward about this, and..." He heaved a sigh. "You can meet with the baker."

I tried not to look too excited.

GALIAN

It had been nearly two weeks since I'd spoken to Olivia, and there'd been zero response from her. I'd become adept at avoiding my mother so I wouldn't have to give her a progress report, but I was coming up on a few days off, and I couldn't avoid her forever.

I sat in the lobby of the hospital at the end of a particularly late shift, considering what other options I had with Olivia. The black car rolled to a stop, and Johar came inside to escort me out, just in case. There weren't many photographers; they never liked to hang around past dark, but I got a few flashes as we crossed the short distance to the car. Johar opened the door, and I climbed inside, releasing a loud sigh of relief to be off my feet and going home.

"Good day at work, sweetie?"

"Ah, shit," I crowed, opening an eye.

"Is that any way to greet your brother?" Rhys asked, throwing a bag at me. "Brought you dinner, too. Your favorite."

I glanced inside the bag, already smelling the burger and fries. Without waiting, I shoveled them into my mouth, grunting my thanks at him as I put my feet up on the seat next to him.

"Well, with all your wooing of Olivia Collins, I thought you might be famished." He pulled out a tabloid magazine and showed me the front cover—a photo of me walking into Collins Shipbuilding, along with the words *Lover's Quarrel: Are the Prince and the Heiress Through?'*

"Oh, that's so sad," I said with mock distress. "I really wanted them to work things out."

"So the meeting went that well, huh?"

I glowered. "Don't ask."

"I thought she was falling over you?"

"She was, before I royally screwed it up. Now she knows she's got the upper hand. So she's letting me dangle." I grunted. "Theo doesn't pull this shit. She says what she means and—"

"And you aren't trying to marry Collins, remember?" Rhys said. "So don't torture yourself by comparing the two of them. Did you try begging for forgiveness?"

I nodded. "She basically kicked me out of her office."

"Ah. Sucks, doesn't it?" Rhys said with a laugh. "Bet you've never had a woman refuse you before, huh?"

"I'll have you know Theo threatened to shove a stick up my...manhood once."

"Oh, is that why you're so fond of her?"

I ignored him and took a huge bite of the burger. "I mean, I don't know what to do. I went to her office, I asked for her forgiveness. She won't give it. Can I just give up now?"

"Do you think Theo's given up yet?" Rhys asked.

I tried to say, "Apples to oranges," but my mouth was too full of food.

"Chew, Gally, then talk," Rhys said, procuring a small envelope from his pocket. "As luck would have it, I might have a way for you to get into Olivia's good graces again. We just received this invite from her mother's organization—apparently, they won't talk to us, but they'll take our money. She's hosting an auction to raise money for the victims of the Duran flood."

I stopped chewing. "But didn't Grieg say he didn't want to help them?"

"The Kylaen treasury, officially, will not send aid to the city of Duran, yes," Rhys said, passing the invite between his fingers. "But the queen has a rather large art collection. And she's able to donate whatever the hell she wants to whomever the hell she wants without going through the royal treasury."

"Yeah, but," I said, remembering Martin, "what about the consequences? Won't Grieg be pissed? Won't he do something?"

"He might, but we're willing to bet he's got other things on his plate right now," Rhys said, growing a bit more somber. "What those things are, we have no idea."

The food in my mouth suddenly tasted bland and I swallowed hard. "Really?"

"Really," Rhys said with a nod. "He's been taking meetings with some of the more hawkish ministers lately, and that worries me. But with Kader gone to Rave and Johar tasked to the barethium producers, we can't seem to get information about it." He paused and tapped the invitation again. "Which is the other reason you're going to this party."

My pulse skipped. "You want me to get information?"

"I want you to go be your charming self, and if you *happen* to overhear anything about what Father's got cooking, you'll report it. But don't go inviting yourself into conversations, and don't go announcing that's what you're after."

I nodded, mouth too full to argue.

"Tonight, and every night until the auction, you and I are going to be reviewing each of the ministers who *might* show up at this thing," he continued. "You'll be educated enough to know what you're listening for, but not so much that you'll give yourself away."

"After all, you're an idiot to these people," Johar piped up from the front seat.

"An idiot with a medical degree," I countered.

She caught my eye in the rearview mirror. "An idiot just the same."

THEO

The day I was to meet with Odolf the baker, Kader had me up before dawn. We would wait out the morning in a house across the street to wait for the streets to clear. It was a risk to have me out in broad daylight, but Kader seemed confident we could avoid being spotted.

I felt like I hadn't smelled fresh air in years, and even the stink of hot trash that permeated the city didn't bother me. Even Kader seemed in a better mood, taking advantage of the empty streets to coach me on what we needed to say to Odolf.

"The good news is you won't be lying—too much," he said, his voice low. "We are here to offer money, we are here to get Bayard out of power and replace him with someone who's a bit less willing to sacrifice his own people. But the origin of the money is where it gets tricky. So, if possible, gloss over that."

"A wealthy Jervanian backer who wants to remain anonymous," I recited.

"And that sounds absolutely rehearsed," Kader said with a smile. "Try...the backer doesn't wish to be identified. Which is also a truth, and will flow easier off your tongue."

I nodded and tried to ignore the butterflies ricocheting off the walls of my stomach. I was as nervous as when I'd given a speech to the international community, but then I'd also had the benefit of Emilie working with me for weeks. Now, I was walking into this situation with only a day and a few tips. Unprepared was an understatement.

As the sun broke over the city, Kader and I arrived at our destination—only a few blocks away from *Platcha*, the presidential mansion, and the government offices where I used to spend most of my time. My government car had driven down this street hundreds of times, although I'd never left the offices to get pastries. Odolf really was playing a dangerous game if he was within spitting distance of those who sought to quash the rebellion.

"C'mon," Kader said, beckoning me down an alley overflowing with trash.

A gray-haired woman stood in the doorway of one of the buildings, nodding her greeting to us as we approached. "Kader."

"Gibbs," Kader replied. "Any news from last night?"

"No one's come or gone," she said. "Though I can't be sure that the flour delivery man isn't somehow connected. Thought I saw them throwing the rebel sign to each other, but could've been a trick of the light."

"What's the rebel sign?" I asked Kader.

He tapped a closed fist to his chest. "Once for Rave." Two more taps with two fingers extended. "Twice for traitors."

Even in the sweltering heat, I shivered.

We bade farewell to Gibbs, who was going to a safe house to sleep before returning to provide cover for our meeting, and Kader led me up a back stairwell into a storeroom filled with boxes and smelling of leather. The storeroom belonged to a shoemaker, who, like most of Veres, had escaped the stifling heat for cooler climates. The room overlooked the front door of the bakery across the street.

"I'm going to scout the area," Kader said. "If anyone comes in, hide."

I nodded and leaned my elbows against the window pane,

watching the city come to life. As the sun grew brighter, the streets became more populated, and I recognized a few people from my time at the public relations office. What did they think of me now? Did they know what Bayard had done with me, or, like the rest of Rave, did they think I'd simply bowed out from a public life?

Around midday, Kader returned, sweating and red-faced, with Gibbs in tow. He handed me a bottle of water before guzzling down his own. "It's too damned hot in your country."

"Sorry," I said, sipping on the water. "Everything clear?"

"As far as I can tell," Kader said. "But I did hear some interesting chatter about Bayard today. Gibbs says the people are getting restless, and there've been a few riots in the south end of the country. Apparently, he's promised money to a lot of people, and the Raven treasury hasn't had the money to give."

"Because he was building a secret weapon in Malaske?"

"That, and he'd been counting on aid from Jervan and Herin. Thanks to Grieg's diplomatic freeze, they're starting to distance themselves from Rave, so the money has been dwindling."

"They probably aren't too happy with Rave either, considering all their money ended up at the bottom of the Madion Sea," I added.

"That too," Kader said. "So the good news is, once Anson gets his footing, he might not have to work very hard to win over the populace. They seem primed for a change in leadership. Or a change, anyway."

He left unsaid the rest of our problems: even if we put Anson in power, Grieg would still be on the throne in Kylae. But that, as he said, was a problem for Korina and Galian.

I glanced at the sky and cursed. I hadn't even *thought* about Galian in days. I tried not to dwell on what that might mean.

Kader, on the other hand, had turned to Gibbs, and they were soon discussing contingency plans, escape routes, and all the different ways this meeting could go horribly, horribly wrong. Not wanting to worry myself unnecessarily, I stood and walked to the other end of the storeroom, running my own scenarios of what Odolf could ask me, and how I might respond without ruining our entire operation.

"You're going to do fine," Kader said, meeting me on the other end of the room. He handed me a pair of sunglasses and a hat. "Just relax. Odolf will know if you're nervous."

I stopped fidgeting and yanked the hat onto my head. "I think this is more stressful than delivering that speech."

"You only think it is because Galian's not here to help you clear your head...and other things."

"*Kader*!" I gasped, glancing to see if Gibbs had heard.

But his joke had worked, and some of my nerves dissipated as he continued poking fun at me and my *amichai* and our short-but-steamy meeting at a hotel in Jervan. He told me to stay in the alley as he strode onto the street, casually scanning the road for anyone who might be interested. But the sun was broiling the city, and no one was outside if they could help it.

Kader whistled and looked to the sky, the signal that I was to join him. Forcing my shoulders into a slouch and my gaze at the ground, I walked as casually as I could to meet him. He tossed his arm around my shoulder and we completed the journey across the street with little fanfare.

The sign in the window indicated the bakery was closed, but the door was unlocked when Kader turned the handle. He walked inside first, then nodded for me to join him.

Inside the bakery, the scent of yeast and sugar made my

stomach rumble. Loaves of bread lined the back wall, and delicate, fluffy pastries sat cooling in a glass case. There was no one at the front, although sounds of activity came from the backroom. The curtains hanging from the doorframe rustled, and a man limped out. He was older, thick and short, with gray hair that stuck up around his head.

He surveyed me suspiciously, and shuffled from behind his display. The source of his limp was a wooden leg. It had probably saved his life as a young man, ending his flying career. Most likely, he'd been assigned to the kitchen until his conscription was complete. I tried to place his age—maybe fifty, which meant he'd been out of the military for twenty or so years.

"Take off them sunglasses," he demanded.

I looked at Kader, who glanced around the shop once more before nodding to me. My heart skipped a beat as I pulled them off, revealing my face.

Odolf gave me the once-over and nodded. "Yeah, he said you might be calling after a while."

"Who did?" I asked.

"Anson," Odolf replied, wiping his hands on a nearby towel.

"Can you arrange a meeting?" I asked, stepping forward. A stern glance from Kader reminded me to dial back my excitement a little.

Odolf smirked. "Not just yet. I need time to talk to some people. To be honest, I wasn't completely sure you'd be affiliated with this *esmaill* here—"

"Come on," I said, glancing at Kader, who either didn't know to flinch at the slur, or didn't care to. "There's no need to call him that."

"He's got some Kylaen pretty close to the surface," Odolf said, eyeing him. "Makes me wonder who you're getting this money from."

"A wealthy Jervanian businessman," I said, hoping it didn't sound forced. I'd meant to say that my backer didn't want to be identified, but the other had come out before I could stop it. "He's interested in facilitating peace between Kylae and Rave—"

The baker choked then howled with laughter. I resisted the urge to look at Kader, as that might betray my nerves.

"What business does Jervan have in the squabbles of Kylae and Rave?" Odolf asked.

"War is bad for business," I said with a shrug.

"Then he needs to get into a better business." He chuckled again, but then heaved a breath. "Fine. Next time I speak with my...person, I'll try to arrange a meeting." He paused. "Come back next week and I may have news."

Although I wanted to argue, to get more information about who, where, and why, I nodded. Kader handed the man a fat wad of banknotes—nearly half of what we'd come with—and shook his hand.

Without another word, I followed Kader out of the shop, hoping we hadn't just pissed away more of our time and chances.

SIX

GALIAN

I never knew just how woefully uninformed I was about my nation's leadership until I began meeting with Rhys after my shifts to learn which ministers did what and which side they were on. As king, my father was the head of government, but there were twelve ministers who comprised his secondary leadership—home, defense, business development, treasury, health, and justice, and six for the main provinces of Kylae. They were evenly split on their views of the war— the six ministers Rhys had dubbed "doves" thought independent Rave and peace was the best option, while the six "hawks" thought we should increase our bombing to retake the colony.

As Rhys quizzed me on each of them, I felt like I was back in military strategy class. Only this time, Rhys was doing the teaching and Digory wasn't throwing spitballs at the back of my head.

"Focus, Gally," Rhys said, handing me a photo of a fierce-looking woman with a hawkish nose and gray hair. "Who's that?"

"Minister Cavillion, Trade and Business Affairs."

"No, Defense," he said, snatching the photo away from me. "You don't remember meeting her at your commissioning ceremony?"

I'd been hungover during my ceremony, trying to drink away the reality of going to war. "Sure."

"And is she hawk or dove?"

That was easy. "Hawk."

"Right," Rhys said, returning to his photos. "Who's this?"

"Minister..." I drew a blank. "But he's in charge of Health, I know that. I see his photo every morning when I go to work."

"Maybe pay attention to the placard under his name," Rhys said. "Biasak."

"Biasak, yeah, I knew that." I didn't know that, but considering I'd been on my feet all day, my mind on patients, it was a miracle I was getting even some of them right.

"And Biasak is—"

"Dove."

"No, Hawk."

"Really?" I said, tilting my head. "You're telling me the head of our health services *wants* to continue war with Rave?"

"The refugees in the slums use the health services," Rhys said. "They don't pay taxes, ergo, he's losing money for every little dark-skinned child you put a bandage on."

"Fine, hawk. But when you're king, I hope you replace him with someone who has a soul," I said, glaring at the photo still in his hand.

"That's a long way off," Rhys muttered. He picked up another photo. "Who's this?"

"Minister...Kopec from the Benter province?"

Rhys nodded and looked at the card. "You should know, you

slept with his daughter."

I flushed and grabbed the card, scanning the man's face. "I don't remember."

"You didn't sleep with *him*, you slept with his daughter."

"And...why is that memorable?"

Rhys sighed and took the photo back, adding it into the deck. "She was sixteen."

"And?"

"You were twenty-two."

"Ah." I shrugged. "Not terrible. Theo's twenty."

"Theo's ninety in Raven years," Rhys said, pulling out another photo. "Who's this?"

"Rhys, is this really important?" I asked. "I mean, it's an *art auction*. I doubt Minister Biasak is going to be hobnobbing with socialites."

"You'd be surprised," Rhys said, grabbing a new set of cards. "Once we get the ministers right, we'll move onto their spouses. Then, where applicable, their lovers."

"I can't look at any more photos tonight," I said, leaning back into the chair. "Let's study something else."

Rhys didn't miss a beat. "If you happen to meet with a hawkish minister, what are the two things you want to convince them of?"

I watched the ceiling. "One, it's important that the barethium miners work with Collins on his new shipbuilding line. Two, it's important that they press Father to lift the trade embargo with Jervan."

"And?"

I looked at him. "That was two."

"And it's most important that they put pressure on Father to restart aid to Duran, or else there's no point to any of it."

"Right." I winced. "That's important."

"Our goal is to convince the hawks that barethium is no longer a viable resource, and it's in Kylae's best interest to move away from it," Rhys said. "And as for the doves, we have to rebuild the bridge that Father's destroyed. They're the ones advocating for a Kylaen democracy—"

I sighed. "And so how does any of this bring about an end to the war? Or have anything to do with what Theo's doing over in Veres?"

"We need to make the ministers happy—all of them—in order to put pressure on Father to negotiate a potential treaty. Our bet is that when Bayard gets deposed, Anson will be a little more amenable to peace, especially when we tell him all his money came from Kylae."

"So we're going to blackmail him."

"If needed," Rhys said. "But Mom hopes he'll be willing to negotiate peace."

"There's really nothing to negotiate, since we've been the aggressors," I said. "Unless it's a 'don't retaliate' treaty."

"There's a whole country of Theos who've been bred to hate us. Bayard was able to coordinate with Herin and Jervan to build a bomb that could've wiped out a tenth of our population. Any treaty has to put an end to the war—completely." He ran his hands over his face. "But before we get there, we need the ministers to convince Father to seek peace. And before they'll do that, they need to like us. Showing up at this auction, donating a piece, goes a long way to convincing some of them." He smirked. "But you'll still need to use some of that princeling charm that won Theo over."

I glared at him. "Only Theo gets to call me that."

"Let's go again, *Gally*."

For once in my life, I didn't don my fancy suit with dread. I took extra time adjusting my tie and combing my hair, making sure there was nothing out of place. I wasn't doing it for Olivia; the prospect of doing some *actual* espionage made me schoolboy giddy.

When we arrived at the art gallery, the photographers wasted no time crowding the car, and Johar had to be a little rough with them to push them aside. Their questions were centered on Olivia and me, which meant that tomorrow's paper would have something along the lines of *Prince Galian Tries in Vain to Win Back Collins*.

Once past the crowd outside, I was refreshed by the cool air in the gallery and the soft murmuring of patrons. There were large paintings propped up on easels, waiters carrying trays of champagne and small bites to eat, and Kylae's richest sons of bitches standing around, writing checks to one another.

I made a beeline for the piece my mother had donated. I'd memorized everything about it, along with the rest of my studying, so I could help sell it to a high bidder. Knowing it was royally touched should've been enough to raise the price, but seeing as everyone was less enthused with the Helmuths lately, I readied myself to do some charming.

"Your Highness!" I didn't recognize the woman who'd placed her hand on my shoulder, and thought, perhaps, connecting names from photos was going to be a bit more challenging.

Luckily for me, she didn't acknowledge my blank stare. "Sire, it's just wonderful to see you out and about again. Your mother tells me the hospital keeps you busy."

Friends with my mother, check. "The good news is, I'm back on day shifts, so at least I know what day it is!"

She laughed and patted my arm. Most people who were unfamiliar with me were scared to touch me, but now I was convinced she'd known me since I was a child. "I have to say, I'm impressed with the way you've turned your life around. Melinda often says—"

Melinda. Girl I slept with. Minister Kopec's wife. Benter province. "And how is Melinda?" I asked, adding a bit more charm to my smile.

"She's married," Mrs. Kopec replied with more than a little disappointment. "But spends most of her time at the university and not making me any grandchildren."

"And your husband?"

She tutted and frowned. "Always in an uproar. This Collins mess is just that—a mess. He told me I wasn't to come to this event, but I told him if he thought I was going to miss this, he had another thing coming!"

I nodded and handed her another glass of champagne. *See, Rhys? I'm listening.*

"All those people in Duran, do you know they're living on the streets? Like those filthy creatures in our slums. Those Ravens don't know any better, but the people in Duran didn't do anything to deserve their hardships."

I sipped my champagne to hide the response threatening to bubble through my lips.

"But I'm glad to see you're here, darling," Kopec said, again, patting my shoulder. "You've always had a kind heart, like your mother. Do tell her I said hello. I've had to decline her invites to tea for the past few weeks."

The tension around her eyes told me that her husband had, at least, gotten his way there. So Mom was also getting frozen out of meetings.

Interesting.

"Oh! There's Camil Severino! Come, you must hear all about his latest sculpture. The Collins commissioned it just for this event!"

Kopec nearly tore my arm out as she dragged me over to an artist, who seemed bored even to be in the same room as I was. After a tedious few minutes as he described his process, I excused myself and went to find another interrogation subject.

Finding something useful from the mouths of socialites was difficult, but the more I listened, the more I began to see a rift happening in the Kylaen upper class. Kopec was the only wife of a hawkish minister that I'd spoken with and, from what I could tell, the only one there. More than one person commented on how so-and-so's wife was missing from the event, and how, like my mother, they hadn't had tea in weeks.

And those who were in attendance made no secret of their feelings for the royal family.

"This is the problem with unchecked power. One man making all the decision ignores the will of the people." Lesli Mansela was the newly appointed governor of the southwestern province, Wanic, and was a year or so younger than myself. Like most of the provincial ministers, she'd been born into her title, and had taken over for her father the year before. She spoke with an eagerness that said she was still trying to gain her footing.

"Be careful, we're in the presence of royalty." Weatherly Bassett was the husband of the minister from the Shoon province, which lay on the other side of the mountains on the western half of the country. He and his wife were old and feeble, but held onto their provincial position nonetheless. They were doves; if I hadn't already known that, I would've guessed by the way he was warily watching me.

To put them both at ease, I offered an easy smile and patted Mansela on the shoulder. "I'm not the one you have to worry about. Too busy at the hospital to cause any trouble anymore. I think the tabloids have become tired of me."

To that, they all laughed and the mood broke, but Mansela kept her eye on me, studying me as if calculating how she could use me to her advantage.

"And how are things with your father, Your Highness?" she asked, after a brief pause. "He wasn't...displeased that you accepted the invitation?"

"To be honest, I don't know," I said, sensing my opportunity to find out more information. "With me so busy at the hospital and he doing...well, the business of ruling a country unchecked," I winked at her, but her face didn't budge, "we haven't even sat down for a dinner together in months. You've probably seen more of him than I have."

Bassett clicked his tongue and kept his gaze on Mansela. "Have you heard anything about this...special project he's been working on?"

I twitched, and hoped neither of them saw it. The last "special project" I'd known about ended up being a bomb with Theo inside it.

"Not a word. Not even confirmation that there is one," Mansela said. "I heard Gren mention it might be just a ruse. Grieg's getting old, like his father, and soon Prince Rhys will take his place. Then we'll really have something to worry about."

I sipped my champagne lightly, hoping to remind her that she was speaking of my father and brother.

"Sorry, Your Highness," she said, the tops of her cheeks turning red.

"Lesli hasn't yet learned the art of keeping her tongue, have you?" Olivia's light voice drew all our attention as she gathered the minister's arm in hers, patting it lightly.

"Liv, it's a pleasure, as always." There was nothing pleasant about the way Mansela glowered at Olivia, but Olivia ignored it.

"I just wanted to thank you for your generous donation, Your Highness," Olivia said with a bright smile. "And, of course, for helping to drive up the price. It's our top item, so far."

"Please. Galian," I said with a wave of my hand.

Mansela and Bassett took the opportunity to excuse themselves. As they walked away deep in conversation, they threw glances back at the two of us.

I turned to Olivia, toasting her with my glass. "I wouldn't have missed this for anything."

She glanced at my champagne glass. "I hope this won't be a repeat of the last art opening you went to."

I frowned. "What are you talking about?"

"The fact that you don't remember it should be an indication of your sobriety."

"Ah," I said, waving off the platter of champagne flutes that happened to appear in front of my face. "Well, I hope I wasn't too embarrassing."

She didn't answer, but took a glass for herself. "So are you here to ask me out again?"

"No," I said. "I'm simply supporting a good friend of mine."

"Hm," she said, glancing at the nearby painting. "This is a charity auction, you know. Might be *more* supportive if you were to bid on a piece."

I glanced at the oil painting, struck by an image of what Theo might say if she found out I paid so much money for the painted woman, but I gently brushed it away and smiled at Olivia. "You know they don't pay well at the hospital. That price tag is about half my year's salary."

She nodded and daintily sipped her drink. "And you don't have access to the royal treasury?"

"My policy disagreements with my father *tend* to limit my access," I said. "But, maybe a case could be made if there were a good cause."

She nodded, a mischievous smile curling on her face. "Like, say, the aid to Duran?"

"Ah-hah." I said with a nod. "So we're not dancing around that, are we?"

She snorted. "I'll admit your little apology had me fooled for a second, but I can't believe your mother would donate such an expensive piece of art simply to get you back in my good graces. I don't consider you an idiot, Galian, so I ask you to extend me the same courtesy."

I let my pretenses fall away, offering a genuine smile. "Fine. Yes, Rhys wanted me get you to stop hating us so we could continue negotiations."

"Negotiations for what?" Olivia asked. "Galian, we can't entertain even the possibility of working with the barethium miners until our headquarters is rebuilt. And we can't do that until your father releases the aid."

"We're trying, Olivia. But Father's not really listening at the moment—"

"But he could be persuaded by the members of his cabinet," Olivia said. "I've gotten Ministers Bassett, Mansela, and Gren on our side, but, unfortunately, they've been frozen out of all the meetings recently, so they can't possibly bring our message—"

"If they aren't invited to play in the first place," I finished. This wasn't news, but it sounded like Olivia had an idea.

"And I've been unable to get a meeting with those who are on your father's good side," she said with a frown.

"The hawks," I offered.

"Hawks?"

"The...never mind," I said. "So you're trying to get a meeting with them?"

"They won't accept Dixon's call. But I know for a fact they will be at the Midsummer's Ball."

Her smile grew strategic and I practically saw the wheels turning in her head. The Midsummer's Ball was one of the largest galas of the year, and getting an invitation from my mother was seen as the height of social standing. But, apparently, it was also a sign of favor from the king.

"Most of the ministers will be in attendance, and I think it will be the perfect time to discuss proposals to restart aid. Collins Shipbuilding is prepared to do whatever it takes to get our city back to the way it was. But first, I need an audience with them."

I had no doubt she'd bring a thirty-page report on the benefits of sending money to Duran strapped to the inside of her designer dress. "I'll see what Mom can do. And between myself and Rhys, I'm sure we'll be able to facilitate some conversations."

Olivia smiled and toyed with the rim of her glass. "It'll be...fascinating when he takes the throne one day. He's very unlike Grieg. I worry that he's a little too...relenting. A couple of powerful ministers get on the wrong side of him—"

"I don't see him as relenting. I see him as...more willing to compromise," I said. "It's hard to achieve anything when both sides dig in their heels." I looked at my champagne glass and chuckled, remembering my early conversations on the island with Theo. "Sometimes you have to just forget about what's happened in the past in order to move forward together."

"Do you think people can do that?" she asked, playing with the rim of her flute. "See past their differences and come together for a common good?"

"I think they can, given the right incentive." I downed the rest of my champagne and placed the glass on a passing waiter's tray. "Well, I guess—"

"Well, what a happy couple you are!"

The voice was familiar, but I'd never heard it in person before. Behind us was Gaetna Zygmont, the presenter and media personality. She wore a simple black dress that fit her mature, but trim body. Her gray hair was pulled back, her manicured fingernails tightened around a pen. She looked as if her birthday had come early.

"Am I to believe the rumors of your dissolution are false?" Zygmont asked.

"There was nothing to dissolve," Olivia replied before I could. "Just the media making up stories. Galian and I are just dear friends."

"That's what they say," Zygmont asked before turning her attention on me. "Shame I couldn't get an interview with you, Your Highness. I know the people are curious about what happened after you crashed your plane on that island."

I swallowed, and caught Johar's eye, hoping she saw my plea for help. "I don't like to talk about it much."

"If you were even there at all," Zygmont replied with a twirl of her pen.

I had to bark a laugh. "Believe what you want. I'm not lying about it."

"That would be a first for your family, I think," she said lightly.

My mouth fell open at her brazen words. "We aren't all like him."

"Then prove it," she said, her eyes narrowing in challenge. "Let me interview you. Live. Nothing off the table. Let's show the country the truth about its royal family."

"Or, how about I cut Olivia a check, bid you good night, and go back to doing my job at the hospital," I replied as Johar appeared at my arm. "If you want to talk about the current spate of summer flu, and how our countrymen can protect themselves from it, then I have all day."

And with that, I let Johar lead me away, thankful I'd gotten out of that one relatively unscathed.

SEVEN

Theo

"Now, don't get your hopes too high," Kader said, as I dove into a strawberry pastry he'd brought from Odolf a week after our first meeting. "Anson wants you to meet with one of his deputies. Then, maybe we can meet with him."

"Deputies?" I asked. "What does that mean?"

"It means he's willing to give you the benefit of the doubt, but he doesn't quite trust you yet. It's a good sign."

I couldn't help but feel a little deflated. "Another step, another week."

"We're making progress, Theo," Kader said. "I have a feeling this might be the break we've been waiting for."

I wanted to feel happy about the news, but I couldn't bring myself to. Everything still seemed so difficult.

"I think Bayard is getting desperate, so he's putting pressure on Anson. I saw more police out in the slums today," Kader said. "There've been a few unfavorable stories in the news, especially since the finance minister announced a major funding gap in the budget. *Apparently*, a couple million crowns went missing, and Bayard can't account for them."

"Not publicly anyway," I said with a snort. "But what does that mean for Rave?"

"Probably that some programs will be cut," Kader said. "Some of your friends in the headquarters may lose their jobs."

"Some, but not all." I hoped Cannon would get the ax.

"But most likely, the poorest will be the most affected. That's usually how it works. The ones with money keep Bayard in power, so he'll shield them from it."

"This could be good for Anson, though, right?"

"He's kept ahead of Bayard this far. I wouldn't bet against him," Kader said. "But Bayard's also held onto power for almost thirteen years, so he won't relinquish it easily."

I thought about Cannon, and how he'd been so sure of his spot next to Bayard. "But he's not going to live forever."

"Neither will Grieg, but you don't see him making preparations. People in power live in the moment. They don't think about their own mortality."

"So you think Grieg will die before he gives up power to Rhys?" That could take a while. Grieg was still relatively young.

Kader smiled, knowingly. "I don't think you'll have to wait that long to be with Galian."

I forced a smile, but I was sure it didn't look convincing. Galian had been a rather uneasy topic in my mind as of late. For being my *amichai*, I thought I should've missed him more than I did, or at the very least, felt more...upset that we weren't together.

But all my mind could focus on was the mission, the

painstakingly slow progress that we were making. Returning to Norose would be a pain in the ass, the reward of seeing Galian so fleeting it wasn't even worth it. And that, above all else, was a guilty dagger straight into my heart.

"But the war won't be over until then," I said, avoiding the subject altogether. "Even if Anson gets into power...Grieg will still bomb us, won't he? Nothing will change."

"That's what Korina and her sons are working to change. If Grieg senses that his people would rather he reconcile, he'll step in and convince the entire world it was his idea." He snorted. "He's an opportunist."

I glanced down at the strategy book, wishing that the answers to my problems were in there and not just the best way to defend a squadron's left flank in formation. "You know, sometimes I miss the days when all I had to worry about was whether my plane would fly and making sure my squadron returned from patrol in one piece. Everything just seemed...simpler then."

"I'm sure it did." He smiled. "I've also arranged for a transport back tomorrow morning."

I swallowed, anxiety bubbling in my gut. "Back? To Norose?"

"The meeting will take the rest of our funds, so we'll need to get more from Korina." His curious gaze pierced me. "Why don't you look happy about that?"

I shrugged and looked back at the book, hoping to avoid a conversation about the guilt eating at me. "Just...it's a lot to get back there. Then to get back here. Might just be easier if I stayed behind."

"I can't vouch for your safety in this house for much longer, especially without me here. Besides, I think Galian would be hurt not to see you."

That, I couldn't suppress a wince at. "Would I see him though?" I said, deflecting. "A kiss, a hand hold, and that's it. Doesn't seem like..." I blew air through my lips. "Never mind."

"Talk."

I clenched my jaw, struggling to gather my thoughts. "I don't... I feel like I should miss him more. And I don't."

"Why?"

The question could've been taken several different ways, but I answered the question I heard. "Because I love him? He's my *amichai* and I can't...I can't..." I sighed and finally came out with it. "I barely even remember what he looks like. And all of this is... I just... *God*, I don't know."

Kader said nothing, waiting for me to finish my thought.

"I'm afraid it means I don't love him anymore," I whispered. "And I'm afraid to go back because..."

"You've seen him what... a handful of times in the past six months?" he asked, and I nodded. "And each time we go to Norose, we're under pressure to stay out of sight, and you have to dress up like your sworn enemy and wear that ridiculous makeup. I'd be *more* worried about you if you weren't dreading it."

"But what if I see him and I don't..." I sighed again. "What if I don't feel the same?"

Kader quieted for a moment, a pensive look on his face. When he spoke, it was soft and wistful. "One time, a mission kept me away from Rosie for an entire year," Kader said. "And when we got back, I barely recognized her. Her laugh was...well, it grated on me. I spent six weeks wondering what had happened to the love of my life, until one day she asked me if I'd always chewed with my mouth open. And we began talking, and we realized that we'd forgotten all of the less-than-stellar things about each other while we'd been gone, so when it came time to reconnect..." He chuckled. "But we got through it. You and Galian will as well. Do you remember how you felt when you saw him in Jervan?"

I struggled to conjure the memory, and gave up with a half-hearted shrug.

"Fine, *I* remember how you looked, and it was clear how you felt about each other," Kader said. "And I believe you'll feel that way again, given a little time with him."

A little time wasn't going to help things. "All I get are seconds."

"Maybe this time we can stay longer. A few days, maybe a week. Then, we'll return to the mission fully engaged."

It didn't escape my notice that he'd said 'we,' and I had a feeling our break was just as much for him as it was for me. But even with his assurances, I still slept uneasily, worried about the meeting, what would come of it, and what would greet me when I got off the plane in Norose.

We set off for the bakery at dusk, as Kader thought it too dangerous to hide in plain sight again. I'd questioned his overprotectiveness, except that the city seemed...different. Police stood on almost every corner, watching Kader and me with such scrutiny I was sure we'd been found out. But with the exception of one patrol that questioned why we were leaving the slums so late (Kader fabricated a good lie about how we were rich Ravens volunteering), we made it to the government sector with an hour to spare.

"It's a curfew," Kader explained, after we watched a few

policemen argue with a young couple. "I heard some rumblings about it yesterday. It's probably limited to the slums, which could complicate our movements in and out."

I glanced around the barren street, not seeing anything that would indicate an official curfew. I also didn't know how Emilie Mondra could've spun such an unpopular idea, but I wouldn't put it past her.

We circled the bakery three times before Kader was satisfied our entry would go unnoticed by the roving bands of policemen. As before, we walked through an unlocked front door, although Odolf wasn't there to greet us inside. The bakery was dark and empty, except for a small light in the backroom. Kader pressed his finger to his mouth and walked ahead of me, keeping me to the side of the curtain as he opened it.

"Come in, come in." The voice was female, commanding. Kader nodded to me and walked through the curtain. When I didn't hear the sounds of scuffle, I joined him.

We stood in a room of long tables, each covered in a light film of flour. As I gazed around the space, I counted five guards, each with missing limbs or burns on their faces, but all as intimidating as Kader. I chanced a look at him, and he stood, unflappable, as if nothing in this room concerned him. I wished for an ounce of his acting ability.

The woman in front of me wore her black hair short and her threadbare clothes hung off her skinny frame. She was middle-aged, perhaps forty, and her eyes roamed over me as if looking for sign of weakness.

"So you're Major Kallistrate."

"I'm not—" I started, but then shook my head. It wasn't doing me any good to mention I wasn't in the military anymore. "Yes, I'm her."

"Come closer," the woman said, beckoning me with her right hand, which was made of plastic. "I'm a *kallistrate* myself. Wilona's the name."

Although she had offered pleasantries, her untrusting gaze hadn't changed as I drew closer.

"Who's your friend?" Wilona asked, nodding to the space over my shoulder.

"A friend," I said, as Kader had instructed. "So did Odolf explain what our intentions are?"

"I always like to hear it from the people themselves."

I nodded, and cleared my throat to steady my voice. "After I returned from Mael, Bayard promised me a lot of things, none of which he ever followed through on. Besides that, I started to see...well," I tapped my fingers on the table, "a lot of things that didn't sit so well with me. Like why most of those in the government offices had never seen a day of battle in their lives."

Wilona nodded approvingly. "Pretty shitty realization, isn't it?"

"Yeah." I chewed my lip for a moment, letting my real emotions play on my face. Kader had said it would help the lies go down easier. "When I delivered that speech in Jervan, I met a wealthy Jervanian benefactor who promised me he'd give me safe harbor if I defected."

"Who?" Wilona asked.

I winced. "I can't tell you that. See, war is bad for business, but if anyone found out he was aiding the Raven rebels—"

"And how much aid are we talking?"

"As much as you need, provided there are results," I said, glancing over my shoulder. Kader stepped forward and placed the last of our crowns on the table. "This is just a small fraction of what we can give you."

Wilona reached across the table and picked up the wad of bills. "Impressive." She handed it to one of her associates behind her. "So what does this anonymous benefactor want to give us money for?"

"His end game is peace between Kylae and Rave."

Wilona snorted. "He is aware there's a second party involved, correct?"

"Yes, of course. He's been making overtures to the Kylaens—"

"And they're listening?"

"*Yes,*" I said, unable to resist the urge to glance at Kader again. His face was a mask of indifference, and I took that as a good sign. "The Kylaen king isn't the only one with power in that country. There are factions as eager for peace as we are."

"Then why come to us?" Wilona folded her arms over her chest. "Why not go directly to Bayard?"

"Because Bayard isn't interested in peace," I said, again allowing some of my real emotion to bubble up. "He's spent millions of Rave's already limited funds on a weapon in Malaske—"

Her face shifted. "You know about Malaske?"

My heart skipped a beat; I hadn't known the rebels knew about the bomb either. They must've had some fairly high-up connections in that case. "That tidal wave—"

"Was the bomb failing to detonate," she finished for me. "Well, well, *kallistrate*, you do know more than you let on. Anson was right." She leaned onto the table. "Tell me what he said to you last winter, and you've got a deal."

My mouth fell open in surprise then fear. "W-what are you talking about?"

Her smile grew even larger. "Last winter, when you still worked for Bayard, Anson met with you personally. He gave you a message, and if you can tell me what it is, I'll schedule a meeting with the man himself."

"I've never..." A memory resurfaced. A cold day next to the Madion Sea, a strange man wearing a worn coat. And I'd been too afraid of what Emilie would say if she knew I'd been taking with someone affiliated with the rebellion. "I... That was *Anson?*"

Wilona's gaze hadn't changed. "Yes, it was. He likes to evaluate people himself," she said. "So? What message did he give you?"

My heart pounded in my chest as I scrambled back through my memories. I could see him clearly, hear the tone of his voice, feel the spray of the water on my face. But as far as the words? The only thing coming to me was how much I wanted to forget he'd ever spoken to me.

"Don't remember?" She chuckled at my obvious nerves. "Well, *kallistrate*, when you remember—"

A loud crack echoed through the room, and I flew out of my seat in an instant. "What was that?"

Voices, yelling, more cracks from outside the bakery. Gunfire.

"Everyone *out!*" Wilona barked, turning and running out the back door, her associates in tow. The door on the other side of the room flew open, and three Raven military members rushed in.

One of them, a young woman barely older than I, locked eyes with me, and recognition dawned on her face.

"*You!*"

Before I could say anything, Kader clamped down on my arm and yanked me forward, tugging me out of the bakery and into the back alley. I knew nothing but to follow him, pushing my legs harder than I'd thought possible to keep up with his long strides. Our footsteps echoed on the empty streets so loudly I was sure they had heard us, or were close in pursuit. Kader turned a corner sharply and we ducked into an alley, waiting. But no one had followed us.

I leaned against the side of the building, gasping for air. "W-what the hell..." I said. "Was it a setup?"

"Don't think so," Kader said, as if he ran that hard and fast every day. "Just bad timing. Or they have a mole."

I cursed. "They saw me. Bayard knows I'm alive. Or he will soon enough. What...what does that do?"

Kader clicked his tongue against the roof of his mouth. "Maybe nothing. We've got our way in to Anson now, assuming his deputy gets out of there alive."

"There's just one problem," I said, closing my eyes. "I have *no idea* what Anson said to me."

EIGHT

GALIAN

"Galian, you might as well ask me to put an end to the Madion War," Mom said, with a sad shake of her head. "The Midsummer's Ball has been my headache for three months."

I'd come to see her first thing in the morning after the auction, to tell her what Olivia had said and see if she could get an invite to some key members of Collins Shipbuilding. But I should've known that nothing was ever as easy as I'd hoped.

"Your father's insisted on approving every invitation this year," she said. "And he's been clear that Collins is not to be invited, nor the more peaceful members of his council. He says both have acted in ways that negatively affect Kylae, and they will not be rewarded." She sipped her tea as if we were discussing the weather. "I've heard rumors that he's looking to replace some key ministers with those who are more loyal to him. Bassett is in her late seventies. She should've retired years ago, but she's holding onto life and her position, to spite your father. Mansela is another he's looking to replace. Grieg thought she'd be a bit more malleable, but she's proving willful."

"I could tell," I said. "So when you say replace...what are we talking about here?"

"That's what I can't get out of Grieg," Mom said. "Best case, he simply fires them publicly. Worst...well, Mael may be closed, but there are other ways."

I knew full well what other ways there were. "Any progress on the assassination attempt investigation?"

Mom sighed, and I could tell I wasn't going to like what she was about to say. "I've told Johar to stop digging."

"*What?*" I nearly dropped my cup.

"Gally, it's not my preference, but it's very difficult to get the barethium processors to work with us if they think we're also trying to arrest them," she said. "If we want them to play with Collins, we have to make some concessions."

"C-concessions? Mom, they *killed* Martin. They almost killed me!"

She placed her cup on the saucer, looking older than I'd ever seen her before. "Politics is a nasty business. Sometimes, you have to lie down with the devil in order to get anything accomplished."

"At what cost, Mom?" I said, standing. "Am I supposed to just forget that Martin's dead? How will I be able to look at his parents, knowing I'm not doing everything in my power to bring his killers to justice?"

She was quiet for a long time. "Would you rather reopen Mael?"

I opened then closed my mouth for a moment. "Of course not. But those *can't* be our only options."

"For now, they are," she said. "The mined barethium is running out, and the builders are getting restless waiting for Collins to make a deal with them. They've begun to pressure your father to reopen the mines, and he's listening. But they said if I called off the investigation, they'd stop and buy us a few more months to work with Collins."

I sank back down onto the couch, something heavy settling on my chest. It was more than just disappointment, it was the reality that my mother couldn't make things better. I'd had the same feeling when she told me she couldn't stop my military commissioning. Then, as now, I'd held on to the belief that Mom could find some magic workaround that would make everything better.

"I'm so sorry," she said after a moment. "I delayed it as long as I could, but your father has made some moves lately that tell me we may be running out of time."

"What kind of moves?"

She set her jaw. "He's ending the transfer of airplane parts to Herin."

My head shot up. "But that means—"

"Our path to Rave has become a lot trickier," she finished for me. "As is the path home."

My heart went to Theo, and, I supposed, Kader, and worry gnawed at me. "But they will be able to get home...somehow, right?"

"Kader has a contingency plan he can use in case of emergencies, though I doubt we're there yet. I've sent word through the usual channels, but sometimes that can take weeks. The last shipment is going out tomorrow but..." Finally, the line between her brows relaxed and she offered me a small smile. "Let's not worry unless we have reason to. For all we know, Kader and Theo are meeting with Anson right now—"

"We aren't."

Kader's gruff voice jolted us both, and we spun to the doorway. Kader stood in his usual guard uniform, Theo by his side in pale makeup and wig. They both looked exhausted, harried, and Theo...well, Theo wouldn't even look at me.

"Eli, Theo," Mom said with a bright smile. "Welcome home. Good news, I take it?"

Kader glanced at Theo for a brief moment then strode forward, leaving her to stand against the doorway. "Yes and no. We secured a meeting with Anson's deputy."

"That's incredible!" Mom said, although Theo's gaze stayed on the ground.

"Anson has apparently met with Theo before, and gave her a code phrase. But..." Kader cleared his throat. "She's having a problem remembering exactly what it is."

Theo flinched and shook her head, the muscles in her jaw tensing.

"You've met with Anson?" Mom asked, clearly shocked.

"It was before my speech, before any of that," Theo said, her voice hollow. "A man approached me while I was out for a walk, and I was so..." She snorted. "I was too far up Bayard's ass to remember it."

"What do you remember?"

Theo placed her hand on her face. "It's all a blur. I've been trying for days, and I can't...I can't..."

"I think we just need a few days of rest," Kader said. "It's been a difficult couple of weeks—"

"Unfortunately, we don't have time," Mom said. "We've gotten word that Grieg is ending shipments to Herin. Starting...well, the last shipment leaves tomorrow morning."

Theo sucked in a loud breath, the worry evident in her face.

Even Kader seemed put out by the news, as the lines around his mouth had tightened. But he nodded and ran his hand over his face. "Your Highness, can we talk?"

"Of course," Mom said with a meaningful look to me.

She and Kader went to the other side of the parlor, leaving Theo and me alone. Slowly, I crossed the room, but didn't move to touch her. There was something about the way she held herself away from me, how she wouldn't look at me.

"Hi," I said, finally. "I missed you."

She nodded, and, to my surprise, moved even further away.

"You'll remember what he said. I know you will," I tried, but she turned away and walked to the window.

"It's not...it's..." She had something on the tip of her tongue, but for some reason, she wasn't willing to share it with me. Finally, she shook her head and said, "It doesn't matter. Maybe if we just bring the entire Kylaen treasury..."

I laughed, although it came out forced. "I'm sure that could be arranged. We certainly aren't doing anything with it."

She leaned against the window. "I just... I wanted to..."

"Hm?"

"Theo," Kader's voice echoed across the room. "We need to get going."

She nodded, as if she'd been waiting for the order all day. Then, without as much as a goodbye glance, she crossed the room, nodding to my mother before walking out the door with Kader.

The air left my chest, and I stared at the space she'd vacated. "Theo was just here, right?"

"That poor girl," Mom tutted, joining me at the window. "Kader says she's a mess. They both are."

"She didn't even look at me," I said hollowly.

"Darling, Theo's got a lot on her plate right now," Mom replied, placing a gentle hand on my back. "She and Kader were both looking forward to a few days of rest. Theo is very upset that she can't remember what Anson said."

That could've been it, but I didn't think so. There was something else she wasn't telling me. And I'd be damned if she'd go back to Rave before she told me what it was.

"Where are you going, son?" Mom asked as I marched toward the door.

"I need Johar to give me a ride."

THEO

"Well, shit," Kader said as we sat in his car.

Shit indeed. As if my nerves weren't frayed enough, now there was the additional pressure of knowing our already risky journey into Rave was even more difficult. I couldn't even think about what it meant that Grieg was ending the last bit of trade with Herin; my mind was too full of other worries.

Our entire mission rested on a stupid memory I couldn't recall. I'd spent six months wishing I could be helpful and now that I had the chance, I was coming up short.

For the billionth time, I brought myself back to that day. The coldness of the wind, the worry that I was squandering my chance with Bayard, the fear when the man had approached me...then everything got fuzzy. I couldn't even picture his face.

Kader had stopped offering platitudes somewhere over the Madion Sea on the way back to Kylae, as I'd snapped at him that he wasn't helping. I'd been looking forward to a few days in Rosie's guest room to sleep, think, and relax. But now, all I would get was a few hours of restlessness before we had to get right back on a plane.

"Don't worry about the airplane part shipment. We'll figure something else out," Kader said, breaking the silence of the car. "We've been sneaking into Rave for decades. There's more than one way."

I nodded, but couldn't find it within me to say anything.

"Theo, you'll remember. I have faith in you." When I didn't respond, he said, "And the queen gave me enough crowns that even if you don't, we can bribe our way in."

The car rolled to a stop at an intersection. "When do we leave tomorrow?"

A sigh, almost inaudible. "Early."

We drove the rest of the way in silence, each of us trapped in our own worlds of worry and frustration. When Kader parked the car underneath his apartment building, I almost didn't want to get out. I couldn't possibly watch him greet Rosie, not when I'd left Galian without as much as a goodbye.

Even worse, I couldn't feel guilty about it.

The pressure in the back of my skull built and I struggled to keep my frustrated tears from falling as we walked into the lift. How many hours of sleep would I get before he'd be shaking me awake? Not nearly enough. The elevator doors opened and I followed Kader into the hall, already dreading Rosie's questions, the concern that might break the dam on my frustration, and the sound of her disappointment when Kader told her we'd be leaving in the morning.

Kader unlocked the door, and I scratched at the makeup on my skin. Perhaps a shower wouldn't be so bad, after all. Maybe I could drown myself in it.

"Hey, beautiful."

I nearly tripped over my feet, sure that I'd misheard. But unless my eyes were playing tricks on me, Galian was sitting in the center of Rosie's apartment, sharing a glass of wine with her, and offering me a bright, if not a little coy, smile.

"What are you doing here?" Kader asked, sounding similarly surprised.

"Since you two can't be bothered to stay at the castle, thought I'd come to you," Galian said, sharing a knowing look with Rosie.

She pecked him on the cheek and stood. "Eli, dear, we're going for a walk," she announced, threading her arm through his. Kader's confusion was mirrored by my own, as we glanced between our respective other halves. But Rosie tugged him gently out the door, with a wink to Galian as she closed it behind them.

I turned back to Galian, who stood with a second glass of wine in his hand. "Well? What's bothering you? We've got exactly three hours to hash it out."

Out of emotional energy, I burst into tears.

GALIAN

Theo stood before me, shaking, her face buried in her hands. I set down the wine and crossed the room, gathering her into my arms.

Relief washed over me when she returned my embrace. I'd been a little scared she'd push me away again.

"I'm sorry, I'm so sorry," she whispered, her lips puffy and trembling.

"There's nothing to apologize for," I said. "Just talk to me."

"No, I just wanna kiss you," she said, pressing her lips to mine.

She tasted of chalky makeup and salty tears, but it had been too long since we'd been together like this. I crushed her to me and found the warm skin under her shirt. But there was something off. Her kisses seemed almost *too* desperate; there was a fake passion behind them.

"Theo," I said, pulling away. "Let's talk first."

"No," she murmured, not meeting my gaze as she tried to kiss me again.

"Theo, something's bothering you."

"Just kiss me—"

I sighed. "I'm not going to force you to sleep with me."

"No, I want to." But the tone of her voice was anything but breathy, her eyes focused on the floor with a faraway look.

"It's kind of hard to take you seriously when you keep crying," I said, although I was only half-joking. "Theo, you wouldn't even look at me. Are you...are you mad at me?"

"No, it's not you..." She sank down onto the couch and buried her head in her hands. "I'm just... I don't know, Galian."

Galian. It was the first time she'd called me that in... "Theo, please don't shut me out. Tell me what's going on. Whatever it is, I promise...I promise I won't be mad or upset. I just want to know."

She took a shaky breath. "When I was over there, I didn't ever look at the moon."

"Come again?"

"You told me to look at the moon when I was sad, but I didn't because all I could think about was the mission and Anson and worrying about whether I was being useful, and some part of me wonders why..." She rubbed her face, glaring at the makeup that came off with it. "And now you're here and...and I can't stop crying. I should be happy. I should be kissing you and forgetting all my troubles. But I can't and I just..."

I released a loud sigh of relief. "Theo, for fuck's sake. *That's* what you're worried about? The fact that you didn't think of me while you were sneaking around Rave?"

Teary-eyed, she finally looked at me, and I plopped down next to her with a smile.

"If you think for one second that I feel bad I wasn't at the forefront of your mind this whole time...well, then...you don't know me very well at all."

"B-but what if...what if..." She released a loud sigh. "What if it means I don't love you anymore?"

I shrugged, ignoring how that nearly stopped my heart. "Then I'll just make you fall back in love with me. I did it once before. And you actually *hated* me then..."

Instead of making her laugh, my joke just made her cry more. "I don't even know *what* I feel right now. I'm so...so damned *frustrated.*"

I placed my hand on the small of her back and rubbed gently. "That's why I came, Theo. I want to help you. We'll figure this out together, okay?"

She rubbed her face, looking at the makeup smearing off. "I've *been* trying. I can't remember anything about it. I just remember..." She growled.

"Okay, okay," I said gently. "Let's start with something easy. What did you have for breakfast that morning?"

She snorted. "Funny."

I was heartened, a little bit. "Fine, that's too hard. Tell me what happened that day? How'd you end up wherever he met you?"

I thought she might snap at me, but instead she said, "It was my day off. I wanted to take a walk because...because I was worried about a lot of things, and the apartment was suffocating."

"Good start." I took her makeup-covered hand in mine, and she didn't pull away. "What were you worried about then?"

"I was worried about you," she said, her voice even. "Worried that you weren't doing enough, but at the same time, *I* wasn't doing enough. I was frustrated because Bayard seemed to say one thing and do another. I was already noticing the disparity in the country, and it made me uneasy."

"Uh-huh."

"Then this man approached me. He said..." She furrowed her brow.

"It's okay, don't push it," I said, drawing circles on her palm. "What did he look like?"

"Not like a rebel leader. He looked like a regular guy. Long hair, patched up jacket. But he seemed...I guess I should've known he was someone important. His face was... I don't know how to explain it, but looking back on it, I remember him being somewhat curious."

"How did he approach you?"

"I think he said something about it being a cold day," she said, shaking her head as if that weren't right. "But he started talking about Bayard's unfulfilled promises, and I knew that he wasn't someone I needed to talk with. So I left as quickly as I could."

I doubted that the message had anything to do with Bayard. "What did he say about the day?"

"It wasn't the day," she said slowly. "It was the Madion Sea. It looked kind of like it did on our island." Her eyes flew open. "Something about trouble. It was poetic. I mean, that fits, right? He's always using symbols. Maybe it was a line from a poem?"

A memory from long ago jumped into my head. "Wait a second," I said, closing my eyes and thinking. "Something like...Madion Sea is calm, but dangerous underneath?"

I heard the sharp intake of breath. "Y-yes. Where—"

"It's a poem, I think," I said, standing and pacing the room as I jogged my memory. "Remember the teddy bear Digory threw into the ocean?"

"Maybe?"

"I had this teddy bear," I said with a small blush. "And Dig threw it into the ocean. I never forgave him for it. But when I was a kid, I read a book of poems about the Madion Sea, and that line—about the dangers—I always had this vision of Mr. Gumbles hanging out with some evil sea creatures..." I trailed off at the amused look on her face.

"Mister...what?"

"Gum—It doesn't matter what his name was," I said, my cheeks burning as I sat down next to her. "The point is, I remember the line. It's something like—"

"There's always something dangerous beneath the ocean—even when the surface is calm," she said, a bright smile growing on her face as she stood. "*Amichai*, I think that's what he said. Or close enough to it."

"That's—" I couldn't get the rest of my sentence out, because she kissed me, the fiery, passionate kind of kiss I'd come to expect from her.

She sat back and her eyes sparkled with excitement and relief. "You're brilliant, do you know that?"

"Yes, I am aware of how incredible I am," I said with a cheesy grin.

Her eyeroll was dramatic and welcome. "*Woooow*. And here I thought you were done with the pompous princeling act."

I grabbed the front of her shirt and pressed my lips to hers, but she pushed away almost immediately with a disgusted look on her face as she licked her lips.

"This makeup is gross."

"Want some help getting it off in the shower?" I asked innocently.

"It or me?"

My mouth fell open. She slid off the couch, taking both of my hands and leading me toward the bathroom with a sly, devilish grin.

NINE

THEO

I was drunk with happiness and relief, and hopeful for the future for the first time in months. I was brimming with gratefulness for Galian, for his patience, for his unwavering belief in me. Once again, he'd taken my jumbled mess of fears and anxieties and helped me through them. And now there was nothing left to do but make good use of the hours given to us.

Because for the first time in six months, we actually *had* a few hours. Just that thought alone pooled warmth between my legs as I guided him toward the small, cramped bathroom.

I hadn't even closed the door before I found myself pressed against it, Galian's mouth over mine and his hands dancing along the skin of my lower back. I shivered and my breath grew shorter as he removed my shirt, unbuckled my pants, and slid my underwear down to the floor. He stepped back from me, an amused look on his face.

"What?"

"Look at yourself in the mirror."

I craned my neck around him and saw my naked body. My face, neck, and collarbones were pale, although they'd become streaked from the tears. I was a multicolored freak.

"How about we get you nice and clean?" he said, turning on the water in the shower.

I grinned and pulled him back to me, helping him remove his clothes, which joined mine in a pile on the floor. I couldn't help myself as I ran my fingers along the ridges and valleys of his chest, reminding myself of the man I'd fallen in love with. His scent, so familiar and comforting, wrapped me up in a warm embrace as I breathed him in.

The water was warm, and the rest of my worries washed away as I leaned against the tile wall. Galian retrieved a washcloth and wet it under the shower head. Then he drew close to me, placing a warm hand on my hip and sliding the rough texture of the cloth along the sensitive part of my neck. With long, deliberate strokes, he wiped away the remnants of my makeup. Every few moments, he paused to press a kiss a spot or, God help me, run his tongue along my skin.

He tilted my head down to meet his gaze, and held it as he wiped away the tears and makeup on my face. There was playfulness in his eyes, but also longing. And love. The warmth in my chest grew hot, and I closed the distance between us, but he pushed me back to the wall gently.

"I'm not done yet."

He lifted my right hand, where most of the makeup washed off already, and cleaned it as slowly as the rest of me, kissing the tips of my fingers. When he finished, he placed it on his chest and began working on the left. But I was no longer content to be toyed with without reciprocation, so I slid my hand down the front of his body, dancing along the lines of his groin before circling his erection.

He sucked in a loud breath and swallowed.

"Are you all right?" My voice came out in a whisper, and it must've proven too much, for he closed the distance between us, pressing himself fully against me and crushing me against the slick tile. His kisses came ferociously, hungrily taking all that he'd missed the past six months. And I returned them with my own, threading my hands through his hair and pulling him closer to me as I wrapped one leg around him.

"I want to make this last," he panted against my lips. "But it's been a long time..."

"And Kader and Rosie might come home soon," I replied with an eager smile.

"*I* might come soon," he said. "But...I don't want to—"

"I don't want to wait anymore," I said, and I meant it. I guided him toward me and as he slid into me, I gasped in pleasure and relief, and he moaned softly. Tilting his head, he caught my gaze, and the sweet moment quickly turned playful as he grabbed my other leg.

"Do you trust me?"

"No," I said, gripping his shoulders anyway.

He hooked a hand under my knee and lifted my second leg around him, a devilish look on his face.

"Is this going to work?" I asked, deciding against asking if he'd done this before.

"We'll find out, I guess." It took a moment to figure out the rhythm and the balance, but once we found it, I never wanted it to end. The sound of his groans in my ears, the feel of him, the warmth of the water and the steam, proved too much and stars exploded behind my eyes as my body rolled with pleasure. He thrusted twice more before groaning and slumping against me.

Gently, he set me on the ground and we held each other, panting and enjoying the aftermath. But the steam of the shower was growing uncomfortable for me, and, based on the redness of his cheeks, probably for him, as well.

He turned off the water and grinned, a boyish smile that made my heart skip a beat. "Shall we continue this in your bedroom?"

I grabbed a towel for myself and tossed one at him, drying my hair quickly before wrapping it around myself. "You know, we're hopelessly out of alignment."

"Not neck, are we?"

"N...*neck*? You mean *niec*?"

"Yeah, neck. That means square, doesn't it?" He shrugged and smiled playfully. "Because, yet again, I've come to save the day?"

"I'm serious, *amichai*. I don't like being in your debt."

His playful smile faltered. "You called me ay-me-key."

"So?"

"You didn't before."

I opened my mouth to question it, but the look on his face stopped me. It was still playful, but there was something deeper, too. Almost a little bit of relief, mixed with desperation. And it struck me that Galian needed me just as much as I needed him. For all his joking when I'd told him my fears that I'd fallen out of love with him, it had scared him.

"*Amichai*," I said quietly. "I'm sorry."

"For what?" The jovial princeling was back. "You'll just have to figure out a way to make us neck."

I rolled my eyes. "*Niec*. Ni-yeck."

"Nope, sorry. I just love Ravens, I can't speak their language. My tongue doesn't work that well."

"Your tongue works just fine, if memory serves."

He grabbed my hips and pressed me against the bathroom door. "Why don't I refresh it?"

"Why don't we take this to the bedroom?"

"Are Rosie and Kader back yet?"

I spun in his arms and cracked the door to the apartment. When I saw no one, I grabbed his hand and we scurried to the bedroom.

GALIAN

We flung our wet towels on the ground and climbed onto the bed, stealing kisses as we went. I knelt over her, taking time to imprint her on my memory again. Our time together was so beautiful, and so infrequent, that the memories had to sustain me for the in-between. Her wet hair splayed out around her, her skin soft and supple from the shower. But the look on her face sent a dagger right to my heart, and I fell in love with her all over again.

I pressed a kiss to her stomach, intent on showing her just how well my tongue worked, as requested, but I stopped when she said, "I want to talk."

My heart stuttered, and I lifted my head to stare at her. "About?"

She smiled at me. "About what you've been up to. About your life. About anything but me returning to Rave in..." She groaned. "Tell me how your effort with Olivia is going."

"You want me to talk about Olivia while we're naked?" I asked, glancing at the bare skin under my lips.

"I mean, I assume you didn't sleep with her..."

"Hah! She kicked me out of her office."

"Did you use some of that princeling charm on her?"

I glared at her and crawled back to the head of the bed to lie next to her. "It worked on you."

"No, your selflessness did," she said, brushing a lock of hair off my forehead. "So what happened?"

I curled her black hair around my finger while I told her about my attempts to woo Olivia, from being kicked out of her office to what she'd said at the art auction, and how Rhys and I were now hoping to get the warring ministers under the same roof during the Midsummer's Ball. But the levity left me when I told her about Martin, and Mom's decision to call off the investigation. In all the excitement of seeing Theo, I'd forgotten about it, and the weight settled back onto my chest.

"*Amichai*, I'm sorry," she said, sliding her nails along my scalp. Then, gently, she added, "But I think it's the right decision."

"I know it is, and I hate that it is," I said, pressing my head against her shoulder. "It's like...some part of me knows that this is the best option. These guys deserve to rot in a jail cell, but at the same time, they hold too much power over my father and the economy. And when I think about the possibility that they'd reopen Mael..." I sighed. "But how can I live with myself knowing that I just let them...*walk?*"

"I didn't say you had to love the idea," she said with a small smile. "But sometimes, you have to put aside your own feelings for the greater good. It's like how I allowed myself to become your friend on the island, despite what your father had done. There were—still are, really—sins to be addressed, wrongs to be righted. But I had to look past that, even for the short term, so that we could survive."

"That seemed easy compared to this."

"Because you didn't have anything personally invested," Theo said with a small chuckle. "To you, I was just some nameless, faceless Raven. But to me, you were someone I really had to work hard to like...then love."

"So you still love me?"

I was too cowardly to look at her, but she gently tilted my head to meet her gaze. There was love there, mixed with adoration, relief, amusement. My Theo, the most amazing woman I'd ever met, the person who made me a better man.

"I love you, *amichai*. With all my heart. And I'm so sorry I ever doubted what we have."

"We have been through a lot," I said with a smile. "What was it you used to say? We wouldn't have made it this far just to be separated, right?"

She sighed and shook her head. "I just wish we could stop leaving one another. It would make it a lot easier to handle."

"Well, once you talk to Anson, what's left for you after that?" I asked, propping myself up on my elbow.

"What do you mean?"

"I mean, all Mom wanted was for you to get money to Anson. When you talk to him, and he agrees to take the money..."

"Huh..." She looked at the ceiling. "I guess you're right."

"And *that* means..." I kissed her collarbone. "More of this. Every morning and evening. In our lake house in Jervan."

"You really like Jervan, don't you?"

"I mean... We can't stay here. Not with His Royal

Dickheadedness. And we can't go to Rave either, not until it's safe for you there. And Herin's just too damned cold."

"We could go home."

She didn't have to clarify where home was. "You'd want to go back to the island? Even with the...the lab there?"

"It's kind of symbolic, in a way," she said. "A lot of things happened there that I don't want to think about. But when I went there last year, I felt like..."

"Coming home?"

She nodded. "The only thing missing was you."

"And indoor plumbing. And food. And—"

She made a frustrated sound and pursed her lips at me. "Stop poking holes in my dream. It's my job to be realistic. And you're a prince. I'm sure you can figure something out."

Theo had a point. If we *could* work out a way to make the place habitable, it would be kind of nice. There'd be no photographers, no politics. No ministers to have to sway. No parties. Just she and I, making love by the fire every single night.

"Fine, I'll consider it," I said. "But we're going to have to bring cows or something because I'm *not* eating rabbits for the rest of my life."

"As I recall, you were pretty squeamish killing those rabbits, how are you going to manage to kill a whole bovine?"

"I got over my squeamishness, *Captain*—"

"I was promoted to *Major*, thank you very much—"

I found the ticklish spot on her hip, and she shrieked with laughter. My assault was merciless until she was wheezing, begging me to stop and let her breathe. So I silenced her with a kiss, which turned the fire back on. We still had a few hours, and I was done talking.

I began my journey down her body, kissing, nipping, and taking cues from the way she gasped and moved under me.

"I think I promised someone a refresher course," I said, chancing a glance up to her. She was beautiful, breathless, and I was ready to claim my prize between her legs.

"We're back!"

Rosie's chipper voice cut through the mood like a knife and I released a loud groan that was anything but pleasurable. With a frown, I crawled back to the head of the bed and snuggled up next to Theo.

"Guess all good things come to an end," she said, a little glumly.

I pulled her back into my arms. "But you're okay, right?"

"Thanks to you," she said, tucking her head beneath my chin. "*There's always something dangerous beneath the ocean—even when the surface is calm.* Damn that Anson. I never would have remembered something like that without you."

"Just add it to the reasons you love me. What with my charm, charisma, sexual prowess—"

She snorted. "Pompous princeling." And before I could respond, she added, "And yes, I know. I'm the one who fell in love with you."

I laughed as Kader rapped hard on the door. "Johar says you need to get a move on, and we do too, Theo." He sounded less gruff than usual. Perhaps I wasn't the only one who'd just gotten laid, but I dismissed that mental image as fast as humanly possible.

"I don't want to get out of bed," Theo whispered. "Can we stay here forever?"

"Whatever you want, ay-me-key—"

"*Amichai,*" she said with a smile.

"I don't think I'm ever going to get it, Theo," I whined as she crawled on top of me. "Help me."

"Ah." She kissed my left cheek.

"Ah," I recited.

"Meh." She kissed my right cheek.

"Mey," I said.

"Meh, like..." She thought for a minute. "Well, like meh."

"Meh."

"Ch—

Rap-rap-rap. "Galian. Get downstairs."

I sat up, but Theo pushed me back down to kiss her once more. We played this game for a while, until another impatient knock on the door ended it.

"Your clothes are by the door. Get them on and get the hell out of here."

Theo sighed as I retrieved the clothes we'd left in the bathroom. I pulled my shirt back on as she went to her dresser to start packing new things to take with her. That was when I saw the black lacy item that she'd discarded in her underwear drawer.

"What are *these*?" I asked, pulling them out before she could stop me. They were nothing but lace, and it sent my already sexual thoughts into overdrive. "And why weren't you wearing them?"

"I forgot," she said, snatching them away from me with a flush on her face. "I'll wear them next time."

I kissed her neck, but Kader swung open the door and glared at me. So, sadly, I gave Theo one more extremely passionate and inappropriate kiss then patted Kader on the shoulder as I passed.

"Take good care of my girl," I said. "And yourself."

"Go home."

"Love you, too."

I met Theo's gaze and she smiled at me—a genuine smile that was happy and sad and resolute and rejuvenated all at once. And I closed the door to the apartment, finally feeling like I'd done something useful for the first time in my life.

TEN

The ghost of Theo followed me around for the next few days. Every so often, I'd taste her skin on my tongue, I'd get a whiff of something that smelled like her hair. Our time together had been far too short, but enough to keep me going until she was back. The promise that there was finally an end to our separation put a spring in my step and a smile on my face.

In the meantime, I redoubled my efforts to bring all the ministers to the Midsummer's Ball, and try to bridge alliances between the hawks and doves. Rhys and I met to discuss strategy over coffee, breakfast buns, and the photos of all the ministers we needed to speak with.

"Our best bet is to focus on the provincial ministers," Rhys said, between bites. "Bassett and Mansela are on Collins' side, but Kopec, Serret, and Faltan are hawkish. But Kopec could possibly be swayed if we could get the trade minister to raise tariffs on Herin, thus making Kylaen oak cheaper. I also know there's an air base in Norgate that needs fixing, so we could make sure to pressure Serret to write the contract stipulating the materials must be Kylaen."

I rubbed my face, already lost. "All this work, just to appease twelve people so they'll stop being dicks."

"Welcome to politics."

He played chess with himself for a moment, moving pieces around as if the ministers would do what he wanted if he ordered them just so.

"So does that mean you're on board with Mom giving up the investigation into Martin's death?" I asked, after growing tired of his mumbling.

His gaze darted to me for a second before he busied himself with pouring more coffee. "It's not ideal, and it's not forever—"

"What if they'd actually killed me?" I asked.

"Then things would be different."

"Why is my life worth more than Martin's?"

Rhys sighed. "Because as shitty as this sounds, no one in Kylae cares about some faceless, nameless sergeant who died in the line of duty. But you? You're Prince Galian, handsome doctor who gave up his partying for medical school. Even without our help, the country would be in an uproar."

"Were they?" I asked. "When I was on the island, were they in an uproar?"

"We mourned for two months," Rhys said. "Look, Galian, would you rather avenge Martin's death but potentially kill thousands more?"

"Isn't there another, less shitty option?"

"If there were, we would've found it, I promise you. I don't want you to think that we made this decision lightly." He picked up the cards and began to reorganize them again. "Now, let's get back to these ministers."

I'd never been more glad to go to the hospital and stand on my feet for twelve hours, the strain of diagnosing disease and patching up injury less stressful than dealing with Rhys' calculated schemes. But when I returned to my room, Rhys was waiting with the photos and a new plan of attack he'd dreamed up while I was at work. I didn't even remember falling asleep on my uncomfortable antique couch, but I sure remembered him poking me awake at seven and ordering me to look presentable for our meetings.

"I just don't see His Majesty budging on this issue." Minister Perks oversaw the Meigart province on the southern end of the country. He was at least seventy, but his love of country (and hatred of traitors) kept him spry. "He's made it clear that Mansela and her ilk aren't invited to the ball. After all, they've got treasonous dissenters in their ranks."

I shared a glance with Rhys, whose mouth twitched at the sound of the work "ilk." This was our third meeting of the day, and every time, Rhys would leave decrying that the word needed to be stricken from the common tongue.

"At the end of the day, we're all Kylaens," Rhys said, with the patience of a saint. "And we need to do what's best for the country, even if it means compromising on a few things—"

"Compromise? On what?" He sniffed. "Letting the Ravens go free? Giving up all the barethium that is our birthright?"

I pinched the bridge of my nose.

"We don't need barethium anymore," Rhys said. "Our building industry can get along with building shorter towers, and our manufacturers can move to different industries, like shipbuilding—"

"Are you suggesting that we allow the turncoat Silas Collins to take *more* of our money? After he made a deal with the Jervanians and Herinese?"

Just six months ago, Silas Collins was heralded a hero, and the treaty he'd gone ahead with was lauded as a major step in Kylae's economy. Apparently, opinions were fickle.

"The deal is good for us all—" Rhys began.

"They would've seen Norose obliterated," Perks said. "That is unforgivable."

And that was the end of that. These hawkish ministers were so horrified that someone *else* would think to bomb Kylae (after we'd been bombing the Ravens for half a century) that the idea of compromise was abhorrent. Trying to get them to see reason was a lost cause. I wasn't sure why we continued to press them, although Rhys swore he was trying different strategies.

"It's like talking to a brick wall," he said as we walked out of the minister's offices together. "How'd you get Theo to stand you on the island again?"

"My animal magnetism."

"Seriously."

"Honestly?" I stopped in the middle of the hall. "We had no other choice. She couldn't walk, and I had no idea what I was doing."

"So that's it then..." Rhys said. "We just need to put all the ministers on an island and hope for the best."

I smiled at his joke, but shook my head. "It was more than just that, Rhys. Once we realized we needed each other, we began to see each other as human beings, not as nameless, faceless creatures. That man in there thinks anyone who disagrees with him is an idiot. It's hard to win someone over when they don't even see you as a person."

Rhys rubbed his chin and kept walking. "Animal magnetism sounds a lot easier. Maybe you can try your luck at getting *him* to sleep with you."

"Funny," I said. "You know, it wasn't *that* many girls before Theo. Two, *maybe* three."

"I counted five," Rhys said with a sly look. "Are we counting the girls you took out, or the ones you slept with?"

"Jealous?"

"That you got to swagger around university and pick up any girl you wanted? A little, yeah." But there was no animosity in his face. "I haven't even had time to think about finding a girlfriend, let alone a queen. Do you know how much pressure is on me? Mom's a lot to live up to."

"That she is," I said, then came up short.

My father was walking down the hallway with his defense and home ministers. Rhys straightened his shoulders and walked straight ahead, bowing his head slightly in deference. Although it ate me up, I also tilted my head in his direction, to which he plastered an almost-too-pleased smile onto his face.

"My boys, it fills me with delight to see you've grown so close," he said, loud enough for the ministers to hear. "Galian, this is the second time I've seen you visiting ministers with Rhys. Does this mean you'll be taking another sabbatical from the hospital?"

I cleared my throat. "Not at all. Just trying to help Mother with the Midsummer's Ball."

His eyes flashed, and I felt Rhys' warning glare. Before I got into any more trouble, I tilted my head. "Father, Ministers."

Rhys' footfalls were close behind me, and as soon as we were out of earshot, he yanked me to a stop. "You need to be a *hell* of a lot more careful."

"You saw that look on his face. He knows *exactly* what we're up to," I said.

"He knows it's easy to push your buttons, Gally, and that's what he's doing," Rhys said. "He and Mom are in a very difficult dance about this stupid ball right now, and the less we get involved, the easier it'll be for her to sway him."

"You don't think Perks is going to walk out of his office and tell Father we were in there?" I said.

"There's a difference," Rhys said. "Perks will go to Father in confidence. You just skirted a fine line of disrespect in front of his ministers. You, above all, should know how much he values his image."

I couldn't disagree with that, nor could I disagree that seeing him always set me on edge. I hated having to pretend I respected him after all he'd done to me and, more importantly, Theo.

"If you can't handle these meetings, maybe it's best you go back to the hospital," Rhys said after a long silence.

"No," I said, with a small shake of the head. "I can do this. I'll behave."

"Good, because we've got to go meet with your boss from the health ministry next. And I *guarantee* Biasek's going to try your patience."

The halls of the castle were silent, save for my footsteps along the tiled floor. It had been the most ridiculous day—five meetings with five ministers who were firmly entrenched in their positions and unwilling to move. Rhys hadn't even bothered to see me to my rooms, too frustrated with his failed strategy to try anymore. I, too, was restless, so after the sun set, I took a stroll around the castle to release some energy.

The moon was visible out of the windows I passed and I took a moment to gaze at it. Theo would be home in a few weeks (I hoped) and I would have nothing to show for my efforts.

Our tangled web of politicking confused and frustrated me. More than once today, I'd had to walk myself back through the complicated dependencies of peace. It seemed like so much effort when there was one person who could make it all go away.

Against my better judgement, I ventured toward the other end of the castle. As I drew closer, the halls became populated with unfamiliar guards who stared but said nothing as I passed. It struck me how different his side of the castle was than my mother's, and I couldn't remember the last time I'd been in my father's private residences. My mother had moved out when I was very young, and since I'd always wanted to limit my time around my father, I'd never sought him out.

The entrance to my father's private apartments was guarded by two men, the left one giving me a stern look.

"Your father is not accepting any visitors at this time," he said.

"Yeah, but...it's me," I said with a shrug. "Let me in."

"I will see if he's willing," he said, and disappeared through the large, wooden door. His partner moved to the center of the doors, and I waited patiently.

After an almost-too-long of a wait, the guard returned and left the door open for me, saying nothing. I offered him a kind smile and my thanks as I passed him.

The simplicity of the small sitting room surprised me, especially considering the amount of gold and silver built into the public rooms.

But the walls were empty, the furniture simple. Not at all what I'd consider a king's bedroom to be.

"To what do I owe the pleasure?"

He sat in a thick, leather chair on the other side of the room, his feet propped up on a footstool, his body slumped in a red, velvet dressing robe and matching slippers. In his hand, he held a glass of brandy. The bottle sat next to him, half-empty, although his gaze was clear.

"Have you come to speak to me in your mother's stead?"

"Wouldn't have to if you'd talk to her," I said. There were no pretenses in this room, no need to dance around the truth. Nobody was watching except Grieg and me.

"Tell me what's on your mind so I can get back to my evening."

"You know why I'm here," I said, walking toward him. "Invite the damned doves. Make up with Collins and give aid to our people in Duran. Stop acting like everyone's got to stroke your ego. You're a king, not a god. You're going to tear this country apart."

"You think too highly of me, son. I'm but one man. I can't tear an entire country apart." He swirled the brandy in his glass. "The ministers simply give voice to the deepest fears of the people, and I must bow to the will of the people, as needed."

"The people aren't always right."

"Now who sounds like a god?" Grieg replied with an infuriating smirk. "Believe me, just as much as you'd like the war to be over so you can be with your Raven girl again—yes, I'm aware of her and your guard's ministrations, I'm not so easily fooled as you might think—I would love to make peace with the Ravens. But what would we do with our economy, which has been married to the war effort since before even I was born? Now that barethium is no longer mined from our mountains, we've lost one third of our workforce."

"Pair them up with Collins," I said, tired of this same song and dance.

"But, son, how will I explain to the ministers, who know the real reason behind the tidal wave, that I've decided to let bygones be bygones with Jervan and Herin? They'll tell the media the truth about the bomb, inevitably whipping our population into a bloodthirsty frenzy, and asking for retaliation against the Ravens."

"And you'll do nothing to stop it," I said. "You've got an entire media arsenal at your beck and call, and you can't possibly find a way to spin this to avoid that outcome?"

"And what outcome would you have me choose, son? Shall I imprison our own people for speaking out against me? Or should I send our Kylaen bombs straight to the heart of Thormondia, where your precious Theo and Sergeant Kader are holding out, trying to speak with the rebels? Or should I just allow Minister Mansela to call for my head and take the throne from me, descending our country into chaos?"

He tilted his head at me, as if he'd do whichever option I told him to. The problem was, I couldn't see a good solution of any of the outcomes he'd painted.

"Lest you think I spend my days lounging about making decisions about lives and property without merit, I've considered all the options, and I'm taking the lesser of all evils." He sighed and finished the rest of his drink. "Much as your girlfriend has when she takes my money to those rebels in Thormondia."

I swallowed. "If they're successful, if Anson overthrows Bayard, would you consider peace with them? An independent Rave?"

I'd expected him to throw the brandy in my face, to say he'd never consider such an awful idea. That Rave was his, and his alone, and independence would happen over his dead body...but instead he simply smiled. There was something behind his silence, something that honestly made me afraid.

"In the spirit of Midsummer, I shall extend the invitations to your Rave-loving ministers, with the warning that if they step a toe out of line, I'll reinstate our hanging policy and string them up in the town square. Collins will get her invitation, but not her aid, and should consider, perhaps, telling her father to move operations to a country which will allow him to take such liberties with property that is not his."

I blinked at him, still thrown off by his non-answer about peace with Rave. But my mind quickly caught up. "You aren't going to rebuild your own city?"

"Kylae will survive without Duran, as it has for many years before Collins decided to waste his money on it," he said simply. "Well, son, was that the end of it? Any other grievances you wish to air? Or may I return to my evening?"

I had plenty, but I thought it best to keep them to myself for now. Whatever my father was planning, it had put him in good spirits, which I didn't think boded well for anyone.

ELEVEN

THEO

The trip back to Rave was thick with talk about the cessation of the Herin-Kylae treaty, and what that meant for their respective countries. I said nothing, but listened intently to the concerns about where Herin would get iron for their ships, and where Kylae would be getting money to replace the millions of crowns they received from Herin. After the first hour, the conversation settled, and my thoughts wandered back to my *amichai*.

I hated the fact that we weren't *niec*. On top of that, he'd saved my life a few times, and the imbalance was palpable. The next time we were together, I would level the scales. And I spent the rest of the flight daydreaming how I would accomplish such a feat.

"Get that grin off your face," Kader had said when we walked off the plane in Herin. "You're conspicuous."

Although I could've argued that Kader, too, had been in a much better mood since we'd left Kylae, I did as instructed.

Our safe house on this trip was back in the slums, but for once,

I didn't mind being left behind. Kader returned before the sun set with the best news: my message had been received, accepted, and Anson wanted to meet the next evening. We spent the rest of the night dissecting what I would say and how, and I was so excited at the prospect of finally making a giant step forward that I forgot to be nervous about it.

But the next morning, a loud throbbing woke me and in my sleepy daze, I worried we were under attack. I scrambled to the window and listened for the screams; instead I heard laughter. It wasn't a bombing I was hearing, it was music.

The door behind me opened, and Kader walked in with two cups of coffee and a bag of breakfast.

"What's going on out there?" I asked, gratefully taking the coffee from him.

"Not sure," he said. "But there's hundreds of people in the streets. Dresses, dancing, some kind of paint—"

"It's *Prima Anela*," I said in amazement.

"What?"

"Our summer festival!" Despite myself, I hurried past him to look out the window of the row house. Young women in frilly pastel dresses strolled by, their hair braided and laced with bright orange phoenician flowers. Their faces were daubbed in greens, blues, and purples, chalk that they'd also be showering on those deemed *plaice*, or lucky.

"I've never heard of it," Kader said, peering over my head.

"That's because we haven't had a *true Prima Anela* festival since...since before independence. We learned about it in school, about the meaning of the colors and the traditional dances. It's supposed to celebrate fertility and the summer crop..."

"So, the same thing as Kylaen Midsummer?"

"No, not the same thing as *Kylaen Midsummer*," I said with a purse of my lips. "*Prima Anela* is celebrated with paint and pastries and chocolate and dancing and—"

"I thought you said you've never had a true festival?"

"We haven't, but we'd have a small party at the base, and we'd always get a little chocolate and paint to throw at each other. And...."

My words died in my throat as an older man pushed a cart of shiny, fluffy pastries, filled with ham and cheese and the traditional Raven spices. My mouth watered and I pressed my face against the glass.

"So that's what I was smelling," Kader said. "Where are those?"

"*Jamo*..." I said with a bit of a whine. "We'd get them at the orphanage, so I haven't had one in ages. But I remember they tasted like heaven. Buttery and gooey and spicy."

I turned back, but Kader had disappeared. A few minutes later, I saw him jog to the man with the cart, purchasing no less than ten *jamos* and a couple of wrapped chocolate balls. My stomach rumbled in anticipation as he returned to the safe house.

"What's the greeting?" Kader said, handing me a greasy bag.

"*Savo Prima Anela*," I said, inhaling the scent of the bag and memories of my childhood.

Gingerly, I retrieved the first hot, buttery dough-ball and took a huge bite. The sweet ham and sharp cheese melded beautifully with the potent spices, and memories of *jamos* given at the orphanage I'd grown up in returned. But the delicacies from my memory didn't hold a candle to the mix of flavors and textures in my mouth.

"You need a minute?" Kader asked with a chuckle after I let out a small moan.

I opened an eye at him. "Huh?"

"You look like you're having a nice time over there. Galian'll be jealous."

I couldn't even be bothered by his comment as I took another huge bite, licking the gooey cheese off my lips. "Fis ish heaf'en."

He unwrapped a *jamo* and ate half of it in one bite. "Smart of Odolf to set up a meeting today. Bayard declared it a national holiday, so there'll be a lot of folks out in the street."

"Waa—a nafional howiday?" That was odd. There'd never been a national holiday in all my years in the military, and I couldn't remember any before either.

"Bayard must be getting desperate," Kader said gruffly. "Festivals are a good way to boost morale and make people forget they hate you."

My initial elation evaporated. Like everything good Bayard did, there was always strategy behind it. I swallowed the *jamo*, which suddenly didn't taste as good. "You're probably right."

"But that doesn't mean we can't enjoy it a little, today," Kader said. Without warning, he threw a bag at me, and the chalk exploded in my face.

I coughed, cursing him and wishing my mouth hadn't been wide open when he'd launched the attack. I wiped the paint out of my face and glared at him.

"What the hell was that for?"

"Disguise," Kader said, dumping a bag of blue-green onto himself. "Thought you might want to enjoy the festival."

I glanced down at my arms, now covered in purple chalk paint. "You know, Kader, tradition says if someone throws paint on you during the festival, they want to marry you."

"I'll leave that to Galian," he said. "Come on. We might as well try to figure out what's prompted Bayard to throw such a big party."

The chalk made for a great disguise, and for the first time in over six months, I could finally walk around my country during daylight hours. I would've been *more* obvious if I hadn't been covered in paint, as everyone was a mix of blues, purples, greens, yellows, and pinks. By midday, I'd already been hit with two more bags by passing young men, both of whom had shrunk away in fear when they saw Kader standing next to me.

The city was vibrant, more alive than I'd ever seen it before. Everyone wore bright smiles and chatted easily with their neighbors. Street urchins ran between people's legs, laughing and giggling. But as the day wore on, I noticed the absence of children between the ages of twelve and eighteen. Most of those carrying bags of *jamo* and glasses of *ambessa* were twenty or older. Even covered in paint, it was clear their hair was clean and their clothes new—and, most jarring, their bodies whole.

Around mid-afternoon, more beggars began infiltrating the crowds, and the disparity was clearer. They carried burns, scars, and missing limbs, survivors of a war that hadn't affected a large part of the country. Those with means ignored the cries for food and money, the same way I had when I'd lived in a fancy apartment in the city.

The *jamo* settled poorly in my stomach. This wasn't a festival for those people; this was a festival for those who already had plenty. As far as Bayard was concerned, the dregs of society were simply there to fight and die in his war.

A twenty-five-year-old woman, her stomach swollen and her eyes dead, begged a trio of well-dressed, older men for food as they walked by her. I'd always thought when a soldier got pregnant, the military would pay for her care and feeding. But since I'd been in the streets, I'd seen at least fifteen expectant mothers, all begging for food with small children around their feet. I'd never been thankful to grow up in an orphanage until that moment.

Kader followed my gaze and his eyes narrowed. "Come on. Let's see if we can convince some of these drunken idiots to tell us what Bayard's up to."

I nodded, but smiled when he gave the woman our leftover *jamos* and twenty crowns before we left the square.

GALIAN

"I've tried all the usual channels, Your Highness," Johar said, her mouth tense and body rigid as she stood before us in the formal Kylaen military uniform. "Whatever Grieg is planning, it's big and kept close to the vest."

It was the longest day of the year, Midsummer, and based on the number of cars lining up outside the castle, the party downstairs was already in full swing. But my mother had called a meeting of her confidants to discuss what I'd learned the night before. None of them had been pleased that I'd sought out Grieg personally, but my news of him planning something had set them on edge.

"None of the ministers were in their offices today," Rhys said. "No one would meet with me in their homes either."

"Your father refused to meet with me all day as well," she said, placing a perfectly manicured hand on her other arm before looking around the room. "Johar, your team did a sweep, right?"

She nodded. "We found one new recording device, and we've updated our security protocols so it doesn't happen again."

"It's fine, we all make mistakes. I should've been more vigilant," Mom said. "In any case, we've got to reassess what this means for Kader and Theo's mission. Perhaps nothing, if they're successful in meeting with Anson. Perhaps everything."

With a soft rap at the door, Filippa appeared. "Your Majesty, His Highness is asking for you."

Mom nodded, not even bothering to hide her worry. "We will be down shortly. Thank you, dear."

I envied Johar as she disappeared to the first story to watch the ball from behind screens, while I had to follow my mother and brother down the hall toward the music. When Rhys and my mother headed for the top of the stairs to be formally introduced, I darted around to blend into the crowd.

By my mother's estimation, two hundred of the richest Kylaens were in attendance, although I felt the tension in the room from the warring factions. Mansela stood in a red dress, watching the room as if she expected an executioner to spring out of the punch bowl. The hawkish ministers laughed loudly and wore easy smiles.

Something was definitely not right.

After the official introduction, Mom broke away to mingle with guests and welcome them to the party, while Rhys did the same. Since there didn't seem to be anyone under the age of thirty in the room (besides Mansela), I was left alone. That was, until I spotted Olivia, standing against the wall, a vision in pastel green.

"I was unhappy to get your message," she said, although she hugged me for the cameras taking countless amounts of photos from their roped off area on the side of the room. "And curious to still receive the invite. If your father wanted my company to relocate, why invite me to the ball at all?"

"No idea," I said with a shrug. "But I'm not giving up. Duran's still part of our country, regardless of what your father's done to piss mine off." I found Rhys at the front of the room, and he nodded approvingly. "Rhys and I are seeking alternate funding sources for aid. Perhaps a provincial governor. Maybe even working with Jervan."

"Careful, Galian, I might think you have a thing for me," Olivia said with the ghost of a flirtatious smile. "Could our engagement be back on?"

I had to laugh at that. "Tell me that wasn't you."

"I avoid the papers if I can," she said, glancing at the photographer taking shots of us talking. "I thought it might've originated from you, trying to temper your...image."

I swirled the champagne in my glass. "So you never...you really didn't like me at all?"

"Oh, I did. But I'm not the kind of girl who'll be jilted more than once. You were very clear that I wasn't *her*, so it's fairly clear that whoever she is..." She averted her gaze and offered a smile to a passer-by. "She has your heart."

"That she does," I said, absentmindedly worrying about Theo over in Rave. I just hoped whatever Grieg had planned wouldn't impact her.

"Well, if it isn't the two lovebirds." Rhys joined us, a thin smile on his face as he held his hand out to Olivia. "You're a hard woman to get hold of."

She made a noise and sipped her champagne. "I was just telling your brother about the upsetting news. Your father has decided against sending aid to Duran?"

"For now," Rhys said, almost a little too quickly. "But I'm sure we can change his mind."

"Are you?" Olivia said, sounding harsher than I'd ever heard her before. "Because from where I stand, *Your Highness*, it seems like you're doing a lot of bowing and not a lot of doing. You're to be king one day, and you let your father just do as he pleases, without check—"

"Now hold on a second," Rhys said, the tops of his cheeks turning red. "I'll remind you that you're speaking to the crown prince —"

"Oh, please," Olivia said with a sly smile. "Do your worst."

I glanced between them, and sipped my champagne to try to stay out of the line of fire.

Rhys's face was now the color of his military jacket. "Maybe we won't bother with you anymore. Move operations to Jervan for all we care—"

Olivia shrugged and leveled her gaze. "And what will you do with your barethium miners? I know your mother wants them to ally with us. Would you turn back on the smokestacks in Mael?"

"Shipbuilding and barethium mining aren't the only industries in Kylae," Rhys retorted.

"But they comprise nearly forty percent of the gross national product," Olivia replied with a raised eyebrow. "*Surely* the crown prince knows that."

"Of course I know what our GNP is," Rhys said, grabbing the champagne out of my hand and downing it with a frown.

"Well, *Your Highness*, I hope for all our sakes that you grow a little backbone before you take the throne. The captains of industry in this country don't roll over for just anyone, and so far, you've been underwhelming."

Rhys' mouth hung open as Olivia turned her attention to me. "Galian, always a pleasure."

"Back at you," I said with a small chuckle as she took her leave. I glanced at Rhys, who still wore a stunned expression. "You might want to close your mouth."

"I can't believe...the *nerve* of her—"

"I think she likes you," I said lightly. "Hey, maybe you could marry her? She'd certainly make a hell of a queen..."

"I need more champagne," Rhys muttered, storming off.

Before I could process what had just occurred, Mom was by my side, a hand on my elbow as she led me toward a less-populated area of the ballroom.

"What's going on?" I said, keeping my voice low.

"I don't know," she replied, glancing back inside the room. "But your father has informed me he'll be announcing...*something* at nine sharp."

"Fifteen minutes," I said, glancing at my watch. "What's got you so worried?"

"It's how he told me." She chewed her lip, rubbing off some of the color. "He wanted the family to be present, to look excited. But specifically, he said the news was about you."

"M-me?" A litany of scenarios ran through my mind. "You don't think he's pushing me back into the military?"

"To be honest, son, I have no idea what he could be planning, but I wanted you to be on your guard," she said. "Whatever it is, we'll deal with it. But for the cameras, and for your father, I just want you to be calm, cool, and collected. Don't show any emotion, don't react. Just pretend you're pleased by the news."

I nodded, wishing the butterflies in my stomach would go

away. "And you have *no* idea what—"

"I've sent Johar to ask around, but..." She sighed. "I think I've stretched my resources a little thin."

There was a weariness about her, and it made me a little less angry with her than I had been. "It's fine, Mom. Like you said, whatever it is, we'll deal with it."

Johar appeared beside us. "Your Majesty, he's asking for you to join him now."

We made our way toward the front of the room, my mother putting on a fine act of smiling and welcoming those who stopped us mid-way. We met Rhys near my father's throne, and the three of us shared a look of uncertainty, before turning to the crowd.

"Welcome, welcome, to our Midsummer's Ball!" my father's voice boomed behind us. The audience clapped, but slowly their expressions melted into confusion, even horror.

And as I turned around to see what they saw, my jaw hit the floor.

THEO

The city's drunken euphoria continued as the sun set, and it became increasingly obvious that Kader and I were the only ones *not* drunk. If Bayard had wanted to improve morale, he'd certainly achieved it, at least in Veres. But Anson had also been smart to set up the meeting during the debauchery; the police would have their hands full keeping the peace.

With all the people clogging the streets, I lost track of where we were in the city, but I guessed it was somewhere in the slums, for the partiers grew more scarred than the ones in the richer district, and the police more prevalent. Kader made sure no one was following us, circling a few buildings and waiting in alleyways, before we finally found the small, rundown building that was supposedly Anson's headquarters. Even in the dark, it was dilapidated, probably unlivable. But I recalled the phrase about dangers lurking under the surface, and I knew he'd probably built a palace underneath.

I felt someone's presence, and glanced around the rubble, jumping when I saw a woman not much older than I watching me. Half her face was disfigured, and her left arm was gone at the shoulder. I kept her gaze, unsure whether I should say something to Kader, but she nodded and pointed at a pile of rubble.

"Kader," I said, nodding in the direction of the girl.

"What?"

I blinked and she was gone, but I hadn't been mistaken. "Come on. I know where we're going."

We approached the pile, and I almost missed the shape of the trapdoor. Kader bent down and rapped on it three times.

The door inched up and a single eye looked out at us. Then the crack opened wider and a teenaged boy climbed out, hobbling on a wooden leg as he held the door open for the two of us. I shared an uneasy look with Kader and we descended a set of dark stairs.

Two guards met us at the base of the staircase—one man missing his left arm, but holding a gun in his right, the other missing a leg. The legless man checked us for weapons while his partner kept a gun on us. I stood perfectly still, offering a half-smile as the legless man ran his hands along my sides. When he was satisfied both Kader and I were weaponless, he stood aside and we were allowed to continue inside.

Instead of the palace I'd been expecting, it was just a small room with the man himself seated at a desk. He sat back in his chair, surveying me in the same manner as he'd done all those months ago. His long hair was pulled back, and his face void of hair or scars. But I could tell that he still didn't trust me, even as he held his hand out to greet me. "Major."

"Thank you for meeting with me," I said, wishing my voice sounded stronger.

His eyebrows twitched and he released my hand, offering Kader and me a seat while he took his own. "I'm pleased I was memorable enough to remember," he said with that same enigmatic look on his face. He gestured to the dark room around us. "You'll forgive me for being cautious. It's taken me almost a decade to build the infrastructure of my network. I don't fancy myself a despot like Bayard, but there's something to be said for an image. It would be most unfortunate if I were to die."

I nodded, unsure what to say.

"Images are important, as I'm sure Emilie Mondra made clear. She's a brilliant one, able to shape the hearts and minds of the Raven people to accept just about anything. But I have something a bit more potent."

"What's that?"

"The truth," he said. "This war could've ended decades ago, but we lack true leadership in Rave to do what needs to be done."

That smacked too closely of Bayard's bomb. Sitting forward, I asked, "What would you do differently?"

"You're wondering if I agreed with that bomb? No, I didn't. I thought it was crass and a move of a desperate man running low on options to retain his country." Another smile. "Funny what desperation does to a person, isn't it? I'm sure you know a little something about it, considering your history."

"History?" I blinked. "I was plucked from an orphanage, same as every other *kallistrate*—"

"I'm talking much more recent history," he said, leaning back in his chair. "Tell me about this *mysterious* benefactor who wishes to give me money in exchange for my alliance."

I glanced at Kader; something felt wrong. But I chalked it up to my nerves. "When I was in Jervan, I met with a Jervanian businessman who offered me asylum in his country. After I found out about Malaske..."

I trailed off. It was clear from the look on his face that Anson didn't believe a word I was saying. His eyes glittered with an unspoken amusement that set me on edge. I wasn't nearly that amusing.

Out of the corner of my eye, I saw that Kader had shifted, and my pulse began to throb. I needed to speed things along so we could get out of here.

"This benefactor seems incredibly generous," Anson said, filling the silence. "But I suppose being the lover of the prince of Kylae has its benefits."

A gasp escaped my lips before I could stop it.

TWELVE

THEO

"W-what?"

I would've thought I'd heard incorrectly, except for Kader's uncharacteristically shocked expression. My heart thudded in my chest and the back of my neck grew warm with nerves.

"Your lover? Prince Galian? It's all over the radio tonight, although I'm sure you two were properly distracted by the festivities. It's fitting that Bayard chose a night when half the country was drunk to announce he was selling out."

Selling out? I shared a worried glance with Kader, but realized we had more pressing issues. Namely, how were we going to get out of this room alive?

"I've been very curious about you," Anson said. "To turn so quickly on Bayard after all he'd done for you. And suddenly you were flush with an unlimited supply of money that you handed over without any questions asked."

"Anson—"

"Please," he said, sitting back. "I'd love to hear what the Kylaen royal family told you to tell me. Are they interested in peace?"

I shared a glance with Kader, and he nodded. "The queen is—"

A throaty laughter erupted from him, and from the others in the room whom I'd forgotten about. A quick glance told me what I already knew—we were outnumbered. As good as Kader was, I doubted he was *that* good.

The only thing I had left to salvage this situation was to convince Anson I wasn't there to betray him.

"If I'd known you had such...elevated connections," he said. "I would've agreed to meet with you sooner. Here I thought you were a plant from Bayard. Imagine my surprise when I saw the news this afternoon."

"Mind enlightening me on the topic?" I asked with more than a little venom.

"See, that's the problem with working with Kylaens. They don't see you as human, so they're more than willing to betray you at the drop of a hat." He tutted and waved to his guards. "It's a shame, really, but I'm sure the prince will move on to another girl soon enough. And this treaty—"

"Treaty?" I gasped as his guards pulled me upright and tied my hands with rope. "W-what treaty? Anson, what the hell is going on?"

Anson laughed and patted me on the cheek. "We'll make sure to return your body to the Kylaens. Show them we aren't total barbarians. I'm sure your princeling will mourn for a bit before moving on."

"Anson—*Anson!*" I cried as one of the guards shoved a bag over my head and the room went dark. Disembodied hands pulled me from the bright room backward into the dark hallway. I prayed they wouldn't separate Kader and me, because then I'd *really* be in trouble.

I stumbled my way up the stairs and heard a car engine nearby. The door opened and I was shoved inside, my shoulder banging against a hard seat. When I didn't hear Kader next to me, I began to panic.

"Kader!" I cried.

"Right here," came the gruff response from outside the car. "Hit the floor."

I barely registered what he'd asked when I heard two bodies slamming together, then a loud crack. I screamed his name, but then remembered what he'd said and pushed myself off the seat to lie flat on the floor. More cracks, more grunts and cries. I wriggled on the floor to get the blasted bag off my head, but there wasn't much room.

"Kader!" I cried helplessly. If he was injured or...God forbid...I needed to get to him. I needed to get him back to Rosie.

The car started and shot forward, throwing me back into the seat. There was more gunfire behind us, but it faded quickly. I tried to get up, but between my bound hands, the bag over my head, and the way the car careened through the streets, I couldn't get my footing.

Finally, I shimmied around to sit on my butt and dipped my head between my legs, holding onto the bag and pulling it off.

I released a sigh of relief when I saw the bald, shiny head at the wheel.

"Kader?" I asked.

"Hrn," he grunted. "St-stay low."

I pushed myself to the front. Kader had one hand on the wheel, the other gripped against his shoulder, which was a dark, crimson color.

"Oh my God, you're hurt," I said.

"I'm fine," he said, glancing into the rearview mirror. But when he turned the wheel, the grimace was unmistakable.

God, if only Galian were here, I thought, staring at Kader's injury.

"Get the bag that was on your head," Kader said.

Hands still bound, I scooted to the backseat and picked it up with my mouth, handing it to him. He grunted in appreciation and pressed the burlap to his wound.

There was nothing but our two headlights on the dirt road and the stars and moon in the sky. I kept my gaze on the white orb, drawing strength from it, and praying that Kader and I would make it back to Norose alive. I wanted to process everything—Anson's enigmatic comments, that he now thought me a dirty Kylaen traitor—but Kader's situation was more pressing.

"How did you...I mean..."

"I always keep a razor blade in my pocket," he said. "Can't feel it when they search you. Cut the ropes, took care of the two guards, and gunned it." He grunted. "Could've done without the gunshot wound."

I chewed my lip.

"Theo, stop looking at me like I'm going to die."

"B-but—"

"I've had worse, and I'll have worse again, probably. We'll be at the safe house soon, and there's a med bag with wires to stitch me up."

Although he smiled at me, it wasn't nearly as confident as usual.

The car was swerving by the time we reached the dark house. Kader sat in the front seat and cut my binds with the razor blade.

"You're...gonna have to carry me inside," he said.

I moved under his uninjured shoulder, and he leaned all of his dead weight on me. My knees nearly buckled, but together, we made it inside. I flipped on the light and helped Kader to the large kitchen table.

He collapsed on top of it, clutching the bloody shoulder which I now saw in the full light. His shirt was drenched in red, and it dripped down his arm. His face had grown paler, but he still retained his cavalier expression.

"There's...a bag...in the pantry..." he grunted out. "And grab the whiskey, too."

I rushed to the tall door in the kitchen and procured a first aid kit and half-drunk bottle of alcohol. I handed the latter to Kader, who pulled the cork with his teeth and muttered something about Gibbs drinking all his good booze.

"W-what do you need me to do?" I asked.

"Didn't Galian teach you anything?" Kader asked with a wry smile after he'd swallowed a large gulp of the whiskey. He gritted his teeth and poured half the liquid on his open wound, screaming as it burned him.

"Kader!"

He chuckled, although it was clear he was still in pain. "You've got to get the bullet out."

"How?"

"Put on those gloves," he said, nodding to the open bag in my hand. "There might be...tongs in there too... But use your finger..." He gulped down more of the whiskey.

Trembling, I stared at the hole in his chest, but didn't move.

"Theo," Kader met my gaze, "it's okay. It'll be worse if you don't get it out."

I nodded then with a deep breath, dug my finger into the wound. Kader inhaled loudly, but he didn't cry out. It took a few slow, painstaking minutes, but I found the bullet.

"L-l-let me look at it," Kader said, grabbing my bloody hand

and pulling the bullet close to him. "G-g-good. Didn't f-fragment. N-now sew me up."

I tossed the bullet away and picked up the sutures. My shaking hands made it difficult to thread the needle, but I managed. I couldn't look at Kader, so I plunged the needle into his ripped skin and threaded it to the other side. Back and forth, I tugged the wound closed, praying I was doing this right.

When I'd finished, I could finally stomach looking at Kader, but his eyes were closed. His chest rose and fell deeply, so that, at least, was welcome news.

I pulled the bloody gloves off and sank to the floor, running my hands through my hair and letting my terrified tears fall.

I must've fallen asleep, because when I awoke, bright light shone in my face. My clothes were stiff with blood and stuck to my body uncomfortably. I was on my feet in an instant, staring at the bloody, empty table.

"I'm in here," Kader called softly.

I followed the sound of his voice and found him, shirtless, on the couch, the wound in his shoulder clean and the sutures holding. He was still pale, but some of his color had returned.

"Are you okay?" I asked.

"Look better than you," he said, nodding to my bloody clothes. "Might have a change of clothes upstairs."

I ignored him and sank into the chair across from him. "You almost died last night."

"Wouldn't be the first time." He chuckled. "For either of us."

He shifted, wincing and placing a hand on his shoulder. "But thank you. Galian will be proud of the stitch job."

"At least you didn't need a transfusion, too," I said with a half-smile. "Not sure I could've managed that." I stared at a bird, which had flown to the window. "How did Anson know about me and Galian?"

"I have no idea," Kader said, staring at the ceiling. "And until we get back to Norose, I don't think we will."

"We're going to have to wait until you're better," I said. "You can't possibly sneak onto a Jervan-bound plane with a wound like that. And we have to get all the way to Herin—"

"Good thing I've got a pilot here to fly me straight to Norose."

I stared at him. "And what am I supposed to fly?"

"You're going to steal a plane."

"You can't be serious."

"It's the last contingency plan Korina and I agreed on. If everything goes to shit—and apparently, everything has—we'll steal a plane and get back to Kylae that way."

"Just one problem," I said. "How is a Raven plane going to get into Kylaen airspace without getting blown out of the sky?"

"We've got a code—all the radar operators know what it is, just not what it's for. It'll get us a landing clearance."

"But that'll...Grieg will know what we've been up to, won't he?"

"Something tells me he always knew."

I didn't want to think about what that meant. Instead, I busied myself with making Kader comfortable. I found some blankets and helped Kader get comfortable, knowing that this part of our escape was up to me. So while he recovered, I sat upstairs in the bedroom and considered our options over a map of Rave.

The obvious choice, to me, was to take a plane from Vinolas. Being a forward operating base, it would be less secure because most resources were focused on defending Rave from Kylae. Besides that, it had been my home for nearly a decade. I knew where the fences were broken, which hangers held which planes. Lanis and I had stolen a two-seater plane before, and there were at least two more available.

Or, at least, I hoped there were. My information was six months old—and, in the case of the fence—even older. But Kader needed medical attention, and he certainly wasn't going to get it in Rave.

When night fell, I helped him get into the backseat of the car, and we set off for Vinolas. I'd flown a plane since I was twelve, but driving a car took a bit of adjusting. To boot, the dark roads made it difficult to know if I was even going in the right direction. Just after midnight, I spotted the lights, and the shape of the air control tower looming over them.

I turned off the headlights and pulled over. Kader was fast asleep in the back of the car, so I left him while I searched for a way in. I walked the length of the barbed wire fence, kicking it every few feet until I found a hole. Most of them had been put here by the new pilots, hopeful they could run away and escape the grim realities of war. But eventually, they all returned when they realized food wasn't as plentiful off base.

I squeezed through the opening without much trouble, and I made my way to the hangar. I knew this place in my sleep; at this hour, the staff would be light. Perhaps a mechanic or two. I crept around the dark perimeter until I found a stack of old wooden crates that I could climb to peer into the windows.

I searched the hangar for the two-seaters and found a pair of two-seater planes parked in the back. They were slower than the one-seaters, but we'd have the benefit of a head start. It would take them a few minutes to scramble after us, but they'd eventually catch up. Then I'd just have to hope I remembered enough of what kept had me alive for seven years.

I climbed down the crates and made my way back to the car. Kader was awake, and looking a bit more alert. "What's the plan?"

"We're going to sneak onto one of the two-seater planes," I explained, and told him the layout of the hangar. "So we'll either need to be discreet or create a diversion."

He grunted. "Diversion would be better. Give us more time to escape. Set fire to the fuel lines, maybe. It'll distract them and prevent them from coming after us right away."

My chest seized out of instinct more than fear. "You want me to blow the fuel lines? B-but that would...then the planes would be..."

He raised an eyebrow.

"Rave would be *defenseless*!" I gasped. "I can't possibly—"

"Theo, it's one fuel line in one hangar."

"But it..." The thought of disabling *that* many planes was horrifying. Especially knowing how little Bayard cared for the base itself. They might not get money to repair it for months, leaving the pilots at risk. And if Grieg found out...

But the night was slipping away fast, so whatever we were going to do, we needed to do it quickly. I half-carried Kader to the fence, then helped to protect his wounded shoulder as he slid under the hole. When we reached the hangar, I left him against the wall on the ground and climbed back onto the crates, peering inside.

My gaze kept drifting to the fuel lines. It would do what I wanted—but at what cost?

I jumped down and nodded to Kader. "Can you walk?"

"Enough," he said, pushing himself to his feet and leaning against the wall.

"Do you know what a two-seater Raven plane looks like?" I asked then added, "I mean, the difference between—"

"Yes, Theo."

"They're in the back, behind the fighter planes. As soon as I..." I swallowed. "I'll join you. I just hope they've been maintained."

He squeezed my shoulder and handed me a lighter and his knife. "It'll be fine."

I nodded and wished I believed him. "Get ready to move."

A thousand angry voices screamed in my head as I crept closer to the bright hangar opening. Fifty planes, the same model as my girl, sat in the center of the room. There were twenty fuel lines from the main tank in the center, about half were already connected to planes.

Oh my God, what am I doing?

I snuck into the hangar, keeping out of sight of the two mechanics talking with each other as they worked. Luckily for me, they weren't expecting a traitorous former Raven major to be skulking around, so I crawled along the oil-stained floor to one of the unattached fuel lines.

"Just a shame, you know? Do you think it's true?"

"She was a bit screwy after her time in Mael. Bet they brainwashed her."

I froze. They were talking about me. I swallowed all the questions I had and listened for the sound of their wrenches to start moving again. I clicked the fuel line into place and waited for them to notice.

"Kallistrate's too smart for that. Bet she got a nice retirement, too. Too bad she has to bed the princeling. Can you imagine?"

Glancing to their shadows on the ground, I quietly scurried to the next plane with a fuel line nearby and waited. The two mechanics continued discussing their wild theories about why I might've done this horrible thing I had no idea about and I was able to connect three more planes.

"*Hey!*"

I craned my neck to the source of the sound, and my heart dropped. They'd spotted Kader on the other side of the hangar. He met my gaze under the plane and then ran for the two-seater as the mechanics called for security.

"*Shit,*" I hissed. There were only a few connected, but it would have to do. Begging forgiveness from my country and the planes I was about to destroy, I sliced the nearby fuel line and let the liquid gold spew out onto the ground. Backing out from under the plane, I clicked the lighter, threw it, and ran like hell.

Beep. Beep. Beep.

The attack alarm began to squeal, and I had flashbacks to my younger years, hearing and dreading that sound as it had meant the Kylaens were attacking. Only this time, the enemy was me.

"Fire! *Fire!* Get the hose!"

"No, stop them!"

I ignored the voices and jumped onto the wing of the two-seater. Kader was already in the backseat, his gaze on the visage behind me. I slid into the pilot's seat and my breath caught as I took in the destruction I'd caused. Large, yellow-orange flames danced to the ceiling of the hangar, and a thick billow of black smoke was filling the room.

"Theo, we need to go before—"

"I know," I said, rushing through my ingrained flight checklist as fast as my brain would work. The twin-propellers began to turn, and the sound and smell of a plane brought me small comfort. I released the brake and we rolled forward, cutting through the smoke and fire and exiting the hangar into the dark night of the runway. I saw pilots scrambling from the dormitory building, and I knew if we didn't get out of there soon, we'd be done for.

Without looking back at the destruction I'd caused, I punched it, and we took off into the dark sky.

I watched the sun rise over the Madion Sea, and let quiet tears fall down my face. Kader and I were safe, for now, but larger questions remained. What would we do about Anson? How would we possibly get Rave to peace with Kylae if even the rebels wouldn't listen? And who had told him about me and Galian?

The plane glided easily through the air, reminding me of a time when this was all I knew. Flying and defending my nation. I knew who was right, who was wrong, and what I needed to do to survive. And now, I didn't know which side was right, or if I was on it. I'd destroyed a hangar full of Raven planes. I'd attacked my own people, my own *'neechais* and *'niichais.*

And for what? My own self-preservation? Saving Kader's life?

"Incoming aircraft, identify yourself."

I jumped; I hadn't realized how close we'd come to Kylae already. But before I could answer, Kader's gruff, but weak, voice came through the microphone, *"This is S.O. Nine-Twenty-Seven."*

There was a too-long pause then a new voice came on the radio.

"Kader? Thank God, are you together?"

"Rhys?" I said.

"We were so worried about you. You're cleared to land. We've got...a lot to talk about. I'll wait until you get here to fill you in."

Gone was the jovial prince who'd poked me into revealing my deepest secrets. The voice on the other end of the radio was tense. Something truly horrible had occurred, so bad that I almost wanted to turn the plane around. But I didn't have enough fuel for that, and Kader needed medical attention.

Conscious of my injured passenger, I landed the plane as gently as I could onto the airfield, amazed at how much nicer it was than those in Rave. As soon as I taxied off the runway, two Kylaen guards were waiting for me, directing me to wheel my plane into a large hangar.

My heart thudded against my ribcage. The guards motioned for me to stop in the middle of the hangar, and I shut off the engines, unstrapping quickly and climbing on top of my seat to help Kader out of his restraints. He was pale, but lucid, and smacked my hands away when I tried to unhook him.

"I'm injured, not dead," he barked, although he allowed me to help him out of the plane.

"Theo!" Galian's voice drew my attention, but the smile died on my face when I saw who stood next to him. Rhys, their father...

...and President Bayard.

THIRTEEN

Theo

It seemed a dream, a nightmare. Maybe I'd fallen asleep piloting the plane. Maybe I was dead. That seemed more logical than seeing the president of my country standing next to the king of its mortal enemy.

Kader, still standing inside the plane with his arm over my shoulder, made a noise. Against all my better judgement, I helped him out of the plane and toward the impending disaster waiting for us.

"Welcome back, Major," Grieg said, and my skin crawled as he spoke to me. "I'm glad you and Sergeant Kader arrived safely. Or, as safe as can be expected." His gaze landed on Kader, and presumably, the red blotch on his shirt.

"W...what's going on here?" I said, finally finding my voice. "And what *the hell* are you doing here, Bayard?"

"Manners, Major. I'm still your commander-in-chief," he said, with a smugness that sent my pulse into overdrive.

"Like hell you are," I snarled. "You put me into a bomb, if you'll remember. You were going to *hang* me for treason, you son of a bitch."

"And I still might," he said lightly. "But as it stands, I have good news for us all. Or, rather, Your Majesty, I'll allow you the honors."

"We've agreed to an immediate ceasefire between our countries," Grieg said with the sort of smile that said he was a man who'd just gotten everything he wanted.

Bile rose in my throat. I knew what was coming next, but like this whole scene, I didn't want to believe it was actually happening. "Under what conditions?"

"After long last, Rave is returning home to Kylaen rule," Bayard said.

It took everything in me not to vomit all over the floor. I couldn't believe this. I just *couldn't*. Not after being pulled from an orphanage. Not after the years of flight training, never knowing if I'd make it home. Not after parroting lies about Rave and independence and sacrifices. Not after looking at hundreds of scarred, maimed soldiers who had given up their bodies and souls to a cause that was bigger than they were.

Bayard had thrown it all away out of desperation.

"We'll be signing the treaty in three months," Grieg said and then, when I couldn't possibly have thought myself horrified at anything else, he added, "At your wedding."

The air left my chest. "W-wedding?"

"It will be perfect," Grieg said. "The two of you as a symbol for the reunification of the Kingdom of Kylae. Kylae's third son and Rave's daughter."

I took a step back, covering my mouth to keep the contents of my stomach from spewing out.

"I thought you'd be happy, Theo," Bayard said, crossing his

arms over his chest. "You were *so concerned* with brokering peace between Kylae and Rave. Now you have it, and you can be with your *amichai*."

The room was spinning and I realized I wasn't breathing. But how could I? The world was moving too fast, this made no sense, and yet it made *complete* sense, and how could we not have seen this coming and how could Bayard *do* this to our country, and...

"Tend to your fiancée, Galian. She's about to faint."

I turned to my left and saw him standing next to his brother, his face white and Kylaen, and I hated everything about him in that moment.

GALIAN

When I'd heard from Rhys that Theo had radioed in, I'd had mixed feelings of relief and horror. Selfishly, I'd wanted her out of Kylae, away from this mess. It might've even been better for her if she'd died, rather than hear what was to become of her country. And if she was returning to Kylae, she clearly had no idea what was waiting for her here.

I'd watched my father's gleeful delivery of the news, powerless to stop it. Then she'd looked at me as she had the first day on the island, when she'd hated me, and my heart broke.

"You *fucking asshole!*" she screamed, her voice echoing in the room. "You—you're going along with this?"

"Theo, no," I said, rushing over to her.

"Don't touch me," she snarled, backing up. "Don't you *ever* touch me again."

"Come, Tedwin," Grieg said, as if Theo hadn't just exploded at me. "Let's let our two lovers hash out their quarrel. I'd like to continue our discussion on the barethium mines."

"As you wish, Your Majesty," Bayard said, following my father out of the hangar like the little lapdog he was.

"Kader, we need to get you to a hospital," Rhys said, speaking up for the first time.

Kader, to his credit, agreed, and hung his good arm around Rhys. Together, they slowly limped toward the doors my father and Bayard had left through.

Then, it was just me and Theo.

"How could you do this to me?" Theo whispered, her gaze faraway. "How could you..."

I stepped forward, even as she backed away from me. "I had nothing to do with this—"

"Then why are you here?" she screamed. "How could you sit here with the rest of them and just...say *nothing*—"

"Oh, trust me, I said plenty," I snapped back. "But I was more concerned about *you* and—"

"Galian," she sank to the floor, a tear running down her face, "what've they done? Why did this happen? Why didn't anyone stop it?"

I knelt in front of her, wiping away her tears. "I don't know, Theo. I found out at that *stupid* party. Grieg made the announcement in front of everyone and introduced Bayard and... God, Theo, it was all I could do not to be sick."

"But you...." She shook her head. "But you're here now?"

"Because we hadn't heard from Kader in days," I said, finally letting some of the fear creep into my voice. "Because the news broke that you and I were...and you were supposed to be meeting with the rebels...and, *God,* Theo, I didn't know what to think. I'm just so thankful you're all right."

She stared at me like I had two heads. "I'm *not* all right, Galian. This...this treaty..." Her breath came in short puffs, and I placed a hand on her back as she buried her head in her hands and cried. "W-what happened? How did we not *know?*"

"Mom's still trying to figure it all out," I said. "But I want you to know, I...I need you to know I wasn't a part of this. I don't..." I swallowed the ache. "I don't want to be a part of this wedding. I don't want to be a pawn in their media game."

Her sobs came harder now, and I couldn't help myself as I pulled her close to me. Relief washed over me as she let me comfort her. There was a new wedge between us, but she wasn't unreachable yet.

"We have a problem." Rhys came running into the room.

"Is it Kader?" I asked, lifting my head.

"No, it's..." He sighed. "Father's tipped off the media. There's hundreds of photographers out there. They saw Father leaving with Bayard, but they...they want a photo of you and Theo."

Theo hiccupped against my chest, her red eyes wide with shock, and didn't seem to be in the room anymore.

"No fucking way," I snarled, holding her tighter. "Bring the car around here."

He closed his eyes. "Father's ordered—"

"Fuck him. Hasn't he ruined enough today?" I said, wishing I could magically transport Theo and myself far away.

Rhys shrugged off his coat and tossed it at me. "That's the best I can do right now. We just need to get back to the castle and...and try to figure out where to go from here."

As expected, the crowd outside the hangar was ten people deep. I shielded us with Rhys's coat as best I could, following Johar's footsteps and keeping Theo pressed tightly to me. She still wore the stunned expression, as if she'd mentally clocked out, but sat down in the car, moving to the other side as Rhys and I climbed in behind her.

Once the door was shut, she pulled her knees to her chest and buried her head in them, saying nothing.

I stared at her for a moment before wrenching my gaze to Rhys, who ran a hand through his mussed hair. "Fucking animals."

"What do you expect? They haven't had a story this *juicy* in ages," I said.

"Don't blame me," he snapped back. "This wasn't my fault—"

"I'm having a hard time believing that. How the *hell* could something like this have happened without us knowing about it?"

"Enough, both of you," Kader barked from the front seat. "We knew Grieg was getting better at covering his tracks. And your mother wouldn't have kept this from you if she'd known."

"Shouldn't you be going to the hospital?" I said, with a dirty glare at Rhys.

"I'll go to the hospital after I know what you know," Kader said. "Because we knew nothing until we were ambushed at Anson's."

"So you met with him?" Rhys said.

"That seems like awfully shitty timing," I said, folding my arms over my chest.

"I think it was just that—shitty," Kader said. "Bayard had declared the day a national holiday. Anson was just taking advantage of the distraction. As was, apparently, Bayard."

"What did you find out?" Rhys asked.

"A whole lot of nothing, except that Anson knew we were there on behalf of the queen," Kader said.

"I'm just thankful you two are safe," Rhys said, looking at Theo, still curled in a ball on the other side of the car. She hadn't moved at all. His face grew softer. "Theo, we're not giving up. This is just a setback, not a surrender."

"What did Bayard get in return for delivering the country?" Kader asked.

"What do you think?" Rhys said with a grimace. "Lifetime appointment as Rave's governor. And full access to the barethium stores."

The car went silent. But my gaze remained on Theo, my hands itching to check her pulse for signs of life. I tried to take her hand in mine, but she snatched it away.

The castle was swarming with photographers, but they remained on the other side of the gate as Johar pulled the car around to the residential side of the palace. With assurances to me and Rhys that she'd call as soon as Kader was admitted, they left us to head to the hospital.

Stony-faced and silent, Theo followed me and Rhys through the castle, ignoring the curious looks from the staff. I led her into my apartment, and opened the door to my bedroom. Without a word, she passed me into the dark space, and I heard the squeak of the mattress as she climbed onto it.

"I'll be right outside," I said, lingering in the doorway. When she didn't respond, I turned and closed the door behind me.

"This fucking sucks," Rhys said, helping himself to some whiskey I'd kept in my liquor closet. Bypassing a glass, he swigged directly from the bottle.

I didn't disagree, but I kept my attention on the closed door, and the girl who lay on the other side of it. I didn't care how selfish it was: the treaty, Bayard's betrayal, barethium, the war—all of it paled in comparison to knowing Theo hated me. As often as I'd envisioned the first night she spent the night in my bed...this wasn't it.

"She's just in shock," Rhys said after a while. "I would be too."

I nodded and stole the booze from him.

"Well, congratulations on your wedding," Rhys said hollowly.

I snorted. "Do you even know how much it kills me to say I don't want to marry her? Rhys, that's all I've wanted to do for a year. And now he's ruined that. Incredible."

He made a noise and sat up. "Except he hasn't. I mean, he doesn't have to."

I took another drink. "What?"

"Why don't you two just go get married now?" he said with a smile on his face. "That way, he won't have that hanging over you. I mean, unless you had your heart set on having a big, televised wedding."

"There's just one little problem with that," I said dryly. "Theo can't stand me."

"Use some of that princeling charm and win her back," Rhys said. "She fell in love with you once, didn't she?"

The phone rang, and I crossed the room to answer it. It was Johar, telling me that Kader had been checked out by Maitland and didn't require any further surgery.

"Eli's asking you to come down so you can tell Rosie he's fine to be released," Johar said with a chuckle. *"She doesn't believe Maitland."*

"I'll be right down," I said, wondering which of my mother's guards could give me a ride as I hung up the phone. I told Rhys what Johar had said and ran a hand over my face. "I don't want to leave Theo but..."

"Go," he said, settling the bottle next to him. "I'll be here if she needs anything."

I found Snyder downstairs, and he was more than willing to drive me to the hospital, even though he confessed he wasn't too great at driving around photographers. Secretly, I was hoping he'd sideswipe a couple. But, sadly, we arrived at the hospital without any incidents.

When I stepped out of the car, I was peppered with questions about Theo, my engagement, if I was happy that I was being forced to marry a Raven woman I barely knew. I ignored the questions, as usual, and entered into the comparatively silent hospital. Even though the questions had stopped, the hurried whispers as I walked by continued, so I almost sprinted to the nurse's station where I found Rima.

"Dr. Helmuth, surprised to see you here."

"Which room is he in?" I asked.

"Room four," she said. "About this wedding—"

"Save it for later," I said, waving her off and making my way down the hall. A couple other nurses tried to stop me, but I ignored them. When I reached room four, I rapped on the door with my knuckles.

"Come in," Rosie answered.

I cracked the door and peeked inside. Kader was sitting up, looking very healthy and not the least bit like he'd been shot a day or so before. Rosie, however, was pale and her hair a mess of frizz.

She stood when she saw me, her hand over her mouth. "Theo's not with you?"

I shook my head. "She's...well, she's..."

"Understandable," Kader said, waving me inside.

I closed the door and crossed to the bed, where I gripped his good arm and smiled. "I'm glad you're okay. I was really worried about you two."

"Eh," he said with a snort. "I've been through worse—"

"And you won't again," Rosie said, smacking him lightly on the arm.

Their married bickering put me at ease, so I sank into the chair next to the bed. "This is a mess, isn't it?"

"That's putting it mildly," Kader said. "I never thought Bayard would go this far." He paused. "And I never considered your father to be a forgiving man."

"This benefits him more than Bayard," I said. "It effectively shuts up the peaceful half of the ministers, and the warmongering ones get what they want, too. Rave's back, and the fighting has stopped."

"Any of them upset about the particulars of the ceasefire?"

"I'm sure some are, but they're not willing to speak out about it just yet," I said, glancing out the window at the Madion Sea.

"I need to speak with your mother—"

"You'll do no such thing," Rosie snapped. "We had a deal, Eli. Next injury you sustained, you're out."

Kader cleared his throat and patted her gently on the hand. "Of course, Rositanna. Do you think you could go see the nurse about getting lunch?"

Rosie softened, just a bit, before releasing his hand and walking toward the door. Before she left, she turned to glare at me. "And don't you *dare* release him before tomorrow morning."

Almost reflexively, I saluted her. She seemed satisfied and closed the door behind her.

Kader let out a breath. "Could've done without you calling my wife. Do you know how many injuries I've hidden from her over the past five years? This is nothing."

I plucked a pair of gloves out of the nearby box and examined the wound. "Kader, this thing is huge."

"Theo did a good job stitching me up. She was scared shitless, but she did it."

I pulled the gloves off and slumped down onto a nearby chair. "She won't even look at me."

"She's in shock, Galian," Kader replied. "After what we went through to get home, finding out all her work had been for nothing was...well..." He blew air out between his lips, and a storm of emotions raged beneath his eyes. "Shocking. What do you hear from your mother?"

I shook my head. "I haven't been able to get time alone with her yet. She's been busy trying to sort out what we know and how we didn't know it sooner."

"If anyone can figure that out, it's your mother," Kader said so firmly that I almost believed him. "And Theo will come around. She always does."

"Will she?" I said, the memory of her shoving me away stinging the back of my mind. "This is different. She hasn't looked at me that way since...since the island. I'm worried she might've been pushed too far, and I won't be able to reach her. And I'm scared...I'm scared of what she'll do."

"You just have to show her that hope's not lost."

"Rhys thinks I should just throw her over my shoulder and marry her already."

"Rhys is a smart man," Kader said with a nod, seeming to like the idea the more he thought about it. "It removes the emotion and turns this thing back into what it actually is—political manipulation. We can fight political manipulation."

"I doubt she'd marry me right now," I said heavily.

"You've just got to get her out of Kylae for a bit. Help her remember why you two fell in love," Kader said. "I'll fly."

"Oh no," I said, standing to gently push him back down. "You aren't going anywhere. You were shot less than a day ago—"

"Just a flesh wound." He cracked a grin, as if to show me he wasn't really in pain, but he was still pale, and I was still a doctor.

"No way."

"Who do you expect to marry you then?"

"Is this just an excuse to get out of the hospital before Rosie chains you up?"

"Yes." He didn't even blink.

I mumbled something about agreeing with her as I peeled back the bandage on his shoulder. The sutures were tight, the skin around it healthy and pink. I replaced the bandage and crossed my arms over my chest.

"Think about it this way," Kader said, with an oddly pleading look on his face. "If you come with me, you won't have to discharge me. I'm still under a physician's care, aren't I?"

I gave him a dry look.

"Look, as much as I want to get out of here, I'm also worried about Theo. You two need a win. Hell, we all need a win right now. And what better way than to celebrate a union?"

FOURTEEN

THEO

I watched the sun's light grow longer on the ground as it moved across the sky. I wasn't even sure how long I'd been there, or how I'd known that this was Galian's room. My mind had shut down when I saw Bayard with Grieg, when they'd told me how they were going to ruin my country.

There were flashing lights when we'd left the hangar for the car. I vaguely remembered Galian using his jacket to shield us, and how he'd protected me from their questions and comments. But once we'd gotten inside the car, I'd kept my distance from him. The journey to the castle, and the subsequent walk to this dark room, were a blur.

Now there was just the dying light on the floor, and the crushing sadness of reality pressing on my windpipe.

When I considered the years of my life given toward the cause of independence, toward Bayard, I felt sick. When I thought of the thousands of children who'd given their lives for him, I wanted to throw something across the room.

What sort of lies was Emilie Mondra feeding the Raven people? Did they, as usual, believe her? What sort of narrative could she craft to make this disgusting treaty go over well with the Raven people, who were so beaten down and weary of war? Or perhaps her strategy was as simple as distracting them with a wedding. It wouldn't be the first time she'd proposed it.

Yet again, I was a puppet, the plaything of politicians, but this time they'd taken something pure and beautiful and twisted it for their evil purposes. As much as I hated to admit it, they might've succeeded. Logically, I knew that Galian had nothing to do with his father's machinations. That if there'd been even the slightest hint that Kader and I had been discovered, Korina wouldn't have sent me back to Rave. But my heart was aching, and Galian was the last person I wanted to help soothe it.

Running away seemed like a good option. I'd never run from anything in my life—not from conscription, not from planes in the sky. But this was an unwinnable effort, that had become clear to me. Grieg was simply too powerful and Bayard too ruthless to succeed against them.

There was a soft rap against the door. "Theo?"

"Go away."

"C'mon, you can't just mope in here all day." Rhys sounded drunk, and when I lifted my head, I saw him leaning against the doorway with a bottle in his hand. "At least come have a drink with me."

"Go away."

"Gally told me to look after you," he said, inviting himself into the room and plopping down on a nearby chair. "Wanted to make sure you hadn't offed yourself yet."

"I'm so glad you can take this situation so lightly."

"Booze helps," he said, offering me the bottle. "Tomorrow, we'll deal with the hangover and get down to business."

I sat up, his attempts at humor falling flat. "I want to leave. I have a plane."

"Do you really think Father would allow that?"

"I don't care. I'll figure out a way."

"I'm sure you would, Theo." He settled back into the seat. "But now's not the time to lose our heads. We've been surprised, and we had to retreat, but the war isn't over yet."

I snorted. "According to Bayard and Grieg, it is."

"There's a ceasefire. That, at least, we can work with," Rhys said. "The rest isn't set in stone. But at least people aren't dying—"

"Yet," I said. "Because it's only a matter of time before Kylae rebuilds their barethium mines in Rave and we're back to square one."

"We won't let that happen—"

"And how do you presume to do that, Rhys?" I said.

"Herin," he said, holding out his hand to help me out of the excessively large bed. "The queen thinks Herin might still have a little leverage, if we can convince them to help us."

I stared at his offered hand, but didn't take it. "Herin has no power. Isn't that why they ended the airplane parts transfer?"

"We're exploring all our options," Rhys said, his hand still outstretched. "Mom's asked her squad to take a VTO over there. With everyone distracted by the wedding fiasco, we might be able to get a ship out unnoticed. Getting back's the hard part, but..." He cracked a grin. "That's up to you."

His meaning was clear, but I wasn't sure how I felt about it. "Are you really allowing me to leave your country and never return?"

"I'm giving you the option, yeah, because I like you, Theo, and not just because my brother's crazy about you." He finally retracted his hand and folded his arms across his chest. "This isn't fair to you, not after what you've already done for us. So if you want to get the hell out of this country, I'm gonna help you do it."

I should've been relieved; instead, I found it even harder to breathe. If I disappeared to Herin, I'd be leaving my country in the hands of Bayard and Grieg. Even after everything I'd been through, it was still my duty to fight for Rave, even if the battle was hopeless.

And then, of course, leaving meant I'd be saying goodbye to Galian forever.

"How about this?" Rhys said after my long silence. "Go to Herin. Take some time to think about what you want. Know that if you choose to come back, we're not going to stop fighting. But if you choose to go, no one would blame you for it. In any case, Johar is downstairs, waiting with the car."

The streets of Norose were filled with people deep in conversation as Johar and I drove by them. Most looked confused, angry even. They huddled in front of shops and cafes with furrowed brows and shaking heads. The people of Kylae were not on board with this treaty, and that, at least, improved my opinion of them.

I'd decided somewhere between leaving Galian's room and meeting Johar that I wouldn't be coming back. Maybe in a few months, I'd send word to Galian, and if he still wanted me, he could come find me.

A few moments later, I'd changed my mind and decided to

return.

But now...now I was sure that I was going to leave forever.

We rolled to a stop at an intersection and I saw my face staring back at me. A television screen inside a cafe bore my photo next to Galian's. Something sharp jabbed me in the ribs and I looked away.

On some level, I hated this manipulation. Grieg must've bargained that my love for Galian would keep me in the country. Knowing this made it easier to leave out of pure spite.

But leaving meant saying goodbye.

And round and round I went.

I almost wanted to strike up a conversation with Johar, if only to stop the angry war in my head, but I doubted we had anything to talk about but the present situation. And I was sure she would offer me no guidance.

The city behind us, we sped through the Kylaen countryside toward the northern base we'd be leaving from. Sleep tugged at the backs of my eyes, but my stress and worry kept me awake.

To return or not.

To be with Galian and unwillingly be a party to a treaty I hated, or to disappear in protest. There was no fighting. Not any fight I could win.

The devil on my shoulder reminded me that I knew nothing of the treaty, that it could be better than I feared. After all, the war was over, the conscription of children had ended. Rave would no longer have to defend her shores—

Because they were no longer hers. They now belonged to Kylae. Even if Bayard remained in charge, he was only concerned with his own wellbeing and self-preservation. He wouldn't blink when Grieg let loose his barethium miners. Together, they'd convince the Raven people that it was best, even as Grieg enslaved us.

How could I possibly consider leaving when my people were facing such odds? I couldn't turn my back on them now. I needed to return.

But how could I fight when I had no weapons? If there was some hope—some small light in the dark—maybe I'd stay. But my faith in the goodness of this world had been shaken. If we'd been this blindsided, how could we possibly fight back? As it was, I might just make things worse.

No, I decided very firmly. I wouldn't return.

That was where I'd landed when the car arrived at the base. We drove straight into the airstrip where the VTO craft was waiting. But when I got out of the car, Johar stayed in.

"I'm not on this mission," she said, speaking for the first time in hours. "But good luck to you."

I nodded my thanks, though I didn't like the idea of getting on a plane with unfamiliar people. But the man sitting on the bottom of the ship was anything but a stranger.

"K-Kader!" I gasped. "Who let you out of the hospital?"

"Me," he grunted, pushing himself to stand. "I'm fine. Let's go."

"You were *shot*. You can't possibly go on a mission. You need a week—maybe two. What about Rosie? What about—"

He waved his good hand to quiet me. "I'll be gone six hours, at most."

I peered inside the ship. There was no one else onboard.

"This isn't a mission to Herin," I said slowly. "You guys are letting me...letting me leave, aren't you?"

He nodded. "I wanted to be the one to take you there."

I was touched, but at the same time, fear shot through me. This was it. I was really leaving. I was putting all of this behind me, and if I went, I could never return. Not without feeling the wrath of Grieg.

"What'll happen to you and Galian?" I asked.

"We'll survive. Though it may take him a few years," Kader said with a small smirk. "I can tell him you said goodbye."

I took a step back before I could stop myself. "Y-yeah. That would be nice. Tell him...tell him I'll send word for him. Eventually."

Kader nodded and glanced at the ship. "Well, it's now or never."

Numbly, I followed him onto the ship and took the passenger's seat beside him. My pulse raced as the overhead engines roared to life, the blades whipping the air before lifting us into flight. I fought back tears as the base grew smaller.

"W-wait," I said above the noise. "Can we make a stop first?"

"We can't take this thing back to Norose—"

"No," I said, swallowing hard. "I want to go...to go back to the island. Just one more time."

Kader nodded. "I had a feeling you'd say that."

I stepped out onto the beach and breathed in the salty air. The green trees greeted me as old friends, the sand crumbling beneath my feet was a sturdy reminder of the person I was a year ago. Everything in front of me was familiar, welcoming. Real.

I was home.

"We don't have long," Kader said behind me. "If we're headed to Herin, even less. So say your goodbyes quickly."

But there was no one to say goodbye to.

The call of nostalgia drew me off the beach and toward our camp. I saw an aged mark on the tree that Galian had made and I pressed my hand against the groove. I half-expected him to be waiting for me around the campfire. And when he wasn't, his absence was palpable.

"What am I doing?" I whispered, sitting down in front of the remnants of our survival. I was running away—that wasn't who I was. Not only that, but I was running from the one person who'd always stood by me.

But to be with him in this way, to have our love permanently attached to this disgusting treaty made me sick. And I was growing disillusioned with my own ability to see the dangers before they bit me in the ass.

I groaned and buried my head in my hands, not knowing what to do, and missing Galian's even-tempered responses. He always knew how to draw my worries out like poison from a wound. He could talk me through the unsurmountable until it seemed silly to have ever feared it.

And I was running away from that? What was wrong with me?

Oh yeah, the treaty. The horrible treaty.

The worst part—the very worst part—was I wanted to marry him. I wanted to be with him until my dying breath. It killed me that I could see the manipulation as clearly as *Prima Anela* had been manipulating the hearts and minds of my countrymen.

I stared at what was left of our fire, and I missed him. Damn it all, I missed him so very much. Enough to ignore the smarter option, which was to run away to a country where no one had ever heard my name. It would, inevitably, lead to less heartache, but...what kind of life would I have? I'd be half a heart without him.

Just thinking about the look on his face when he found out I'd left without saying goodbye drew fresh tears to my eyes, and I let them fall. After all, there was no one else on the island to see my misery, no one to take advantage of it.

"Well, I'm glad you're crying *before* I surprised you this time."

I closed my eyes and balled my fists. "You son of a bitch."

FIFTEEN

GALIAN

I'd hidden out in the back of the VTO, but with the way Theo had shuffled onboard, I doubted she would've noticed me even if I'd been sitting in the front seat. Indecision played on her face for the entire flight, and the way she'd looked when Kader mentioned me sealed the deal. She wasn't going anywhere, but I just had to let her come to her own conclusions.

So I'd let her wander, keeping my distance as she explored our home and watching as she rested against a tree, contemplating her next move. Still, I hadn't been able to help myself when she'd started crying.

"You are a complete asshole, you know that?" she said, although the smile on her face told me she wasn't unhappy to see me.

"What'd I do this time?" I asked, walking into the campsite.

"Let me wallow in my misery. Were you on the damned VTO?"

I shrugged, and she shook her head, wiping tears from her eyes. Then, she stood and in three steps, crossed the camp and fell into my arms. I held her in silence for a moment, amazed at the relief I felt to have her in my arms, in our home.

"I'm sorry I..." she began. "I'm sorry."

I pulled back, needing to look her in the eyes. "Theo, you have to know I had *nothing* to do with—"

"I know," she said, taking her place against my shoulder again. "I'm just so...tired of being played. I'm tired of losing."

"So you decided to run away without me?" I asked. "You know I'd go to the ends of the earth with you."

She didn't respond for a long time. "I don't know what I want. Other than this. Right now. This I want. You and me here on this island. Where there's nobody trying to ruin anything or manipulate us or anything like that."

"Just wolves that want to eat us."

She snorted.

"Let's go for a walk," I said, releasing her from my arms. "I want to see the old place."

She slid her fingers around mine, and we strolled through the lush forest. She stopped at a mark on the tree—one I'd made to show the way back to our camp. "You know, it's been a year since we crashed here."

I smiled. "I know. What a year, huh?"

We continued walking, while listening to the birds in the trees. Even after all these months, these paths were familiar to me. She'd been right that this place felt like home—more home than the castle in Norose, or even my apartment with Martin. Or maybe it felt that way because Theo was here with me.

"So Kader..."

"I think he wanted one more hurrah before Rosie locked him

up," I said with a laugh. I wasn't eager to return to Norose and hear what Kader's wife thought about me breaking him out of the hospital and flying to an uninhabited island.

"So he's out?" she asked, and sounded nervous by the idea. "No more working for Korina?"

"Not sure. He's out for a month, at least." I cocked my head in her direction. "Thinking about returning now?"

"I don't know," she said heavily. "If I return to Kylae, I'm part of their plan. If I don't return, I leave my people to the mercy of the Kylaens."

"Being part of their plan isn't necessarily the worst option," I said slowly.

She stopped in her tracks, giving me her signature "are-you-kidding-me" look.

I couldn't help myself and kissed her nose. "I'm saying it makes you and I *valuable*. They can't have a wedding without the bride and groom. In some ways, they've actually put themselves at risk by making us—their enemies—the centerpiece of their plan."

She still looked unconvinced, but didn't interrupt.

"If this goes like I *think* it's going to, they're going to be parading us in front of cameras nonstop. But what they can't control is what we *say* in front of those cameras."

"Yeah, they can. When I was in Rave, I was barely allowed to speak—"

"You spoke plenty when you went off script during your speech," I reminded her.

She shook her head. "That's different."

"How so?"

"I still said basically what Bayard wanted. If you and I were to stand in front of the international media and talk about how we think Rave should be an independent nation, they'd cut the feed—or worse."

"Ah-hah, but my father's grip on the media has grown weaker," I said.

She considered me for a moment then shook her head again. "*Amichai*, it doesn't matter. If we go left, they'll already be there. We can't win—we've been trying."

"There's one thing we haven't tried," I said, my pulse spiking when she said *amichai*. "Fighting them together."

"And what can you and I accomplish together that we couldn't apart?"

"Hear me out," I said, taking her hands. "Theo, when I landed on this island a year ago, I was...useless. I was selfish and ignorant. More than that, I couldn't even take care of myself in Norose, let alone on an island. But you taught me how to skin a rabbit and make a fire and make drinkable water from the sea. And because of you, I got home. Because of you, I became a better person."

She shrugged. "I wouldn't have been able to if you hadn't saved my life—"

"*Exactly*," I said with a grin. "Theo, we've made a lot of progress apart, but imagine what we can do now that we're *together*. For fuck's sake, we survived two months on an island with nothing but our wits. And more importantly," I brushed a strand of hair out of her face, "we fell in love despite all the odds. You *hated* my guts, remember?"

"Still do from time to time."

"Theo, come on."

She sighed loudly, taking her hands out of mine. "Sure, we fell in love. And that's great. But it's one thing to fall for the person you're surviving with every day, and quite another to convince two whole nations that their leaders are taking them down the wrong path—*and quite another* to get your father and Bayard to scrap the treaty in favor of true independence."

"And I thought we'd starve to death in a week," I said. "Together, we survived two months. Nothing's impossible."

"Princeling, you could win a prize for naïveté," she said with a bit of a laugh.

"You've told me that before," I said. "But you know I'm right. We can do this, Theo. You and me. Fully out there together. We'll show the world that it's possible for a Kylaen and a Raven to get along."

She almost looked convinced, but then her shoulders dropped. "But this wedding..."

"What we need to do is take the emotion out of it," I said as my pulse began to race. "We need to see this wedding for what it is. Pure political bullshit. And if we decide not to show up because they've not done what we asked, then that's that."

She nodded, a little sadly, and began walking, but I tugged on her hand to keep her here.

"But that doesn't mean we can't just go ahead and get married now."

Then, heart pounding, I fell to one knee.

"Theo, you are the person I want to see when I wake up, the person I want to see when I go to sleep. You make me a better man, you make me *want* to be a better man. You inspire me, you excite me, you mesmerize me every day. I want to be by your side fighting every battle with you until the day I die."

I reached into my back pocket and pulled out the simple gold band I'd "borrowed" from the royal treasury.

"Theo, will you marry me?"

THEO

My pulse thudded in my ears and I stared at this man, on his knee, pouring his heart out to me and asking me to be his wife.

I was skeptical. I'd been burned too many times by Bayard's machinations and Grieg's plans. I'd played right into his hands more times than I could count—and nearly lost my life in the process. Galian was crazy to think that simply being together would make a difference.

And yet...the simple act of him kneeling before me, asking me to marry him, knowing that we *could* keep our love protected from the politics and the treachery, somehow filled me with so much hope for the future.

"Theo?"

He sounded nervous, which made sense considering I'd been standing silently in front of him without reaction. Still kneeling before me, he was a picture of nervous innocence. And I knew in that moment I'd be a fool to ever let him out of my sight again.

"Of course I will, *amichai*."

He stood and wrapped me in his arms in one movement, lifting me off the ground. He held me for a moment, and his relief that I'd accepted flooded through me. Or perhaps, it was my relief. In all that had gone wrong, *this* would go right. I would marry my *amichai* in—

"Wait a minute," I said, as he set me down. "You want to get married *right now*?"

"Yeah, and it's a good thing you said yes," he said, pressing his forehead to mine. "Because it would've been a really awkward trip back to Kylae if you'd said otherwise."

I laughed harder than I had in months, filled with so much joy and excitement I might've burst. He grinned and released me, but took my hand and led me back past our camp to the beach, where Kader stood barefoot on the beach, wearing a dress uniform. He held a book in his hand, his face uncharacteristically warm and inviting.

We stopped in front of him, and Galian took both my hands with an eager grin on his face. "Let's do this, Kader."

Kader cleared his throat and opened the book to one of the dog-eared pages.

"This passage was read at my own wedding, and I'll repeat it as a blessing that you two will find the same happiness we did. At least until my wife finds out I left the hospital, and she murders me."

"Your sacrifice will not be in vain," Galian said solemnly, and I stifled a giggle.

Kader rolled his eyes but began to read. "They say love is hard, but love is quite easy. Love is infatuation, love is caring for one another. Love is stepping outside yourself for someone else. But what makes love *appear* difficult is life."

He paused and gave us a knowing look.

"Life is not fair, nor is it easy or predictable. Life is full of circumstances outside of our control and people with their own intentions. This life tempts us with easy solutions to hard problems that simply cause more problems. But when two people truly care for one another, their love can endure even the most difficult challenges. If they work together to overcome them."

Tears had begun to gather in the corners of my eyes, and I turned to my *amichai*. He chewed the inside of his cheek, his eyes revealing the emotion underneath them. I squeezed his hand and caught his gaze. As he smiled at me, I could've flown around the world.

"Galian Neoptolemos Helmuth, do you promise to love and cherish Theophilia Kallistrate? To stand by her side against all enemies, to give her hope when she is without, to care for her in her times of need, as long as you both shall live?"

A chill ran down my spine as he spoke. "I do."

"And do you, Theophilia Kallistrate, promise to love and cherish Galian. To give him the strength to do the right thing, to guide and teach him, and to pull his head out of his ass when he needs it—"

Galian's teary face soured. "Do it right, Kader."

"I just made it more truthful."

"Kader, this is my *wedding*."

I laughed—the vow sounded appropriate to me. "I do."

"Then by the power vested in me by the Kylaen, and Raven, military," he winked at me and my heart fluttered even more, "I pronounce you husband and wife."

Galian didn't wait for Kader to give the word; he was kissing me, laughing, crying, and I couldn't help but join in.

"How long until we have to get back?" Galian asked Kader but with a sly look at me.

Kader made a face. "Three hours."

We dashed off the beach before he'd even finished his sentence.

GALIAN

I didn't need to look at the marks on the trees to find my way back to our cave, but it took us longer than usual because I couldn't keep my hands off my new wife.

My wife.

"*Amichai*," she moaned as I pressed her against a tree and kissed trails down her neck. "We don't have that much time."

"We're almost there," I said. "I love you."

"I love you, but I'm pretty sure Kader will leave us if we aren't back in time."

"I wouldn't say no to that."

"Rabbit," she said, sticking her finger against my chest. "Nothing but rabbit to eat."

I covered her mouth with mine to keep her from saying such horrible things, then dragged her away from the tree. The opening of our cave was covered by new brush, but once cleared, looked exactly the same as we'd left it. Laughing, we descended down into the darkness where we found our mattress and other signs of our time on the island.

"That thing is disgusting," Theo said, poking the bed that we'd slept on for two months. It was grimy, covered in leaves and dirt.

I yanked off my shirt. "You didn't mind last year."

"Last year we *both* looked like that," she said, but peeled off her shirt with a smile. We stripped naked and placed our clothes as best we could on top of the mattress, but I became impatient and pushed her down on top of it, earning a loud squeal of surprise from her.

She giggled and tangled her hands through my hair. "I remember the last time we were in this cave. I think I was in this very same position."

"Did you ever think we'd be back?" I asked, searching her body with the tips of my fingers.

"We should make it a regular thing," she replied, finding my hard erection and stroking it gently. "Though next time, we should remember to bring a new bed. I have a feeling we'll be using it a lot."

I groaned, all rational thought leaving me as she explored my sensitive area. What I did know was I wanted her to feel what I felt, so I slid my fingers between the wet folds.

"*Amichai*," she whispered breathlessly, and after a moment, forgot me in favor of gripping the sides of the mattress. She cried out, and I was grateful there was no one on the island to hear it. That sound of pleasure was for my ears only. A nagging voice in the back of my head reminded me that this was the last time we'd ever get true privacy again, and it only made me want to hear her scream more.

Flushed and panting, she caught my gaze and grinned. "I wonder if I'll ever tire of that."

"Maybe. We *are* an old married couple now," I said, sticking one of my fingers into my mouth and tasting her. "I won't."

"You might."

I moved down lower, trailing kisses as I went. "I won't. I've waited too long. And now I get you every," I kissed the warm, moist place, "single," another kiss, "night."

She writhed as I assaulted the space with my fingers and my mouth, making her scream before she told me to stop. Breathless and shaking, she squeezed her legs together with a smile.

"No more. I can't take any more," she said. "Surrender."

"*Surrender?* I think you're getting soft."

She smacked me hard on the shoulder. "Ass. Now it's your turn."

"My turn?" I said, allowing her to push me down onto the mattress. She took her time, biting and nipping at my skin, swirling her tongue around my nipples, and making me squirm with anticipation the closer she drew to my erection.

Her eyes danced, as if she knew I was about to lose my mind. Then, with aching restraint, she pressed her lips to my member, and my eyes rolled back into my head as the sensations washed over me. She was gentle, her lips feather-light against my skin before she took me in her mouth. I gripped the side of the mattress, nothing but pleasure and love for this woman in my brain.

Just when I thought I might explode, the sensation stopped. I opened my eyes just as she was climbing on top of me. I wished I had some comment about letting her do what she wanted to me, but even I couldn't find the right words that wouldn't ruin the moment. Slowly, she moved against me, watching my expression before losing herself in her own pleasure. The more she moaned, the quicker she moved, and I fell over my edge when her final cry echoed in the cave.

She stilled, her hands clawing at my chest and her breaths coming in short puffs. But the pleased, sly expression on her face was just for me. It was one I'd hoped to see more often.

"What are you thinking about?" she asked.

"How many more times I can make you come when we get back to the castle."

"Liar," she teased.

I pulled her down to lie in my arms. "Oh yeah? And how do you know I'm lying?"

"Because you're my *amichai*," she replied. "And I know."

The first time she'd taught me that word, she'd said it was felt rather than said. It didn't just mean lover, it meant something deeper, a soulmate, a deep connection between two people. I'd thought I knew what it meant then, but now I finally, truly understood.

"*Amichai.*"

PART II

SIXTEEN

THEO

"Sire, I—Oh!"

I jumped at the sound: a new voice in my bedroom. Beside me, Galian lifted his head to blink sleepily at the intruder. "Go away," he said, before settling back down and pulling me closer to him.

But the new voice, whoever he was, wouldn't be deterred. "S-sire, your father has requested your and...M-major Kallistrate's presence at breakfast this morning."

Galian groaned, raising his hand to dismiss the man. "Fine. We'll be down in—"

"Breakfast begins in half an hour," he said.

"Whatever," Galian said, opening one eye at me. "That's enough time."

I snorted at his obvious insinuation. We'd been gracious enough to keep our hands to ourselves on the flight back to Norose, although Kader had remarked more than once how disgustingly sweet we looked. But when we'd arrived at the castle, there wasn't anything that could keep me away from him. We'd made love long into the night until we'd worn each other out, but based on the way his hand played with the skin on my stomach, I was pretty sure he was ready for more.

"V-very well, I'll tell him to expect you."

The door closed behind him, and Galian's lips found my collarbone. "Morning, *amichai*."

I grinned, goosebumps rising on my arms from his touch and that word. "Morning."

"We've been summoned it seems," he said, kissing a gentle trail over my breasts and stomach.

"Does it happen often?" Despite my exhaustion, I perked up, especially as he nipped at the skin on my hip.

"Not usually. But one of the downfalls of being married to the prince of Kylae is that you have to do what the king says."

"Small price to pay for being your wife, I suppose." I enjoyed the way his grin widened every time I mentioned that fact. I'd never assumed my *amichai* would take such pleasure in being married, but he seemed positively giddy over it. And if I were being honest, so was I.

"Now, *amichai*, I have to remind you to be on your best behavior," he said sternly.

I sighed in mock distress as I ventured in search of the erection I was sure I'd find under the covers. "Well maybe if I'm satisfied in bed, I'll be more pleasant at breakfast."

"S-so you're saying," he said, jumping when my fingers made contact, "I have to pleasure you every morning?"

"I think I was promised every morning and every night," I said, running my hands along the shaft. Then I stopped, as if I'd been doused in cold water. "Which reminds me, how do I get contraception in this country?"

He blinked at me for a good minute before responding. "Contraception?"

"Yes. It's hard to get in Rave, obviously, but I'm pretty sure I can just get it anywhere in Kylae, right?"

"Why do you want contraception?"

My eyes nearly fell out of my head. "Did your medical training neglect to teach you how babies are made?"

"I *know* that, but..." He grinned. "It wouldn't be the worst thing in the world, would it?"

"*Yes!*" I exclaimed, sitting up. "*Yes, it would!*"

He swallowed. "Are you... You don't want kids?"

I worked my jaw for a moment. "To be honest, I never thought I'd be around long enough to consider it—and being married to you was always such an impossibility that..." I shook my head. "Yes, fine. *Eventually*, I'd like to have a child. But right now? Galian, now is not the time to bring a baby into the world—especially a mixed-race one!"

"Ah-hah," he said, tucking a lock of hair behind my ear. "But marrying me was an impossibility, and here we are...*married*. So maybe just going for it isn't the worst idea, hm? I mean, maybe having a little mixed-race baby is what this world needs?"

"Contraception, Dr. Princeling." To his pout, I added, "For *now*. For crying out loud, we've been married for less than a day. Let's try to space out our major life changes a little bit more, okay?"

He kissed my nose. "Fine. But can we still...?"

GALIAN

"I see you've come around, Major," Grieg said, as we walked into the room hand-in-hand.

I tried not to grin at my father's choice of words, but failed when I caught Theo's eye. My wife was wearing me out, and I loved every second of it. I couldn't wait to get her alone again.

Not even the tense atmosphere in my mother's private dining room could dampen my spirits, although Grieg certainly seemed up to the task as servants poured coffee and served our breakfast.

"I want to be clear. You will be expected to carry yourselves in a manner befitting the royal family," he began, staring down at Theo and I with his usual lofty sneer. "We will assign handlers to manage your media schedule. You will be expected to engage with them at every wedding-related event. Korina informs me that the top dressmaker has offered his services."

Smirking, I picked up my coffee. "That's so kind of him. I'm sure my wife will be happy to meet with him."

His gaze fell on my left hand, where I proudly wore my wedding band.

I took a sip. "I'll accept your congratulations now."

I glanced across the table at my mother's face, which was emotionless, although I saw the firm lines around her mouth tighten even further. Rhys, too, looked impassive, as if he hadn't been the one who'd recommended I go off and marry her.

"So, you have defied me again," Grieg said, throwing down his napkin. "Will you make me a fool in front of our kingdom when I have to tell them you *eloped* instead of having an official Kylaen wedding?"

"Father, you can have your dog and pony show," I said. "But our wedding was not about you."

"Watch your tone with me, boy."

I shrugged and squeezed Theo's hand under the table. Her palm was starting to sweat. "And also, we have some issues with that illegal treaty you're about to sign."

My mother's eyes flashed at me across the table.

"I'm sure you do," Grieg said, standing and knocking over his coffee. "But you listen here, boy. You two had better shape up and fall in line or there *will* be consequences. Do you understand?"

I kept his gaze, unwilling to show weakness after the display of strength. Theo's pulse beat against my hand, and knowing I was fighting for both of us kept me stoic.

Grieg broke first, straightening and barking an order to a servant to have his breakfast delivered to his private quarters. And then, with a final warning glare at me, he left the room, slamming the door behind him.

"Galian, *really*," Mom said, after a few minutes. "Was that necessary?"

"Yup," I said, releasing Theo's hand. I finally looked at her; she was pale, but smiling.

"I'll be right back," Mom said, standing and walking out the same door Grieg had stormed through.

"You know, for once, you two could make our lives a little easier," Rhys said. "I mean, for fuck's sake, Gally, have you learned *nothing*?"

"It was *your* idea for us to get married!" I said, aghast.

"Yeah, but not to *tell anyone about it*!" Rhys said. "Especially not Father! Gally, you've been playing this game a while now. You know better."

"Oh yeah? What can he do?" I asked.

"Send you to the new Mael he's probably planning to build in Rave," Rhys said. "Blow you up in a car bomb."

"I thought you said he wasn't responsible," I said, narrowing my eyes.

"He wasn't, but that doesn't mean he wouldn't try it," Rhys said.

"He won't try to kill us," Theo said. "He needs us. How can he have a wedding without us?"

"He'll have a double funeral instead, and the countries will mourn together," Rhys said. "We've seen it happen before."

That quieted Theo, who shrank back in her chair, wide-eyed.

But I remained defensive. "What happened to fighting back? What happened to *this isn't the end*, and *we aren't giving up*?"

"We *aren't*, but we can't really be open about what we're doing either. Everything's different, Gally. We've gotta be careful. More careful than we have been. There are consequences now, and I don't want to see either of you dead."

At that moment, Mom returned, looking flustered and annoyed. "Well, Galian, your father sends his blessings."

I snorted. "I'm sure."

"And, as to be expected, he also forbids you to tell anyone about your marriage." She picked up her coffee and sipped it as if nothing were amiss. "He's billing this as a true Kylaen wedding, similar in size and scope to ours, and wants us to put the full force of the Kylaen royal staff on it."

I whistled. Obviously, I hadn't been in attendance, but the sheer extravagance that had surrounded my parents' wedding was clear even in photos.

Across the table, Rhys frowned. "But..."

"Darling, you don't even have a girlfriend," Mom said, patting his hand and for the first time, I saw a little jealousy on his face. "And this is less about the wedding and more about the spectacle. Your father wants this wedding to be so exciting that the Kylaens forget we're re-annexing a country."

"And what about Rave?" Theo asked.

Mom sighed heavily. "That's Bayard's headache. I haven't been able to reach my sources since the news broke, but my guess is the country is in an uproar."

"Probably not," she said, glumly. "Half the country just wants to keep their privileged life, and the other will be glad not to have to send their children to war."

"Don't think so little of your people, Theo," Mom said with a smile. Then, glancing around the room, she said, "Johar swept this room last week, but I don't trust your father. We'll discuss this further when we finish breakfast and retire to my sitting room. Unless, of course, you'd like to talk about your wedding dress ideas, Theo? Those will be the only safe topics for us to discuss when not in a secure room. I wore a traditional Kylaen dress, lots of petticoats, long train. Would you like something similar?"

Theo choked on her eggs, and I couldn't help but snort at the idea of her in a poofy white skirt.

Mom chuckled and took another sip of her coffee. "Since I might not get to offer it again, congratulations, to the both of you. I'm not sure what sort of mess you married into, Theo, but we're glad to have you as part of the family."

THEO

My breakfast sat uneasily in my stomach as Galian and I followed his mother and brother into her sitting parlor, and it wasn't just the prospect of wearing a large Kylaen dress. No, my worry was about what Rhys had said. It was true that, without Mael, we'd been a bit brasher, a bit more willing to test Grieg's patience. But knowing how well-versed Grieg was in using national mourning to bolster his cause, Galian and I needed to be more careful.

Inside Korina's study, we found Johar and, to my surprise, Kader, although he wore plainclothes instead of his usual military uniform.

"Rosie let you out of the house?" Korina asked, taking his hand in welcome.

"I am under strict orders to decline any mission requiring me to leave the city," he said with a wry smile and a wink to me.

"Isn't it so nice to have someone who worries over us?" Korina replied kindly.

I shared a glance with Galian and he tucked me under his arm and kissed the side of my forehead. We sat together on the couch as we'd done so many times before, although this time, I wasn't wearing that damned makeup and wig. I hadn't realized how uncomfortable it made me until I sat here, in my own skin.

"I hear congratulations are in order," Johar said, smiling at the two of us.

"Get them out quick," Rhys said. "We're forbidden to talk about it."

"We have a lot to discuss, and not a lot of time do to it in," Korina said, settling in her chair. "Our goals for the next three months are to increase pressure on your father to change his mind and allow Rave its independence while maintaining the peace treaty."

I smiled, grateful to hear those words come from her mouth.

"I've been considering this from many different angles, and I see three avenues. The first is to increase the instability in Rave through our continued efforts with Anson and the rebels."

"Anson won't meet with us," I said, glancing at Kader. "He thinks—"

"He has an opinion of us, one which we'll need to change," Korina said. "Now that Bayard is working with Grieg, it might make Anson a bit more amenable to listen to what we have to say. Johar, I'm putting you in charge of that effort."

"I'd like to be involved," I said, knowing that my leaving Kylae wasn't feasible.

"I know, and that's why you and I will start socializing your interest in some charities," Korina said.

I frowned, confused. "Ch-charities? Like, those silly little art auctions and parties you go to?"

"Hear me out," Korina said, holding up her hands. "There's a chance Anson has key members of his organization here in Kylae, or if he doesn't, he will soon. There are a few charities that need a royal sponsor, some of which help the less fortunate in the slums."

I glanced at Galian, and he said, "That's where most of the Raven refugees end up."

"It will be easy to convince the media that your focus is the plight of your people," Korina said. "Grieg will send along his spies, so we must be very careful. But I'm sure you're up to the task."

I nodded eagerly.

"Eli, if Rosie will allow it," Korina said with a smile, "I'd like you to focus on the slums and find out what sort of network Anson has. That way, when Theo arrives, we can expedite their conversation."

He tilted his head in agreement, so she moved on.

"Our next avenue will be to seek help from Herin and Jervan, but since our travel routes there are limited, we'll have to be creative. Galian, I'll need you to call on your dear friend Olivia to see if she can assist us here."

Galian nodded, looking enthused by the idea. "I think she and I have come to an agreement."

"I also want you to work your normal shifts at the hospital. It tends to give the impression you aren't getting in too much trouble," Korina said, before turning away from us. "Finally, our last option will be with our friends in the Kylaen government. Rhys, you and I will focus on them. We'll have to find a way to convince them—even the hawks—that we can provide a better option than reclaiming Rave."

Rhys sat up. "Mom, I don't think—"

"Son, you're going to be king one day, and if you can't stomach a little bit of political maneuvering now, you'll never make it as a ruler."

He reddened. "Mom, it's not that. Have you talked to these idiots? It's like reasoning with a brick wall."

"Of course reason isn't working," Korina said. "If reason worked, we wouldn't be in this mess in the first place. What I need you to do is figure out what makes them tick. If needed, find their weaknesses and exploit them. The time for playing nice is over."

Pride swelled in my chest as she spoke. Like the rest of us, she'd been thrown for a loop, but she wasn't backing away. She was doubling down, fighting back. I was glad to call her my mother-in-law.

"We won't be able to meet like this," Korina said to Galian and me. "The two of you will be heavily watched. There will be media requests, photographers everywhere. Officially, you two are being forced together, so they'll be looking for signs of discord between you. Try to keep your fights to a minimum, and behind closed doors."

"I think we've worked out our problems," Galian said, with a wink. In response, I elbowed him.

"It would be wise of you not to decline any invitation, especially if it comes from Grieg. In order for this to work, we must remain out of his crosshairs. Especially after your display this morning. We want him to think that your impromptu wedding is the biggest bit of rebellion he can expect from you. Understand?".

"Yes," I said, squeezing his hand. "We'll behave."

"Theo, may I have a word with you, privately?" Korina said, standing.

With a nervous glance at Galian, I followed her, as I'd done so many times, to the other side of her apartments to look over her lush, green gardens.

Before she said anything, she took my hands in hers, then dropped my right to inspect the simple gold band on my left. "Well, I can understand the haste under the circumstances, but we need to see about getting you a nicer ring. At least in public."

I retracted my hand, cradling my left finger with a frown. "I like my ring."

"Unfortunately," she said with a heavy sigh, "your likes and dislikes will have to take a backseat, at least temporarily. In order to make this work, we'll both have to say and do things we detest. But we do it knowing that we're both marching in the same direction. No matter what I say in front of the cameras, I want you to know—in your heart of hearts—that I want your country to be free, as much as I want you to be with Galian."

I half-smiled. "I appreciate that."

"I also wanted to warn you that we will be spending a lot of time together—in front of the cameras—and not all of it will be pleasant. You'll be attacked on all sides, painted as a traitor and a harlot, at best. I fear it's already begun in Rave, especially as you've been named as the primary negotiator of the peace treaty."

"*What?*" Horror and shame washed over me. "But this was...this isn't... *he's* the one signing it!"

"And trust me, that Emilie Mondra is doing a fine job spinning the national conversation to make him the hero and you the villain." Korina paused. "Speaking of which, she will be arriving in the next few days to take over wedding media operations for the Ravens. I will have someone assigned to handle the Kylaen media. You and Galian will have to meet with them regularly."

"I'm not meeting with *her*," I said. "She's vile."

"Remember what I said about having to put on a nice face," Korina said. "We'll need you to be on your best behavior so we can meet with the Ravens in the slums. Part of that is pretending you enjoy vile people's company."

I'd done that plenty in Veres, so very unhappily, I nodded.

"To Emilie and to everyone else, your focus should be the wedding and establishing yourself as a Kylaen princess—"

"A *what?*" I took a step back. "No way. I'm not a p-p—"

Korina chuckled. "That's how I felt the day after I realized I was going to marry Grieg. Don't worry, dear, the title fades rather quickly. Then all that's left is the work."

I glanced at Galian, who was locked in tense conversation with Rhys and Kader. "I suppose I should've expected it, marrying a prince and all."

I jumped when she took my hands again. "Above all else, please know that you and Galian aren't alone. I'm with you every step of the way. If you stay close to me, if we walk this thin line together, I believe—truly believe—we can find independence for Rave."

SEVENTEEN

GALIAN

Morning came too soon, in the form of the alarm ringing. I groaned and reached for it, intent on shutting it off and sleeping more, but then I remembered why I'd set it. I had a shift today, and per my mother's instructions, I needed to go in to pretend everything was normal.

It would've been easier had I not stayed up until well after two making love to my wife.

I glanced down at her; she hadn't stirred. For a moment, I was content just to watch her sleep, thanking whatever stars had aligned for us that we were finally able to be together. Even though I had to go to work, knowing she'd be there when I got back warmed my heart.

I dressed and ate a quick breakfast before meeting my car downstairs. Johar sat at the wheel, her lips pressed into a thin line.

"I thought you were going to Rave?" I asked, sitting in the back.

"Leaving as soon as I drop you off," she said. "Kader's not fit for duty, not even driving your princely ass around."

"Ah," I said with a nod. "I mean, you can trust one of the other guys, can't you?"

"Snyder's going to be taking over until Kader's better."

I nodded. "I like him. I think."

She didn't respond.

"Is he chattier than you?"

I caught her displeased look in the mirror.

"Just trying to make small talk, Johar," I said, turning my ring around on my finger. "I mean, I know you all think I'm scum, but if we're forced to spend time together, we might as well be pleasant about it."

"I don't think you're scum. And take off your ring."

"What?"

"Your ring. Take it off or your father will have a fit."

I glanced at the wedding band on my left hand. With a grimace, I pulled it off and stuck it in my pants. "I wish this wedding would hurry up and happen already."

"I wouldn't mention that to your wife, seeing as that'll also mean her country is officially Kylae's again."

This time, it was my turn not to respond.

We arrived at the hospital to more than the usual amount of attention. The photographers were relentless in their questioning, asking me if I was happy or upset about my engagement. I offered them a neutral smile and allowed Johar to forge a path into the hospital.

"I won't miss that," she said, shaking her shirt.

"Well, take care of yourself," I said. "And thanks for...well, for everything."

She nodded. "I'll see you soon, Highness. Wish me luck out there."

Although she'd probably meant the tabloids waiting to mob her when she walked back to the car, I said a little prayer that she'd be successful in Rave. We needed all the help we could get.

THEO

I awoke alone in the bed, and for a moment, wondered where my *amichai* might've run off to. But a hazy memory of a kiss, a promise to return after work, as well as a handwritten note on the nightstand lessened my fears. Korina had told him to go to the hospital, after all, and I supposed that meant early mornings and late nights.

I lay in the ridiculous bed for almost half an hour, before giving up on going back to sleep. I should've hated all this luxury—after all, everything my body touched belonged to a royal bastard—but, as I ran my bare feet along the silky sheets, I decided I'd be indignant later. This bed was comfortable, as were the memories of what Galian and I had done in it.

I rolled onto my side and let my fingers dance on Galian's pillow. I was rather impressed he'd gotten up so early for his shift, especially considering how late we'd stayed up. After breakfast with his mother, he and I took a tour of the castle, which lasted all of half an hour before we gave up and returned to his room to continue what we'd started before breakfast.

I rolled onto my back and toyed with a lock of my hair. I

wasn't completely confident he would bring me contraceptives, so I made a mental note to ask Rosie the next time I saw her. After all, unlike Rave, Kylae didn't have the need to replenish their people after a costly war—

Which was, in effect, over.

I groaned and stared at the top of Galian's (and, I supposed, my) canopy bed. The despair of knowing my life had been in vain threatened to take over, but I wouldn't let it. I wasn't completely powerless; I had Galian, his mother, and brother. Kader, Rosie, and Johar. There was still a chance the rebels in Veres would be emboldened by Bayard's treachery. Bayard's administration had made the deal, so if he weren't in power, it would be null and void.

Filled with fire and morning vigor, I swung my legs over the bed and walked the length of the large room that Galian called his "bedroom." There were expensive oil paintings adorning the walls and Jervanian cherry wood furniture, including a desk with a stack of papers. The plush crimson carpet I stood on covered most of the room, the stone floors of the castle visible on the edges of the room. A fireplace sat dormant in the corner, and a smile twisted my lips as I thought about how I would stay warm with my *amichai* in a few months.

His massive closet was larger than the living room in my old apartment in Veres. I inhaled the scent of him deeply, allowing myself to sink into the fact that he was mine. My husband. In all my wildest dreams, I'd never thought we'd make it this far. And even though there were miles to go before we could relax, it was comforting to know we'd face those obstacles together.

In the closet, there were even more dresses and shirts than the day before. Galian had said his mother's people would be responsible for buying my things, and although I'd been horrified at the thought of someone else picking out my underwear, I couldn't deny that it was nice to open one of the intricately carved drawers and discover a plethora of clean items.

I languished in the shower, finding it stocked not only with Galian's particular brand of soap, but also a lavender-scented one that left my skin soft and supple. There were lotions and cosmetics in his vanity area, more than I'd ever seen before, and all for me. Korina must've arranged for this finery; I'd have to remember to thank her later. I tried some of the powder on my face, but frowned—it was entirely the wrong shade. I washed it off before foregoing the entire set and leaving the bathroom.

Galian's private suite consisted of his bedroom, closet, and bathroom, but there was a semi-private sitting room on the other side of the bedroom that he called his parlor. There were a few uncomfortable couches, a writing desk, and large windows open to the blue sky. I stood in front of them, gazing out onto the green, lush gardens and allowing the sun to wake me further.

My stomach rumbled with hunger, but I wasn't sure what the protocol was. Did Galian ask for a meal to be delivered to his room? If so, whom did he ask?

The door jiggled and I spun around, nervous for no reason. I was Galian's wife—of course I deserved to be there. But the idea of being in this castle, in enemy territory, without him was suddenly terrifying.

A young Kylaen woman popped her head in, glancing about the room until her gaze landed on me. I think she might've noticed the scared look on my face, because she smiled warmly as she slipped through the heavy doors.

"You must be Princess Theo."

I choked on my spit. *"Who's calling me that?"*

"You're to be Prince Galian's wife, aren't you?" She smiled. "You need to start getting used to the title."

"Please don't ever call me that again," I said, placing my hand over my heart. "Theo is just fine."

"Very well, *Theo*, my name is Filippa. I'm Queen Korina's personal assistant. I've come to see if you'd like your breakfast delivered."

I nodded. "I wasn't sure who I needed to..."

"It's no problem at all, Your Highness."

I winced at the title, but didn't correct her. I'd thought I had to be crowned or something in order to be called that. Before I could say another word, she was opening the doors for a gray-haired woman, who shuffled in with a plate of food. She placed the gold-plated tray on top of a table without looking me in the eye then bowed and left before I could properly thank her.

I stood for a moment, staring at Filippa like an idiot, before I realized that she expected me to eat the food she'd brought. Slowly, I crossed the room to the table, jumping when Filippa held out the chair for me.

"Please, sit," she said with a kind smile.

"You really...this is too much," I stammered, but sat down all the same. She pushed my chair in then lifted the golden cover off the tray, revealing a mouth-watering meal of eggs, bacon, sausage, and some puffy bread I'd never seen before. Filippa poured coffee from a golden carafe into a china cup, and offered me milk and sugar, which I declined. Then she stood, hands clasped behind her back, watching me.

"Er..."

"Please, Your Highness—"

"Theo, please," I insisted. "I'm not, nor do I want to be, a princess."

She cocked her head. "But you're marrying Prince Galian?"

"His royal status was one of his cons, trust me," I muttered, picking up the gold fork and staring at it.

"Is there something wrong with your food?"

"N-no, but...I mean, are you going to watch me eat it?" I felt like a complete idiot.

She chuckled. "Royal protocol is for me to wait until you've tasted the meal. Then I'll leave you in peace."

"Oh..." I picked up a piece of bacon and chomped down on it. The sweet, salty pork melted in my mouth and I tried to keep in a moan. "It's very good."

"Excellent," she said, bowing. "I'll leave you—"

"No, stay," I said, having shoved the rest of the bacon in my mouth. "Please, I'd like some company this morning."

She hesitated, as if she didn't understand. But I figured, if she was Korina's assistant, perhaps she'd be an ally.

"I mean," I swallowed the bacon, "Galian's at work for the next...however long, and I don't...well, I don't really know what to do with myself. And you seem to know what's going on around here. I could use some tips on how not to get beheaded."

She snorted, but then took the seat opposite me. "Beheadings were outlawed over a hundred years ago."

"Good to know," I said, drinking the most delicious coffee I'd ever tasted. "You know, if Galian grew up eating this way, it's no wonder he whined so much on the island." She smiled, but didn't respond, so I inhaled more food, only pausing to remind myself not to eat like a total barbarian in front of her. "The past few days have been completely... I don't even know which way is up anymore. One minute, I'm meeting with the Raven rebels, the next I'm—"

"Theo, dear?" Korina's melodic voice echoed through the room.

In an instant, Filippa was on her feet, her gaze on the floor and her face bright red.

Korina saw the two of us and smiled brightly. "Filippa, darling, thank you for keeping Theo company this morning. I have a favor to ask. Can you please run to Rhys's office and ask him to meet with me at his earliest convenience?"

"Yes, Your Majesty." And before I could say another word, my new friend rushed out of the room, not making eye contact with the queen.

When the door closed, Korina turned her kind glance on me, but there was a little annoyance in it. "Darling, Filippa works for the king. Please be careful what you share with her."

My mouth dropped open, and two crumbs fell out. Then, blushing, I closed my lips and wiped the corners. "I'm so... I didn't..."

"Darling, it's fine. You can't be expected to know all the loyalties of this castle," Korina said, taking the seat vacated by Filippa. "But a good rule is if you haven't spoken to a person before, expect their intentions not to be aligned with yours."

"You'd think I would've known better by now," I said, picking at the remainder of my breakfast.

"Filippa fooled me for a bit as well," Korina said. "I wanted to let you know I've scheduled a dressmaker to stop by today. We won't have time to discuss anything, so please keep your comments brief and your smile bright. I can't say there won't be a photographer here either."

I grimaced, but nodded.

"I will tell Filippa to collect a list of all the charities dealing with the poor and the refugees in the slums," Korina continued without stopping. "With any luck, we should have our first meeting within the week. But I'll ask you to keep any comments on the task at hand. Grieg will have spies, so we'll have to be delicate."

"I will," I said. "And this dressmaker..."

She had the good grace to pity me. "I'm afraid you'll be expected to wear a rather refined set of clothes, in public, anyway. If you want to be accepted in Kylaen society—and, if we want to make anything happen, you do—then you'll have to put aside your military training and learn how to be a lady."

"Fantastic."

Filippa returned, much to my annoyance, and stood ready to answer whatever direction the queen might offer. Korina's countenance changed almost immediately, and she grew colder, her head drawn higher. I supposed this was what she meant by putting on appearances.

"Filippa, dear, we'll need to see about getting my hairdresser here, as well as my esthetician. I can't have her going on camera this afternoon looking like this."

I tried to recall that Korina was playing a part, but she was very good at it.

"Yes ma'am," Filippa said with a similarly haughty glance to me. I only supposed her earlier sweetness was an attempt to draw information out of me and now that she was found out, she'd take her cues from the queen.

It was going to be a long day.

GALIAN

The sun was setting by the time I finally got off my shift. Snyder proved to be much nicer than Johar, and we had a great conversation about his family on the ride home. But even though I'd been on my feet for twelve hours, I was wide awake and eager to see what awaited me when I opened my bedroom door.

To be honest, I'd been looking forward to this all day. The sight of her curled up on one of my couches, holding a steaming mug and reading a book was the most gorgeous thing I'd ever seen. I opened the door fully and leaned against the doorframe for a moment, burning this into my memory.

"*Amichai*," she said, before furrowing her brow. "What's wrong?"

"Nothing," I replied with a smile. "You just... I've been waiting to do this for months now."

"What?"

"Come home to you. Like this."

Her lips parted in surprise, and I closed the door behind me, leaning against it and watching her.

"Um." It was rare for Theo to be at a loss for words, so I enjoyed the way she squirmed and fidgeted.

"Don't you dare ask me how work was, or else I might not be able to take the pure normalcy of it," I said with a grin.

She finally laughed, putting her cup on the table next to her and sliding off the couch to come meet me. "How was work, *amichai*?"

"Uh!" I put my hand over my heart. "I can't take it, *amichai*. Too much normalcy."

She slipped her hands around my waist and kissed me gently. "Say it again."

"*Amichai*?" Her eyes lit up, as if the word were as pleasurable as my lips on her skin. "I've gotten pretty good at it, hm?"

"Just keep saying it," she whispered. "Then I can forget all about the weirdest day of my life."

"Oh?" I said, taking her hand and letting her walk me back to the couch. "How so?"

"Let's see. First I woke up without my husband because the son of a bitch *left* me to the wolves." To my surprise, she climbed on top of me, straddling my hips. "Then I met Filippa—"

"Oh, be careful with her, she works for—"

"I'm aware," Theo said, kissing the side of my mouth. "And then your mother put on her bitch queen face and dragged me from person to person to person so I would be 'presentable.'" She paused and picked at the ends of her hair, which was shinier and smoother than normal. "Apparently, nobody's ever done a Raven's hair before because they spent a good half-hour talking about how *different* it is."

"Is it different?" I asked, threading my hands through it. I supposed it was a bit coarser, now that I thought about it.

"And then this woman waxed every single part of my face, and yet another decided to lather me with makeup." She frowned. "Nobody in this castle has anything close to my skin color."

I swallowed a smile, because she was starting to look upset by the whole thing.

"And all of that happened before I was marched in front of this dressmaker and my measurements were read aloud—in front of this photographer. So I'm sure my waist and bust size will be all over the newspapers tomorrow."

I brushed a strand of hair out of her face. "Where was Mom?"

"There, the whole time," Theo said, sitting back. "I know she said this was going to be unpleasant, but....this was just too much. Galian, I was *humiliated*."

I pulled her down to my chest and held her. "I'm sorry, *amichai*. Do you want me to talk to Mom about it?"

"No," she said. "I know this is just part of it. But how does treating me like a prized cow stop the treaty?"

"Maybe it disarms people?" I said. "I mean, you're scary when you're in full Major Kallistrate mode. Maybe Mom was trying to...I don't know, make people unafraid of you? So that they'd lower their guard around you. I can almost guarantee that most of Kylaen society is going to think you're beneath them."

"Thanks."

"I'm not saying they're right," I said quickly. "I'm saying that's what you've got to expect. And if I could," I grabbed her hips and shifted her closer to me, "I'd whisk you away and we could live on our island. But if we want this treaty to change, we've gotta suck up to these morons. And when you finally do break out full Major Kallistrate, they won't know what hit them."

She toyed with the collar of my shirt. "I didn't like that you weren't here today. I wanted us to do this together, and when you're gone, it's like..."

"You know, you can come visit me at the hospital any time," I said, unbuckling her pants. "In fact, I'd love it. We could have a quickie in the doctors' lounge like I've always dreamed about—"

She smacked me on the shoulder. "Is sex the only thing you think about?"

"Right now? Yes." She moved to smack me again, but I grabbed her hand and pulled her down on the couch, pinning her beneath me. "But I want you to visit me. I want us to try to be as normal as possible."

"Normal."

"Yeah, normal," I said. "Normally, a new husband wants to show his new wife off to all the staff. And have quickies with her in the doctors' lounge."

She poked my chest. "You can't tell them we're married."

"Fiancée, whatever." I stopped my attempts to disrobe her. "But I'm serious. I want us to try to find some kind of balance between the bullshit and ourselves. Because somehow I think you and I will never have a normal life together."

She softened. "So what's normal?"

"Normal is going into that bedroom over there and having some awesome sex before I pass the hell out."

"You are *so* romantic."

EIGHTEEN

THEO

Galian's insistence on trying for some kind of normalcy had seemed farfetched, but when I awoke to the smell of breakfast and coffee, I couldn't argue that seeing him across the breakfast table felt kind of nice. More importantly, it was the only part of my day where I could have a real, honest conversation with another person. Maybe my princeling was smarter than I'd given him credit for.

He had very little to share with me, other than general conversation about patients and his colleagues' constant questions about our relationship. He'd told Maitland about our marriage in confidence, and the old doctor had been thrilled. But Galian hadn't been able to meet with Olivia, or make any overtures toward her. As he gathered his belongings for work, he promised me (with a sensual kiss that left me weak in the knees) that he would redouble his efforts. I was unhappy that he was leaving me (again), but I supposed I understood.

My solitude was fleeting, as Filippa arrived almost as soon as Galian had left. She had taken her cue from the queen and was now treating me like I was a child. I considered what Galian had said about people underestimating me. And if Filippa thought me beneath her, she probably wasn't going to pay too close attention to my activities.

"The queen said you were gathering a list of charities that I was to be...helping with," I said, unsure what my role would actually be.

"Yes," Filippa said with a small curl of her lip. "Unfortunately, I've been unable to get the list yet."

I wondered if that was because Grieg wanted to approve it or was stonewalling me.

"The queen is busy tending to the planning of your engagement party, but she's requested that you begin calling on esteemed members of Kylaen society."

"And...what does 'calling on' mean?"

Filippa raised her chin a little higher. "It means simply that. You will meet with the spouses of the Kylaen ministers. I *assume* you know how the Kylaen government is structured?"

As much as I didn't want to admit my ignorance, I shook my head.

"We have six—*seven* provinces now," she said with a broad smile. "And six ministers to manage six cabinets. Each of them sits on the king's council. There are vice ministers and aides you'll meet with in time. The queen expects you to know all of them."

Filippa ran through a list of times and names and locations of meetings she'd scheduled for me. There was a car waiting downstairs, and I was to wear the outfit that she'd picked, which turned out to be a starchy pantsuit in pale pink that looked utterly ridiculous on me.

I tugged at the sleeves, wincing at the horrible way they clashed with my skin color. Filippa had the same woman from the day before come do my hair and makeup, and, yet again, I stared at a stranger in the mirror.

"And the queen's not going to be coming today?" I asked for the fifth time. "Can I talk with her before we go?"

"Sorry," Filippa said, holding the door open for me. "We're on a—"

"Tight schedule."

I followed her down a set of back stairs, each step filling me with dread. After yesterday's embarrassment, I didn't think things could get any worse. But if it was Korina's plan to make me look like an idiot...she was definitely succeeding.

"O-oh," Filippa said, stopping short. "Your Highness."

I glanced up, and my hopes lifted. Rhys stood against the door, talking with a driver I didn't recognize. He offered Filippa a nice smile as he pushed himself upright.

"Heya, sis!" He glanced at Filippa. "Well, soon-to-be-sis."

"I didn't have you on the schedule," Filippa said with a frown.

"One of the perks of being the heir is that I get to make the schedule," he said with a daring glance. Then, as her face turned bright red, he plucked the clipboard out of her hand. "But we'll make sure to stick to the one you've laid out."

"But—"

"I'm *sure* Mom needs help with planning their engagement party," Rhys said. "Why don't you take the day to help her?"

An argument seemed on the tip of her tongue, but instead, she nodded, spun on her heel, and walked away.

"Thank *God*," I said when she was out of earshot.

"That's the reaction I want every time you see me," he said with a laugh. "What the hell are you wearing?"

"Filippa chose it," I said with a glare. "Can I change?"

"Into what?" Rhys said, holding open the door for me. "You look every bit the princess."

"That's the point," I said, slumping into the car. "I'm not a princess."

"I mean, *technically*—"

My glare cut him off.

"All right, all right. Technically, not yet. But that reminds me." Rhys dug into his pocket and tossed me a small box. "From Mom. Well, supposedly from Gally."

I opened the box and my eyebrows went to my hairline. The bright red jewel stared up at me from a silver ring, carved with the symbol of Kylae.

"This thing is ugly," I said, pulling it out of the box. "And heavy. Tell me I only have to wear this in public."

"Just my luck. The one time I give a girl a ring," Rhys said with a chuckle. "You know, I'd hoped to give that to *my* future wife. Guess I'll get to have the second best wedding of the century."

"You want to get married in three months? Be my guest." I swallowed my disgust as I threaded my finger through the ring. It fit, but still felt strange on my hand. I missed the simplicity of my actual wedding band. "But...thanks for saving me from Filippa." I swallowed a comment about Galian not being there for me. I knew he had to go to the hospital to work, but it was starting to feel like we were back to doing everything separately.

"Well, how could I pass up the opportunity to spend a day with my lovely sister?" Rhys said, glancing out the window.

"How come I sense an ulterior motive then?"

He flashed me a familiar grin. "Fine. I'm also tagging along to chit-chat with some of the spouses who happen to sit on the hawkish side of things. Remind them that everyone has secrets, and I'm in a position to use them, if necessary."

The car reached the front gates of the castle and was swarmed by flashing lights. Reflexively, I curled away from them.

"Relax, the windows are tinted. We don't want them printing stories about how I'm stealing my brother's fiancée," Rhys said with a laugh.

"Yeah, can you do anything about these stories being printed about us?" I asked. This morning's was particularly false, talking about how we were getting to know one another over tea and insinuating that Galian was taking refuge at the hospital. The second part didn't feel too far off from the truth.

"That's Father," Rhys said. "Though I enjoyed the story about how you two bonded recently over a game of squash."

"I don't even know what squash is."

"It's a game... You know what? Never mind. It's probably better if you don't know."

The car drove us to a part of Norose I'd never seen before. Old houses with gold trim, immaculate green yards with iron fences. The air seemed sweeter, the sun looked a little brighter. And, of course, the car pulled up in front of the largest, most ornate house on the block.

"One thing before we get out," Rhys said, taking my hand before I opened the door. "This woman is the definition of Kylaen elitism. She's going to say and do things that will make you want to deck her. But she's also the lead patron of a very expansive charity helping Raven refugees. So if you want to speak to Anson, you're going to have to get her to *invite* you to help out."

"And how do I do that?"

"Just stay silent and let me do all the talking."

Rhys was the epitome of princely perfection as he stepped out of the car, adjusting his suit jacket and helping me out. I tried to emulate the way he tossed his shoulders back and strode confidently toward the house as if he owned it, but I undoubtedly failed miserably. After all, in a few decades, he *would* own this land, whereas I would permanently be a stranger.

The butler was there even before we rang the doorbell, and we walked into the old home, which was decorated with gold pieces and oil paintings that rivaled the castle I now called home. In Kernaghan, the decor seemed sparse and tasteful. Here it just looked like someone with too much money had tried to cram as much as possible into a small space.

That this woman could also be involved in charity work was astonishing.

"Prince Rhys! I wasn't aware you'd be calling on me." The woman who owned the house was dressed like her décor—too many baubles and jewels for such a small woman. The brooch on her lapel was the size of my fist, the pin in her hair held at least six diamonds. If she hadn't been expecting Rhys, perhaps she was trying to intimidate me with her wealth. Perhaps Galian hadn't been too far off about Kylaens underestimating me.

"Mrs. Kopec, always a pleasure," Rhys said, walking into the old woman's waiting arms and pecking her twice on the cheek. "You're looking well."

"Oh, yes. Just wonderful news about this treaty, isn't it?" she said, ignoring me completely and leading Rhys into a small room where tea was waiting. I saw only two cups, and she made no move to ask for a third as they sat across from each other.

"Mrs. Kopec, this is my soon-to-be sister-in-law, Major Theo

Kallistrate," Rhys said, finally noticing me standing awkwardly in the doorway.

"Oh, you don't have to put on airs with me, son," Kopec said, snorting in my direction. "Your poor brother. Forced to marry a Raven to solidify a treaty. The Ravens should be thankful we're allowing them back into the country at all."

I opened my mouth to retort, but a hearty laugh from Rhys cut me off. "You're too kind. Galian's a nice sort of fellow. He'll make a decent husband. Eventually." He glanced at me with equal parts apology and warning.

"It's a shame you couldn't marry first, Your Highness," Kopec said. "But I suppose it's for the best. We've got to keep the royal Kylaen bloodline pure."

This time, I didn't need the warning glance, as I balled my fists against the pastel pink cushions of the chair and focused on the patterns. I kept reminding myself that she was the ticket to Anson.

"As my brother would probably tell you, cut us all up and we look about the same," Rhys said. "Isn't that right, Theo?"

I didn't trust my tongue not to say something I'd later regret, so I stayed silent.

"Speaking of our new Raven citizens, or, I suppose they're back to Kylaen citizens," Rhys said, placing his teacup on the saucer. "My soon-to-be sister needs something to occupy her time, now that she's not flying planes. She was hoping to get involved with your charity."

Kopec turned and smiled, but there was no kindness in it. "Of course. Those poor creatures can't possibly help themselves. I mean, we offered them a chance to rule their own country and see what they did?"

I made a noise before Rhys cut me off again. "Theo and I are just so touched you've taken the time to offer your help to those less fortunate," Rhys said, his gaze boring into mine. "And those less fortunate should *keep quiet and allow her to help them.*"

"They do, Your Highness, they do," Kopec said. "Bless their hearts, they just need all the help they can get."

"I would presume," I said, ignoring the confused look on Kopec's face as I spoke for the first time, "that those *less fortunate* can make up their own damned minds. And they can absolutely fend for themselves given enough freedom to breathe."

Sure, I knew I wasn't supposed to say anything. But I'd taken enough Kylaen arrogance for one week, and I wasn't about to keep quiet anymore.

"Oh, Theo," Rhys said with a forced laugh and a look that could've killed. "Isn't she just a treat?"

Kopec turned back to him and laughed, and soon they were discussing other matters, and I was forgotten. I swallowed and tried to calm myself without appearing too agitated. This woman was either oblivious or too focused on her appearance to take note of our argument. Either way, Rhys was going to discuss this with me after.

"Well, would you look at the time," Rhys said, making a huge show of checking his watch. "I apologize. We've got to go visit Minister Bassett today—"

"Oh, but didn't you hear?" Kopec said, sipping her tea daintily. "She's decided to take a position in Rave. Your father asked her to help Bayard restructure the government."

For the briefest of moments, a sliver of shock passed over his face. But he hid it well, and stood with Kopec to wish her well.

"Theo, dear, would you mind running to the car and telling him we're ready to go?" he said, without looking at me.

I stood, already dreading the conversation we'd have in the car, but grateful to be leaving this woman. Even though she might've been able to get me into the slums, I wasn't sure I could get there without trying to shove her into the Madion Sea.

I was almost halfway out the door when I heard a loud gasp. I spun and hurried back toward the room we'd been sitting in. I heard low voices, so I kept out of sight, straining my ears for the content of the conversation, but came up empty.

I jumped when the door flew open and I came face to face with Rhys, who looked upset. He looped his arm through mine and we walked to the car in silence.

"So—" I began once the car door was shut.

"I thought I told you to keep your opinions to yourself," he said. "It's a good thing Kopec's got a short memory from all the booze or else you would've been sunk."

"Didn't Galian tell you that's not my area of expertise?" I watched her house disappear out the window. "What did you do to her?"

"I did nothing. She's the one who's run up a credit with the Kylaen Royal Bank," Rhys said. "I just informed her that I had the power to call in her debts."

I wrenched my gaze to him, shocked. "You did what? How could you do that?"

"Do you know who she's married to?" Rhys replied. "He's one of the ministers who helped my father negotiate this treaty with Bayard. He'd have the entire country of Rave in chains and working the barethium mines."

I chewed my lip, unconvinced.

"Theo, when you were at Vinolas, you shot down hundreds of

Kylaens, didn't you? So how is this any different? Treaty or not, we're still at war. And in war, you've got to kill or be killed."

I thought it a little rich that *Rhys* of all people was lecturing me on the realities of war. "You're right. When I was in the air, it was kill or be killed. But it's an entirely different scenario when you're looking into someone's eyes."

"I know that. But if you think this was bad...Theo, we're down to our last options here. We don't have time to think about other people. You're going to have to grow into someone who's okay with...metaphorically killing someone while staring them in the face." He sighed. "Besides, I'm not *doing* anything. I just told her that if she didn't get you invited to her next visit to the slums, and if she didn't start feeding us information about what her husband is up to in Rave, we'd bankrupt her. She does what we say, nothing happens."

I stared at him, surprised at his ruthlessness. We sat in silence for a while, until we came to a stop in front of yet another house with gold-plated trim and ornate columns.

"You know, Rhys, you ought to be grateful I couldn't kill a person in cold blood," I said, before opening the car door. "Or else your brother would've been a dead man."

GALIAN

Although Olivia was in the forefront of my mind, at the hospital, my impending wedding with Theo was on the forefront of everyone else's. After two days of talking with patients, most of them fell into one of three categories. The first pitied me, and wondered how my father could force me to marry someone against my will. The second group thought me a monster for preying on an innocent Raven, as I was obviously using her for cheap political points and would treat her horribly. But the third group was merely curious, seeing through the spin and the stories and wondering how I really felt about being permanently attached to a woman from another country who I supposedly barely knew.

I gently diverted all the questions back to the examination, knowing that "no comment" would be better at this point. But even Mom had mentioned that we were due for a splashy media inquiry—a day I was dreading.

"Dr. Helmuth," Nurse Rima called as I walked by her. "You've got a patient in room four."

"O-oh, thank you," I said, glancing at the name and smiling. "Thank you very much."

"I thought you'd want to be the one to examine him," she said with a wink.

I patted the table in front of her and sauntered to the room, knocking briefly before letting myself in.

"About time. I've been waiting for half an hour." Kader sat shirtless on the examination table, the wound on his shoulder still pink and healing with the wire stitches poking out.

"Are you here for an examination or to talk?"

"Both?" he said, and I went to the cabinets to retrieve some gloves. "Feels fine though. You should clear me to go back to work."

"Uh-huh," I said, checking his shoulder for signs of infection. "And how does your wife feel about this?"

"Married two days and you're an expert?"

I shrugged.

"Then perhaps I won't tell you what your friend Olivia said when I paid her a visit on the way to the hospital."

"Oh yeah?" I leaned against the cabinet, pulling off the gloves and tossing them into the garbage. "Fine then, what'd she say?"

"She's got an uncle upstairs who's had surgery, so she'll be popping in to visit tomorrow," Kader said. "Thought you might want to check in on her."

I laughed and leaned against the cabinets. "Thanks. It's been hard to get around."

"It's a good thing I stopped by," Kader said, looking around as if for surveillance equipment. "A lot of ministers are being reassigned. You'll notice some new reporters on the front page of the Kylaen newspapers. Your father's taking full advantage of having a whole country to make people disappear in."

"But Rave's not...I mean, people *know* what's going on there, right?" I said. "He can't say someone's going to work for Bayard and then..."

"Bayard's in your father's pocket, so he'll do whatever Grieg says, whether he wants to or not. The reports we're getting from Johar aren't good. There's been rioting in the streets, and from what I hear on our end, Grieg is mobilizing the Kylaen military to 'help.'"

I rubbed my face. "That didn't take long."

"No, it didn't. Destabilizing Rave might not be our best option after all." He slid off the table and donned his shirt, flinching only once as he pulled it on. "So Olivia getting to Jervan and Herin is more important than ever."

Which would, in effect, result in more bloodshed. More war. More pain.

"Kader..." I said after a long silence. "How does this end?"

"Bloody."

NINETEEN

THEO

"R-rioting?"

Galian had arrived home after I'd already gone to sleep, so our now-familiar breakfast was the first chance I had to catch up with him. I'd intended to tell him all about Kopec and Rhys' methods for pressuring her, but when he'd told me Kader's news about the situation in Rave, I'd forgotten all about it.

"The reports from Johar are fuzzy," Galian said, reaching across the small table to take my hand, running his finger along the gold band. I could only wear it in the privacy of our bedroom. "But...Grieg is sending troops over. Bayard must've lost complete control of the country. Which is good, but...not good."

"Fuck," I said, no longer hungry. "What does that mean? What can we do? What *should* we do?"

"To be honest, we should've expected this," Galian said. "Grieg's ruthless. And if you look at the papers, it's all stories about the wedding—nothing from Rave."

"And nothing about the missing ministers either," I said, remembering the look on Rhys' face. "There was someone yesterday, I can't remember the name, but a minister had been replaced."

"Mansela?"

I shook my head. "Someone else. Bassett?"

"That's two," Galian said. "Guess Rhys'll have to dig up some dirt on whoever's replacing them."

I stared out the window at the gray day as rain splattered against the window. The small hope that I'd had when Galian and I married on the island was in danger of flickering out. Yet again, we were outmatched and outmaneuvered and there were no clear answers.

Galian's squeezed my hand. "Hey, *amichai.*"

I turned back to him, the word still sending chills down my spine and distracting me from from my worried thoughts. "You know," I said, running my other hand over his, "to be honest, I thought I'd never hear you call me that."

"No?"

"I thought it was just something I'd have to accept, falling for a Kylaen. Your shitty country and your shitty accent."

He grinned. "Oh, I'm so glad you lowered your expectations so I can constantly exceed them."

I laughed and his other hand joined my two. Then I slipped my hand out from the bottom of the stack and stuck it on top. He pulled his out and placed it on top of mine. We played this game of whose-hand-is-on-top for a moment, until he went for my side, and I shrieked and nearly fell out of my chair.

"You're such a cheater," I said, guarding my hips against any further attacks from his devious fingers.

"Apparently," he said, holding up his hands in peace. "You

should hear some of these nurses. They're either pitying me that I'm being forced to marry you—"

"As well they should."

"Or pitying *you* that you're being made to marry such a philandering playboy."

"Also, as well they should."

He snorted and sat back. "Little do they know I'm actually the luckiest man in Kylae that I get to spend time with you every morning over breakfast."

My face grew warm, especially when he leaned over the table to plant a kiss on my lips.

"And lucky me that I don't have to go in for another hour. So how about we finish breakfast and then figure out how to get hungry again?"

As he spoke, he'd circled the table, pulling me to my feet and against his body. I giggled as his hands found my rear, lifting me up. I wrapped my legs around his waist and kissed him mercilessly. We stumbled toward the bedroom, banging into the table and knocking over a lamp and nearly dropping me as he tripped over the rug.

But when the door to the parlor swung open, I gasped in surprise.

GALIAN

"W-what the hell are *you* doing here?" Theo said, as she slid to the ground. I craned my neck and saw a slightly familiar Raven woman standing in the doorway, a thick binder in her hand and an amused look on her face.

"I missed you too, *'neechai.*"

"Don't call me that," Theo said through clenched teeth. "And get the hell out of my room. You weren't invited in."

"Theo, you and I both know that neither of us have any say in this country," she said, closing the door behind her and walking over to the sitting area where our breakfast had grown cold. "Now, why don't you put your clothes back on and we'll discuss your schedule for the day?"

I blinked, torn between confusion at this woman's no-nonsense demanding and indignation on behalf of my wife. "Er...who are you?"

"My apologies, Your Highness. Emilie Mondra. President Bayard has offered my services while we deal with the public relations of your wedding."

Theo snorted, but I glanced between them. "P-public relations?"

"It won't surprise you that the Raven people aren't very happy about this situation," Emilie said, and Theo muttered something under her breath. "For them, we need to sell the two of you. Have them celebrate *your* union instead of the union between our nations."

"A union that we didn't want any part of," Theo snapped.

"From the looks of things when I walked in, you seemed pretty happy about it," Emilie said with a pointed glance at Theo's disheveled shirt.

"How can you even stand here when there are riots in Veres?" Theo said, although her face grew even redder.

"I could ask how you can stomach sleeping with your fiancé when his father has killed thousands of our countrymen, but then we'd be here all day," Emilie said. "As it stands, I appreciate that you look a little more alive now that you two are back together. I can only assume that's the reason behind your little spark of life in Jervan, *'neechai*."

Theo's jaw fell in horror, and I stepped in front of her. "Despite what you might hear, our sex life is none of your business."

"Actually, *everything* you do is my business. What you do, who you see. What you say. How often and where you kiss. The next few months will be a carefully planned strategy, which you and Theo will play along with."

"Or what?" I said.

"Or I could tell a different story. I could talk about the building in Malaske, how Bayard had put all the millions in resources toward the defense of our country. But thanks to one lovesick Raven major, instead of ending the war in victory, the bomb went to the bottom of the Madion Sea. And, out of options, Bayard had no choice but to bow to pressure and return the country to Kylae." She tilted her head to the side. "How well do you think that will play with your rebels, *'neechai*?"

Theo's eyes widened. "You wouldn't dare. P-people will see right through that. They'll question why Bayard had the bomb—"

"Because he was trying to end the fighting—"

"By killing half a million people!"

"By any means necessary. Theo, I've been in this game a lot longer than you have, and I *can* make anything look like anything I want, so how about you quiet down and let me help you instead of destroy you?"

"Okay, so I have a question," I said, before Theo could retort. "Not to sound...whatever...but how the hell did a Raven get put in charge of our public relations?" I tossed an apologetic glance at Theo. "Sorry."

"Much like your fiancée, I didn't let the simple fact of my race get in the way of what I wanted. Besides, based on the photos I've been seeing, she wants me here. I brought the right foundation color, at least. And I'll do my best to help her look as professional and put-together." She paused. "Despite what you might think, Theo, I did grow a little attached to you during our time together. I thought of you as a little sister."

Theo quirked a brow. "Then why the hell did you let them put me in a bomb?"

"I didn't believe you'd turn on us," Emilie said with a shrug. "You disappointed me when you left to warn the Kylaens."

"Who you now work for, might I remind you," I added.

"And aren't you so lucky that I do." She crossed the room to sit at the small table where Theo and I had been eating breakfast, moving a plate to put her thick binder down. "The king has been persuaded that Theo embarrassing herself by meeting with ministers who'd rather spit on her than shake her hand isn't the best course of action. And the queen was persuaded that Theo highlighting the plight of poor Ravens in the Kylaen slums is a bad image."

Theo glanced up at me, but said nothing.

"Instead, I've got a better strategy. We're going to showcase both of your strengths. I've got an idea, but it'll take me a few days to get the pieces ironed out. In the meantime, Theo, you and I will discuss your social profile. What I want you to say, how I want you to say it, and to whom." She smiled as Theo rolled her eyes. "It'll be just like old times. Complete with your prince to take to your bed every night."

"Fuck off," Theo growled.

"And as for you, Your Highness," Emilie said, leveling her intense glare at me. "You're free to do as you wish, but I ask that you try to keep your behavior respectable when you're in public." She glanced at her watch. "Speaking of, it looks like you'll be late for your shift if you don't leave now."

"Uh..." I began.

"A word." Theo grabbed my shirt sleeve and dragged me into the bedroom, slamming the door behind her and taking heaving, deep breaths as she paced in front of me.

"What the... I can't even.... *Ugh!*"

"Calm down, *amichai*," I said. "She's just trying to get a rise out of you."

"Put on makeup and parade around while my people are *rioting*?" she said. "And now she's had the brilliant idea of stopping me from going to the slums—*now* what am I supposed to do?"

"We'll think of something else," I said. "Maybe you can persuade her to come visit me at work, and we can arrange a meeting there?"

Theo frowned, glaring at the door and, presumably, the woman on the other side. "Galian, I feel like a puppet again. I hate this feeling."

"Then don't be a puppet," I said with a shrug. "If you know what they're trying to do, you can figure out how to use it to your advantage. You know Emilie's here to prevent you from screwing with this treaty, whether by Bayard's order or Grieg's, so everything she says is designed to do just that. All you have to do is figure out a counteroffensive."

She leaned against the door. "Please don't go to work today. I need you here. Emilie's so much smarter than I am—even if I could come up with something, she'd already be three steps ahead of me."

"I've got to meet with Olivia today," I said. When her gaze darkened, I qualified, "As soon as I meet with her, I'll come right home, I promise."

She released a loud sigh. "*Fine.* I'll deal with Emilie by myself. But you promise—"

"Right home."

"Can't believe you're abandoning me to meet with your ex-girlfriend," Theo said with a ghost of a smile on her face. "But you'd better make some serious progress with Olivia or else there will be *hell* to pay tonight."

I swallowed. "Oh really? What kind of hell?"

Her eyes flashed. "No sex."

"Fine," I said, saluting her. "I'll do my best, ma'am."

THEO

Galian left with a kiss and a heartfelt apology, but I hung on to my annoyance. I knew I was being a bit irrational. We both had our roles in this staged production, and he was playing his. But his promises to work together were starting to ring hollow. Making me laugh in the morning was one thing; leaving me to contend with Emilie by myself was quite another.

When I finally walked out into the parlor, Emilie had already set up shop on the table, and was reviewing her notebook.

"Get that scowl off your face, you'll get wrinkles," she said without even glancing in my direction. "Now, I've got a few ideas for how we can shape your image. You've already got a few requests for interviews, but I've taken the liberty of declining them all, as per the king's request. He's not sure you're ready for the media's glare, and after your performance in Thormondia—"

"Veres, for fuck's sake. Call it by the right name," I said.

"Rave is no longer a country," Emilie said, and I was surprised she didn't show even a modicum of sadness over that statement. "We are now the seventh province of the Great Kingdom of Kylae, so it's back to Thormondia." She tapped her pen against the folder, furrowing her brow in thought. "The queen was fairly adamant that she wanted you to help out with charity. Was that her choice or yours?"

"M-mine," I said, wishing I was better at lying. "If I'm going to be stuck in this damned country, I want to help my people."

"The slums are so...well, I might be able to figure out a way...but I'd have to scout the location first, and make sure the...urchins are clean, at least." She pursed her lips. "Fine, Theo. As a favor to you, I'll see about getting you a photo opportunity with some Raven refugees. You met with Kopec, right? She's the leader of a good one—good reputation, and she rarely gets her hands dirty."

I smiled, pleased that I'd achieved one small victory against her. Maybe Emilie wasn't as impervious as I'd thought. "Emilie... how do you really feel about this treaty?" I asked, hoping to test my luck a bit more.

She glanced in my direction then opened her mouth. "Of course, I fully—"

"Not the spin, just...your honest opinion. I know you have one. Tell me you don't honestly believe this is what's best for our country."

She didn't respond immediately, and when she did, her voice was thoughtful, a little softer than it had been. "No, I don't think this is what's best for our country, and frankly, I think Bayard is making a grave mistake. I personally believe Rave will declare independence in another decade, led by Anson and his little band of renegades, and we'll begin another fifty years of bloodshed with Kylae."

I couldn't believe her bluntness. "So why are you here, then?"

"Because it's my job."

And just like that, she was back to normal.

GALIAN

I hated leaving Theo to her own devices, but she had the spark in her eyes that had been missing these past few days. At the very least, I was sure Theo knew how to handle Emilie. But her arrival had made things far more complex. She'd done Grieg's work for him by vetoing Theo's visit to the slums with logic and reason.

Which meant my time at the hospital needed to be effective, and I spent a good portion of my downtime in the morning making sure I rehearsed exactly what I needed from Olivia. We were on better ground than when I'd asked for her help before, but I still was prepared for her to throw things at me—especially now that I was officially engaged.

But when I found her, sitting in an empty patient room, she was quick to embrace me. "Galian, I'm so sorry."

"For?"

"This whole mess with the Raven girl. Your father has no right to force you to marry her—"

I laughed, unable to take the absurdity anymore. "It's not like that. It's..." I sighed. "Theo was there with me. On the island."

Olivia's eyes widened, then her brow furrowed, and finally she nodded in understanding. "I see. Well, I suppose that makes sense. I did find it hard to believe you could've survived two months on your own."

"Hmph."

"I'm serious, Galian. You're a talented doctor, sure, but...?"

"Well, you're right, I guess," I said, scratching the back of my head. "I was pretty much worthless except that I stopped the bleeding and saved her life on that first day. But after that, it was all Theo." I couldn't help the grin that spread across my face. "She's..."

"She's *her*, huh?" Olivia chuckled to herself.

Glancing around, I retrieved my wedding band from my pocket. "She's my wife, too. But we can't tell anyone..."

"Not with the way your father is promoting this wedding, no," Olivia said with a sigh. "It's quite the romantic story. A prince and a pilot. Warring nations. Forbidden romance."

"It doesn't seem all that romantic," I muttered. "Especially considering how much things have gone to absolute shit recently."

She quirked a brow. "That's an apt description."

"That's part of why I wanted to talk to you," I said. "Our communication lines have gone down. We need to be able to talk with Jervan and Herin. See if maybe they can intervene in some way—"

"Are you talking an escalation to the war?" Olivia asked. "You'd have Herin and Jervan fight your father over a single island?"

"It's not just about Rave. It's about basic human rights. Grieg's going to reopen barethium mines in Rave. He's going to be even more ruthless than he has been in order to maintain power."

"He's already begun," Olivia said wearily. "Mansela is missing."

"She's in Rave—"

"They say she's in Rave, but it's been a week, and neither of her parents have heard from her. We never got along much—being on opposite sides of most issues—but I did care for her. She was a passionate woman who cared deeply for this country." She stared out the window. "Your father may have lost Mael, but he gained a whole country to imprison people in. And that's why I'm headed to Jervan by the end of the week."

"W-what?" I said. "You're leaving the country?"

"It's not safe for me anymore," she said. "I don't think it's safe for any of us. I sent my father away the night of the Midsummer's Ball. I couldn't risk Grieg doing anything..." She sighed. "But I needed to stay behind and get everything in order before we move. Now, it seems even I can't ignore the writing on the wall."

As much as I hated to see her go, I was glad. "If there's anything you can do for us in Jervan or Herin..."

"I'll certainly try," Olivia said. "War is bad for business, but so is your father's power unchecked. I'd prefer it if we could resolve it without more bloodshed."

"Believe me, if we could, we would've done it by now," I said with a small smile. "I just wish you and Theo could've met. I think...I think you guys would've found a lot to talk about. She's...well, she's amazing."

Olivia offered a tense smile. "She must be, to have made you a one-woman kind of man."

"Oh, come *on*, I wasn't *that* bad," I scoffed.

"You were pretty terrible," Olivia said with a smile. "But truly...you're happy?"

Despite everything, I grinned. "Yeah."

"Well, I suppose you and I were never meant to be."

"Hey, my brother's still single..."

"Queen?" She blanched. "I've got my own kingdom to run. I don't need to add Kylae's troubles to the mix."

I laughed and hugged her once more, bidding her safe travels. And as she walked through the door, I prayed that it wasn't the last time I'd ever see her.

TWENTY

GALIAN

"Shit," Theo said, as I relayed what Olivia had told me. It was still early, and I'd awoken with a particular need to make love to my wife. But as we basked in the afterglow, we caught each other up on the previous day's events.

"It could be a good thing," I said, kissing her collarbone. "If Olivia's actually in Jervan, she could help ferry messages for us. She could be an asset."

"Is she willing to be an asset?"

"I think so," I replied, stroking the skin of her hip. "Peace is best for her company. And without my father's money, she can't rebuild her port in Duran."

"Maybe Emilie could convince Grieg that giving aid is best for the country. I have no idea how she managed to weasel her way into his good graces." She frowned. "And Rhys stopped by last night. We got another report from Johar. Veres is burning—literally. And now there's a mandatory curfew from dusk until dawn." She sighed. "I wish I was there. I wish I was doing *something*."

"I'm kind of glad you aren't," I said. "I like you here. Where I can do things to you every morning." To prove it, I traced a finger down the side of her body.

The side of her mouth turned upward. "You're like a dog with a bone."

"We have months to make up for," I said, trailing kisses down her stomach. "And technically, this is our honeymoon."

"Oh *no*," she said, propping herself up onto her elbows. "This is *not* our honeymoon. This is the farthest thing *from* a honeymoon."

"I'll arrange for a week on the island, how about that?" I kissed her hip, her stomach, the inside of her thigh.

"Oh yeah," she said with a grin.

"Your wish is my command, Princess—"

She half-groaned, half-whimpered. "Don't. Ever. Call. Me. That. Again."

"How about I just call you *amichai*?"

"Yes, please." She arched her back, spreading her legs for me. I loved every moment of this game, watching her anticipate my next move, the playful banter. I was rock hard again—

Rap-rap-rap. "Rise and shine."

Theo let out a groan that was most certainly not an orgasm and all blood flow to my groin ceased.

"Tell her to go *away*," Theo cried with an uncharacteristic pout.

Rap-rap-rap. "I can hear you. I'm not going away. We have a schedule today. And His Highness is late for work."

"Are you seriously going to work today?" she asked, cracking open an eye at me. "Are you kidding me? What good is us being married if you aren't here to help me fight off these idiots?"

"But you said you had a handle on Emilie," I said, feigning innocence. In reality, the *last* thing I wanted to do was hang around and have our relationship dissected. Emilie scared the shit out of me, and the less time I spent in her presence, the happier I was.

"Galian."

"Mom wanted me to keep working!" I insisted, crawling off the bed and heading to the bathroom.

"Yeah, and you also said you'd come home *right after* you met with Olivia," Theo said. "And you didn't get back until midnight."

"We got slammed at the hospital!"

"Bull. Shit."

I stood in the doorway. "Theo, come on. I told you this was how it was going to be."

"No, you didn't," she snapped, throwing the bedsheets off. "You said we were going to work together—"

"In-between my time at the hospital. Theo, I need to be there to courier messages."

"Really? Were you couriering messages until midnight last night?"

"No, I was saving lives."

Her eyes narrowed, and her anger was palpable from across the room. She stalked toward me, her lips pressed into a fine line, her eyes flashing dangerously. She swiped her dressing robe off the ground and wrapped it around herself. Then, with one final glare that informed me just how in trouble I was, she stormed through the bedroom doors.

THEO

Oh, that man made me so angry. One minute he was concerned, and the next, he was leaving me to fend for myself.

Well, if he thought he was going to kiss his way out of this one, he had another thing coming. My downstairs was off-limits to husbands who didn't fulfill their end of the bargain.

I slammed the doors behind me and puffed out a breath.

"Stop being so melodramatic," Emilie tutted, sitting at the writing desk in the parlor. An assortment of makeup and brushes lay before her, and she was testing it on her own skin with the finesse of an artist.

"The queen has decided that you *will* be accompanying her on a trip to the slums," Emilie said, checking two dark eyeshadows on the back of her hand. "Against my strong recommendations."

"I'm going to the slums today?" My anger at Galian vanished. This was...this was good. I'd finally be able to talk to some people, maybe even get a message to Anson.

"Yes, in less than an hour, so we'd better be quick. I've put together an outfit for you—red and silver, to match the Kylaen flag—but I'll need to do your hair and makeup." She picked up the foundation, tapping it against her skin first. "Unfortunately, my request to have a Raven makeup artist was denied by the king. So I suppose I'll have to step in and make you look presentable."

"Can't get everything we want, hm?" I said with a daring smirk.

"I can also make you look like a clown, so watch that tone."

I sat down across from her and let her work. My gaze kept drifting to the door, where I was sure my husband would be coming out any moment. Just thinking about him drove a hot knife of fury into my chest.

"You look like you're about to murder me. I thought you'd be happy about this?" Emilie said, painting my lips.

"I am," I forced out, tearing my attention away from my bedroom.

"Well, I'm not. Your first official event with refugees? Do you know how *bad* that looks?" Emilie shook her head. "I haven't even had time to arrange the official engagement photos. The first impression these Kylaens are going to have of you is you hobnobbing with street urchins. They'll consider you one of them."

"Or, it'll show how caring I am."

"No, *'neechai*," Emilie said, taking her brush to my hair. "These people already think you're garbage."

I chewed my lip, tasting the makeup. "What does it matter what they think?"

Emilie stared at my reflection and shook her head as she reapplied my lip stain. "It matters."

"Hey, beautiful." Galian strolled out of our bedroom, his hair still wet from a shower. The smile on his face was adoring, and I wanted to slap it off. As if he was going to get out of this argument with compliments. "Where are you going?"

"Slums," I said, refusing to look at him. "Charity photo opportunity. Aren't you going to work?"

He met my gaze in the mirror and frowned.

"Well? Go on. You were so eager a minute ago," I snapped, turning to Emilie and looking at her eyeshadow with great interest.

He stared at me a moment longer before crossing the room and planting a gentle kiss on my cheek. Then, with one final, uncertain look, he left.

"Oh my goodness, that was awkward," Emilie said, grabbing the blush and applying it to my cheek. "Trouble in paradise?"

"Tell me more about this event," I said, punctuating it with a warning look.

Emilie, thankfully, took the hint. "The queen has asked you to accompany her to visit a food dispensary. She's hoping to bring attention to increase donations from other Kylaens."

"What is a food dispensary?" I asked.

"Exactly what it sounds like. For those too poor to afford their own food, the Kylaen government offers a ration. I'm sure the queen will tell you what she needs from you when we get there."

"I'm not riding with her?" If I wasn't riding with Korina, I wouldn't be able to talk with her in private about why she'd arranged this meeting. I was starting to get annoyed with all these Kylaens promising me they'd help me and then leaving me on my own.

But lucky for me, there was one Kylaen I could count on. Kader was at the wheel of the car that picked me up, which filled me with so much relief, Emilie even commented on it. Good old Kader.

It took us some time to drive to the poorer part of the city, but I knew when we'd arrived. It had the same dilapidated, dirty facades as the buildings in Veres. Street urchins loitered under awnings and in alleyways, watching my car with an unsurprised interest.

"Have fun," Emilie said as Kader slammed the front door.

"You aren't coming?" I asked.

"It's not my preference."

"Why, because they're beneath you?"

Her eyes were sharp. "Because I would prefer that your narrative not be sullied by my presence. In case you're unaware, I'm not that popular anymore."

Kader opened the door and waited for me to walk out. I glanced at Emilie, who had busied herself in her notepad again.

"C'mon," Kader said gently, and I finally stepped out of the car and let him lead me into the building.

Korina was already hard at work, talking with reporters with a genuine smile on her face. They stood at rapt attention, holding out recording devices and soaking up every word.

And pointedly ignoring the other occupants of the room, the refugees. Some were missing limbs, some had burns, but even those who were whole still looked malnourished, haunted. They, like me, were in a country that thought them less than dirt. And also like me, they were slowly running out of places to go.

They stood against the walls in filthy clothes that hung off their thin frames, gazing at the floor but seeing nothing. The photographers walking amongst them ignored them in favor of snapping photos of the queen, and the Ravens seemed content to be ignored. These appearances by rich Kylaens must've been nothing new, and must've done little to actually improve lives.

"So how does this work?" I asked Kader.

"The Kylaen government rations a certain amount of food each week. They're waiting for their turn." He nodded to a child nearby, who clutched a scrap of white paper in his hand.

"And what am I supposed to do?" I asked.

"Nothing. Stand here and smile and have your photo taken."

I blanched. "These people are starving and you expect me to do nothing to help them?"

"Larger goals, Theo," Kader replied, glancing around the room. "I'm going to see if my contact is here." He paused. "On your left."

"My, my, not anything to look at, are you?"

Kader's warning had been for a gray-haired, sharply-dressed woman. She drank in the sight of me like I was the most interesting thing she'd ever seen as she twirled her pen in her hand.

"How does it feel to finally be amongst your people again?" she asked.

"I'm sorry, who are you?" I blinked.

"Gaetna Zygmont, how lovely of you to join us." Korina was beside me in a moment, extending a pale hand toward the woman, who took it graciously. "Though this isn't usually the sort of assignment for a lead news anchor, is it?" She gestured to the room. "A simple photo opportunity?"

"The first with the future princess of Kylae." The woman's beady gaze landed on me, and despite my best efforts, I gulped. "Tell me, was it your idea to spend the day with your kinsmen, or the queen's?"

"Ms. Zygmont, I thought we'd agreed to no interviews," Korina said.

"Just a few questions. The Kylaen public is dying to know more about Major Kallistrate from the woman herself. The press releases the castle puts out are so...underwhelming."

"Well, we do the best with what we have," Korina said with a small shrug.

It was easy to look offended, but harder to remember that Korina was playing a role. Especially in front of this new woman, who I assumed was someone important in the media, it made sense to pretend I was an unwilling participant.

"Theo, dear, why don't you make yourself useful?" Korina said, throwing me a knowing look. "Ms. Zygmont and I can discuss the specifics of the wedding. I know how it bores you so."

Zygmont looked like she'd much rather stay and talk with me, but Korina was insistent and led her to the other side of the room next to the window. Still, I had a feeling that Zygmont wasn't going to give up that easily.

I needed to keep myself busy, because standing in the center of the room like an idiot wasn't helping anyone. Especially because no one was actually receiving food through the small window. Those that I saw on the other side of the wall seemed in no hurry to feed the hungry.

Well, Korina *had told* me to be useful.

There was a small door beside the window, and it was unlocked, so I walked through into the kitchen. It appeared to be similar to the ones back in Vinolas—multiple burners, lots of big pots and pans to make a lot of food quickly, a large icebox. But back in Vinolas, at least, the kitchens were always a hum of activity, getting ready for the next meal. Here, the Kylaens sat around a small table, playing a card game.

"Excuse me—" I started, but their reactions were swift.

"Get the hell out of here!" The woman who spoke was large, with a red face, and she didn't even bother to stand as she addressed me. "Feeding starts in an hour."

"There are hungry people out there now," I said, placing my hands on my hips.

"So wait in line with the rest of 'em," she replied. "Or we'll call the police."

"Um..." I glanced at the closed door. "I'm...I mean, I'm not..." I swallowed and hated myself. "I'm Prince Galian's fiancée."

"And I'm Prince Rhys' shoe shine girl. Get out of my kitchen."

"Excuse me, is there a problem?" My hero, Elijah Kader, appeared behind me through the door.

"This migrant's trynna get more food."

"This migrant will be your princess in three months, so I suggest you give her food to hand out. Or shall I get the queen in here?"

They stared at him, but, apparently, his Kylaen citizenship afforded him greater respect than my impending marriage. Their chairs scraped the floor as they rose to stand, grumbling about dark-skinned idiots and some other insults I chose not to take personally. The one who'd yelled at me—the head of the kitchen, I assumed—went to the icebox and yanked out a bag. She waddled across the kitchen and thrust it into my hands.

"Here. Give this to them if you're so worried."

The bag was cold in my hands, the bread inside icy. "I can't give them frozen food."

"If you have a problem with it, take it up with your father-in-law."

I made a noise and pushed past her, marching toward the oven. I supposed if I wanted anything done, I'd have to do it myself. Unsurprisingly, Kader joined me to help me work the oven, and together, we managed to fill up two large baking trays with the frozen bread.

I stood with my arms crossed over my chest, a frown on my face.

"I know this isn't getting to you," Kader said quietly. "You've been in a bad mood since we left the castle. What's wrong?"

"Galian's being a dick."

He chuckled. "*Galian*, huh? You must really be steamed."

"Remember all that shit he said on the island? About how we were going to do this together?" I motioned to the kitchen. "Well? Where the hell is he?"

"Have you talked to him about it?"

"This morning. He said he was couriering messages." I snorted. "I think he just doesn't want to be around Emilie."

"Is any of this behavior surprising?" Kader asked. "He's Galian. The only time he's ever compelled to do anything outside his comfort zone is where you're involved."

"Yeah, well..." I smirked. "He's about to see what happens when I'm *not* involved."

"Right now, you need to focus," Kader said, glancing at the kitchen staff, who were back to playing cards on the other side of the kitchen. "This was a smart move, wanting to pass out food. You'll be able to talk with the Ravens without looking too suspicious."

"So there's someone I need to meet today?"

"He's wearing a yellow shirt. Be brief and let him know you want to meet with Anson again now that things have changed. Don't linger, especially with that Zygmont woman out there. She'll start digging if she thinks there's anything worth reporting."

The oven dinged, and we pulled out the bread, which was still hard and cold, but at least not completely frozen. Kader helped me put them into a large basket, and then, with a nod, he sent me out into the main room.

First, I searched for the yellow-shirted man, who I found almost immediately. Unlike the rest of the refugees, he seemed to be exactly where he wanted and held my gaze confidently. Conscious of appearing too interested in him, I began handing out bread to those in the room.

As Kader had said, Zygmont's attention zeroed in on me, even as the queen engaged her in conversation. So to keep up appearances, I focused on the children in the room, smiling and asking them about themselves. None of the photographers took photos of it, but I soon forgot about them. For the first time in what felt like months, I was helping my fellow Ravens.

Unfortunately, this sentiment wasn't shared by anyone over the age of ten, as they refused to acknowledge me or take food. I heard them mumble unsavory things about me, so I kept moving. I told myself one day they'd know the truth, and I might be vindicated.

I approached the yellow-shirt man last, offering him bread. "How long have you been over here?"

"Long enough to know not to take bread from a treasonous bitch."

I let it roll off my shoulders. "I had nothing to do with Grieg and Bayard's plan, you know." Narrowing my eyes, I added, "And if Anson thinks otherwise, he's an idiot."

"Don't matter if you knew or didn't know. You're playing along now."

"Sometimes you have to play nice with vile people if you want to get anything accomplished," I replied, forcing a smile onto my face as I caught Korina's eye. "My end game hasn't changed. A free and independent Rave."

"My advice?" He took a bite of the bread. "Stick to screwing your Kylaen fiancé and leave the revolution to the revolutionaries."

Then, before I could react, he spat the bread in my face.

The reaction was swift—Kader had me away from him, a few of the guards cornered the man and cuffed him, Korina and Zygmont rushed over to see what the commotion was. Lights flashed as the photographers finally found something interesting to record for posterity.

The news anchor looked like her birthday had come early, as she twiddled her pen between her fingers. "Well, I daresay not everyone's pleased about the wedding, hm?"

"Some people just don't know what's best for them," Korina said, refusing to catch my eye. "Please ensure that man is reminded what happens when you disrespect a member of the royal family."

"She ain't a royal yet, bitch, and won't be if Anson has anything to say about it!"

"Enough," Kader said. "Get him out of here."

As the royal security took the man away, I caught the eye of a child who'd taken bread from me not five minutes before. And my heart broke when he tossed his half-eaten food in the trash.

GALIAN

I'd been married for less than three days and already my wife was mad at me. She had every right to be; I was basically ditching her to go to work.

If I were being honest, it was because staying around the castle reminded me of all the things left to do. We had a war to stop, a treaty to fix, and...well, when Theo and I were in my room, I could forget all about that. I had my wife. We were getting our happily ever after. And though she was worried for her country, I was too firmly in wedded bliss to care.

That was, until I watched a yellow-shirted man spitting bread into her face on television and saw the horrified, lonely look on her face. She needed me, and I wasn't there for her. Some husband I'd turned out to be.

Immediately, I called for a car back to the castle. I peppered Snyder with questions about what had happened, who'd done it, what had gone so wrong, but he had no answers to give. And as I ascended the stairs to my bedroom, I knew she was already angry with me for leaving her. How badly would I have to grovel to get her to forgive me now?

I found her sitting against the pillows, wearing one of my old shirts with tear stains on her face.

"I came as soon as I saw it," I said, crawling across the bed to her. "Are you okay?"

"They hate me," she whispered against my skin. "The refugees. They hate me. Anson hates me. The world hates me."

"But I love you."

"Do you?" she asked, staring at her hands. "You haven't been doing a good job of showing it lately."

She had me there. "I am so sorry," I said, hoping it sounded sincere. "I could sit here and make excuses but...I'm just sorry. I'll do better. I'll take leave from the hospital. You aren't doing this alone."

"You said that before."

"I mean it this time," I said, hating myself for letting her down.

She sniffed and wiped her face. "I thought things would be different, but it all feels the same. Everyone's making decisions for me. Everyone's speaking for me. When do I get to talk?"

I laughed and leaned back against the bed, pulling her to my chest. "There's an insistent reporter who wants to interview me."

"I think I met her today," Theo said with a snort. "She didn't like me very much. Then again, no one did."

"They just need to get to know you. Fall in love with you like I did." I kissed the top of her forehead. "*Amichai*, I am so sorry that I wasn't there for you today. I want to make it up to you."

"I'm not sleeping with you."

I had to laugh. "I deserved that. But why don't I call downstairs and get us a big, greasy burger and fries and a couple of beers?"

She sat up and pursed her lips. "That sounds amazing, actually."

"Consider it done." I cupped her cheek and brushed my thumb against the wet skin. "You and me, *amichai*. From here on out. I promise I'm not going to let you do this alone anymore."

TWENTY-ONE

THEO

The next morning, Galian called Dr. Maitland and asked for a few days' leave. It made me feel marginally better, although I still didn't trust that he would stay true to his word. Rhys had come to visit us around midnight, and informed us that the event in the slums hadn't been sanctioned by Grieg, and he'd been very angry about me being let out without his permission. I could only imagine how angry he would be when he read the long, complimentary piece Zygmont wrote in the paper about how I was handing out food to children.

"She's buttering you up," Galian said, tossing the paper down in front of our breakfast. "She wants you to think she's on your side, then she'll roast you live on camera."

"But we're not going to be live on camera any time soon... Right?"

He smiled. "Not unless you want to be."

I shook my head.

"Good morning, good morning!" Emilie bustled through the

door, a bright smile on her face and clothes bag in her hand. " *'neechai*, I have a big surprise for you today."

I shared a look with my husband. "What kind of surprise?"

"Oh, wouldn't you like to know?" She handed me the bag with a bright grin. "Put that on and both of you meet me downstairs. Today's going to be *very* exciting."

I unzipped the bag and froze. It was my old Kylaen flight suit—complete with the major's gold star. "What the hell is this?"

"Hurry up! Hurry up!"

Perplexed and a little concerned, I dressed quickly and joined my *amichai* in the car downstairs. Yet again, Kader was at the wheel, but his expression didn't give me much confidence. Nothing could've prepared me for what I saw when we drove into one of the hangars at a nearby Kylaen airfield.

"You have *got* to be kidding me," I gasped, my mouth falling open.

There she was, in all of her glory. My girl—the Raven plane I'd flown for seven years. Or a model similar to it. Sitting in the hangar of the Kylaen air base, pristine and beautiful.

"Are you pleased?" Emilie asked, getting out of the car. "I think she's pleased, Your Highness."

I didn't want to be. Much like the morning breakfast which I'd become accustomed to, and the silky sheets, and sleeping with my Kylaen husband, a part of me hated how much I really wanted to fly that plane.

"Welcome to your first bullshit appearance for this treaty you hate so much," Rhys said, walking up next to us. He looked about as enthusiastic as Galian did. He noticed Emilie's scowl and clarified, "My apologies. Your first appearance for the treaty."

Emilie seemed satisfied and pressed her familiar binder to her chest. "If you'll excuse me, I've got to speak with the media outlets about the plan for today."

"You guys can't be serious," I said, leaning into Galian as he wrapped an arm around my waist. "You want me to go fly this thing around Norose? Get my photo taken next to it?"

"Be sure to smile, *kallistrate*."

Whatever good mood I'd been fighting evaporated when Mark Cannon strolled around the other side of the plane. I hadn't seen that son of a bitch since he'd sentenced me to death and put me in that plane, but he wore the same smug, conceited expression as if he had all the answers and I was just some dumb kid he toyed with.

"I suppose you're responsible for this farce?" I snapped.

"Your future father-in-law," Cannon said, placing a loving hand on the hull of my ship. "And Emilie, of course. We'd like to show the world that Kylae will let Rave live in peace."

"You mean you want to distract them while Kylae enslaves us again," I snarled at him.

"Semantics," Cannon said with a flippant shrug that made my blood boil.

"Fuck your semantics. Don't you care about what's happening to your own people?" Galian asked, and I felt a surge of affection for him.

"Is that any way to address a vice provincial governor?" Cannon asked.

"Tell me how much power you have in the cabinet, and we'll talk."

"More than you, princeling, I assure you. President Bayard sent me here to make sure Major Kallistrate represents our province with all the professionalism she displayed while on active duty."

I narrowed my eyes. "Bayard's not here?"

"No." Something about the way he shifted said there was more to the story than he was letting on. My experience with Bayard was that he never let a good photo opportunity go to waste. So why was he sending Cannon to represent him at such an overtly Raven event? Especially if the idea was to show how well Kylae and Rave were getting along.

"I won't do it," I said, folding my arms across my chest. "You can't make me fly this thing and, you can't force me to participate."

"I thought you might say that," Cannon said. "So Bayard told me to offer you a deal: If you go show us your flying skills like a good little *kallistrate*, then I'll secure the pardon for your friend, the chief mechanic."

My blood ran cold. "L-Lanis?"

"Who?" Galian said looking down at me.

"The mechanic who helped your fiancée escape Rave all those months ago. While you've been eating roasted beef and getting serviced by your prince, he's been sitting in a cold jail cell. All alone. Wondering why you haven't come for him yet."

I knew he was playing my emotions, but it worked. For all I knew, Lanis could've been dead, or worse. And knowing I'd put searching for him aside sent a knife straight to my gut.

"But, if you do what I say, and show all those photographers out there just how you survived seven years in the military, I'll make sure he's in the front row at your wedding."

"I'd like a word." Galian's voice cut through the storm of emotions in my head and, before I could respond, he was guiding me away from Cannon's gleeful face.

"That guy's an ass," Rhys said, as he and Galian stood in front of me, blocking Cannon from my view.

"*Amichai*," I said, placing a hand over my mouth. "Lanis...I can't... Can't we do something? Lanis took care of me. He's in jail because of me. I can't...I can't let him stay there." I chewed my lip.

"We'll send word to Johar," Rhys said. "If he's been incarcerated, we'll pull some strings and get him out. I promise you. After all..." He cringed. "We own the country now."

"But Anson—"

Rhys waved his hand. "Let Mom and me worry about him. Regardless of what Cannon says, we both think it's a good idea for you to do this."

"Why?"

"Because Father wants you to," Rhys said. "And we need to prove to him that you two are playing nice, if only so he'll let you continue to move unrestricted. We'd rather you lose some ground with Anson than get pulled from the game completely."

The familiar uneasy feeling blossomed in my gut. When I'd been in Bayard's team, I'd faced much the same quandary. Do something I disliked in order to gain favor with the man in charge for the greater good. It hadn't worked out so well for me then, and it was hard for me to see how it would work out any better now.

"Let me have a minute with her, will you?" Galian said to his brother, who nodded and went to join Kader on the other side of the hangar.

"*Amichai*, I don't know what to do. Anson already thinks I'm a traitor. Flying around in this thing? That'll just confirm it."

"Well, you have a choice," he said. "Either you fly the plane and risk that Anson won't be willing to listen when you talk to him again, or you don't, and Father won't let you out of the castle to even attempt it."

I winced. "Do you think he'd do that?"

"Yup."

I closed my eyes and leaned into his chest. "Do you know what the worst thing is? I really want to fly the plane. I haven't flown in a plane like this since before the island. I miss it, you know? It was who I was, what I did for almost half my life."

"I know. I saw your face when you walked into the hangar," he said with a chuckle. "And I remember how angry you were at me when I destroyed your plane."

So did I. "Did I ever apologize for that?"

"I'm sure you did." He rubbed my back comfortingly. "Look, forget all this shit with Lanis, forget Anson. Forget that dick Cannon even. Get in that plane and fly it like you've never flown before. Go enjoy yourself. Remember? We're trying to find normal."

I tilted my head up. "*None* of this is normal."

"You in a plane? Seems pretty normal to me." He tightened his hold around me as I laughed, unwillingly. "I mean it. We don't get a lot of wins anymore. And if this convinces Father to ease up...*and* puts a smile on your face, well, I don't see how that's a bad thing."

My attention snagged on a man on the side of the hangar. At first glance, I thought he was part of the Raven ground crew, presumably. But then, as we locked gazes, he tapped his chest.

Once for Rave.

Twice for traitors.

"Galian," I whispered, turning back to my *amichai*. "I think..." But when I glanced back at where he'd been, no one was there.

"What is it?"

"N-nothing."

GALIAN

Theo had seemed spooked, but if we were going to stay ahead of public opinion, she needed something new for her image. Although I hadn't mentioned it to her, everyone *except* Zygmont was talking about the bread-spitting incident.

"They're just ripping into her," Rhys said, as we ascended the stairs to the radar tower. "I'm glad she agreed to do this."

"Me too." But not solely because of the press. Theo needed a little fun in her life.

When we entered the radar tower, Rhys took his position at his normal desk, and I sat beside him, glancing at the others manning the station. Some of them wore disgruntled expressions, although they kept their comments to themselves, thankfully.

The phone in the tower rang and the young sergeant nodded to Rhys, who turned on the microphone.

"Theo, this is Radar Tower One Two Six. You're cleared for take-off."

"Fantastic."

Pride swelled in my chest as the plane engines roared to life. I'd never actually seen Theo fly (other than when she shot me out of the sky), and I was a little excited to see her in action. She was back where she belonged—in the air.

The plane rolled down the runway, picking up speed then

taking off gently. I considered how easy it would be for her to keep going all the way to Rave and beyond.

"You don't think she's going to fly away, do you?" I asked, reaching into my pocket to finger my ring nervously.

Rhys snorted and offered me a wry glance. "Are you that bad a hus...*fiancé?*"

The plane circled the air field, gaining altitude, and her grainy voice came through the speakers. *"How far can I go?"*

"Keep it within the confines of the air field," Rhys said, before turning off the microphone. "Are you two mind-readers or something? Just disgusting."

"You'll find your queen one day," I said, elbowing him gently.

"For my sake, I hope she's half as exciting as your wife."

From the my vantage point, I spotted the photographers lined up along the edge of the runway, their flashes visible even from up here. Somewhere down there, my father was watching the spectacle, as was that bastard Cannon.

"Do you think it's weird Cannon's here and not Bayard?" I asked, hoping the question was innocuous enough not to draw attention.

Rhys glanced at me then shook his head. "I hear he's helping Minister Gren get settled in Rave."

I swallowed. Three of the twelve ministers gone. Three doves. "Who are the new ministers?"

"Don't you read the papers?" Rhys said with a glance behind me. But he knew as well as I did that the reassignment of the ministers hadn't been mentioned except for a small note in the very back.

"Theo and I read it every morning, thank you very much," I said, watching the glint of metal in the sky with my wife in it.

"Yeah, I hear from your guards how much you *read the paper*. You two make me sick," Rhys said, swiping the microphone. "Hey, Theo. How you doing?"

"...Fine."

"Question for you. What's better: flying or my brother?"

There was a long pause of just static.

"Theo? You there?"

"I'm thinking."

A loud chorus of 'oohs' echoed from the radar tower, and I marched forward, yanking the microphone away from Rhys. "Ouch, Theo."

"I love you?"

"Nice try."

I handed the radio back to Rhys, who seemed to find the whole thing funny. I just wished the next time he wanted to change the subject to avoid eavesdropping, he'd leave our sex life out of it. Between him and Emilie, far too many people were making fun of our bedroom activities.

I sat back in my chair and watched the plane zoom this way and that, doing a few loops and fast turns. Theo was actually a pretty good pilot—not that I was any kind of expert in it.

"Okay, Theo, that's good. Come on in," Rhys said after she'd done a few aerial moves. "I think these idiots have enough footage of you to last a lifetime."

"Copy that."

The aircraft zoomed away before turning and descending toward the airfield. But just as her plane neared the runway, her engines roared to life and she shot back into the sky and I nearly fell off my chair at *just* how close she'd come to skimming the concrete runway.

"That was a little too scary, Theo," Rhys said, sharing a glance with me. "You scared your poor fiancé—"

"Rhys, the landing gear is stuck."

My heart stopped beating. "What did she say?"

"Theo, repeat that?"

Her voice had taken on a note of fear. *"The landing gear won't come down. I'll try it again, but..."*

"Can you get it on the ground safely?" Rhys asked.

There was a too-long pause. *"I'm going to take it down as easily as I can."*

"*Fuck!*" I was out of the chair in an instant, dashing down the staircase of the air tower two-by-two, visions of a fiery crash filling my mind. Her bleeding out on the island, the paleness of her skin, the explosion of her plane when I'd shot a flare into it. I burst out of the air tower door just as her plane hit the far edge of the runway.

The plane skidded, the screech of metal-on-concrete piercing. I ran toward the wreckage as it slowed then stopped. Theo didn't seem to be moving, so I hopped on top of the craft and kicked open the glass top. Her head tilted up and she stared at me from beneath her helmet, dazed, but otherwise seemingly unharmed. I unhooked her restraints and she wrapped her arms around me, allowing me to lift her out of the plane. Cradling her, I hopped off the wing and onto the safety of the ground, getting her away from the danger.

THEO

When my mind finally caught up with me, I was sitting in an ambulance, and Galian was pointing a flashlight into my eyes.

"Follow my finger," he said, all business. I tracked the movement to his satisfaction, and he placed his hands on my cheeks, gently moving my head from side to side. "Does this hurt?"

"No," I responded. "*Amichai*, I'm fine."

"Not until I say you are," he said, humorlessly. "Any numbness or tingling?"

Again, I shook my head. "I'm fine. No pain. I've gone through worse."

"You'll feel it in the morning, maybe—"

I took his hands into mine and kissed his fingertips. "I'm fine, I promise you."

"So romantic, Your Highness," Cannon drawled, walking up. "Is this how you won her over on the island?"

In response, Galian turned, reared back, and punched him square in the face. "What the *fuck*, man? Were you trying to kill her?"

I blinked, shocked that my doctorly husband had that kind of fight in him. Cannon looked up from the ground, blood trickling down his face. "*That* wasn't my fault," he grunted, pushing himself upright.

"He's right," I said, taking Galian's arm before he went after Cannon again. "It wasn't him. I saw...I think I saw a rebel in the hangar."

Cannon's face melted into an expression of horror. "A r-rebel?

Anson's rebels?"

"Are you sure?" Galian asked.

"I saw one of them before I took off. I thought I might've been...I didn't know that..." I closed my eyes and rubbed the sore spot on my forehead. "I just thought they were there to...I don't know."

"You didn't think they'd be *that* pissed at you," Galian finished for me before glaring at Cannon. "Maybe they thought this asshole would be flying it."

Cannon shook his head, rubbing his chin. "Damn Tedwin. Does your father know about the rebels? Is he doing anything to keep them out of this country?"

Galian and I shared a look. "Why? Nervous they'll come after you?"

"Damn. *Damn*!" Cannon began walking away.

"Wait!" I called, pushing myself off the table and ignoring how it made my head hurt worse. "What about Lanis?"

"You stupid girl. Who cares about him?" Cannon spat back. "If the rebels are in this country, both of us have a lot more to worry about than some stupid mechanic."

"Cannon," I pressed. "Please, you have to release him—"

Cannon sighed and rubbed his face. "We have no idea where he is. He left the country the same night he dropped you off in Rave."

I released a loud breath, and couldn't even be angry that they'd tricked me. "Thank you. Thank you so much."

Cannon snorted and kept walking, calling for his aides.

"The rebels were able to get onto this base, to get to your plane," Galian said after a moment. "Theo, this is bad."

I chewed my lip. "Maybe it wasn't a rebel. Or maybe your father sent him to make me *think* he was a rebel..."

"You're right. This could've been anyone," Galian said, running a hand through his hair. "It would make a convenient story if the rebels were framed for killing you."

Behind Galian, Rhys was jogging up to us. "Why does Cannon have a bloody nose?"

Galian shrugged.

"Look, you two had better get the hell out of here. The media's going crazy, and a group of protestors is starting to gather outside the base. I'm worried it's going to get bad, so Kader's already getting the car."

We took the hint, and Galian led me to the waiting car, where Kader gave me a once-over, but said nothing. Galian and I settled into the backseat, where the beginnings of a headache formed between my brows. Closing my eyes, I snuggled into my husband's shoulder.

But even without looking at him, I felt the tension in his body, so I lifted my head. His eyes were focused on a point in the distance, his jaw clenched. When I gently touched his cheek, he jumped as if he'd forgotten I was even there.

"*Amichai?*" I asked quietly.

"I almost lost you today, Theo," he said, his voice barely above a whisper.

"Galian, this isn't... It's not the first time—"

"It's never been so..." He sighed deeply and finally met my gaze. "Theo, that was *scary*. And I just...I couldn't do anything to save you."

"I'm fine—"

"But what if you weren't?" he said, his voice thick with emotion. "What if I'd just gotten you back and I lost you for good? I don't know what I'd do." He swallowed and glanced at the top of the car, as if to keep his tears at bay.

As one fell, I kissed it away. "Galian, we didn't make it this far —"

"To be separated," he finished for me. "But people want you dead, Theo, and I can't... I'm not..."

I pressed my lips to his. "I'm fine. And that's all we can worry about right now. We'll figure the rest out, okay?"

He nodded, but the fear in his eyes remained. So I returned to my place in the crook of his neck and let him hold me until we reached the castle.

TWENTY-TWO

GALIAN

Prince Galian Saves Blushing Bride-to-Be
Aerial demonstration goes sour, Prince Galian rescues fiancée from
burning wreckage

"The plane isn't even on fire in this photo," I said, pointing to the newspaper in front of us.

"That's not the point, *'neechai*. Look at the concern. The love. That photo tells it all, don't you think?"

Emilie had walked through the door at precisely nine with a bright smile on her face and flung the newspaper in our face.

"I want to capitalize on this," she said. "I want to tell the world your story, although a carefully edited one. Up until now, the papers have mostly been speculating that this union was one of political strategy, but after this photo, well..." She grinned down at the image of Galian holding me. "Everyone can see this is a love story."

"You aren't going to use this," I said, standing up. "It's one thing to lie to the people about this war, but our relationship isn't up for public debate."

"Debate? Oh, Theo. I'm just asking you and him to go on camera and be your charming selves," Emilie said. "The hand-holding, the flirtatious smiles. The way you subconsciously lean into him when you're seeking support."

"That's creepy," Galian said, stepping back.

"No. I don't want to do it," I said, looking to Galian for guidance.

"See? That's exactly the kind of Theo the people need to see," Emilie said. "Vulnerable. Sweet. The girl who won Prince Galian's heart."

"*Amichai*," he said slowly. "Let's just think about it—"

My eyes grew to the size of saucers, and I took a step back. "You can't be serious."

"Emilie, give us a few minutes," Galian said, without breaking my gaze from me.

"But—"

"Out."

Emilie gathered her things and shrugged. "I've got to speak with the queen regarding your engagement party anyway. But when I return, we will begin discussing your interview."

The door hadn't even closed when I exploded. "There is no way in *hell* I'm going on camera to talk about us. You said that Zygmont woman was going to destroy me if she ever got me on camera."

"I know, but that was before. Now everyone's interested in us, so it wouldn't be the best course of action for her to go negative. Besides that—just think about it. If we did an interview, we could talk about the war. About the treaty. Isn't that what you want?"

"They're going to tell *us* what to say, and anything unflattering about Grieg or Bayard will get cut," I snapped.

"There are still things we can do. Codes, phrases. That sort of thing. We can get our message out to the people."

I folded my arms over my chest, staring at the ground. "I thought the reason we got married was to prevent people from screwing with us. This feels like the opposite of that."

"*Amichai*," he said gently, "all we'd be doing is talking about ourselves—"

"Exactly! I don't want to invite anyone else into our love. I want us to be...private."

He sighed. "Please don't divorce me, but you married a prince. You don't get privacy. None of us do."

"I didn't marry a prince, I married *you*," I said. "Despite your royal status."

"Theo..." He sighed. "Fine. I won't ask you to do anything you're uncomfortable doing. And you're right, if we go on camera, we're inviting the public into our relationship, and that never ends well. But at the same time...this could be a great opportunity to change some minds. They're already talking about us as a couple, and not you getting bread spat in your face."

"This just feels...disgusting to me," I said, rubbing my arms. "I feel like what we have is fragile."

"Fragile?" He chuckled. "Theo, we lasted through four months of not talking then six months of not seeing each other for more than an hour. And you still married me. I'd say we're strong enough to withstand anything."

"But it wasn't all good. We fight all the time..."

"It's not about how little you fight, it's about how well you communicate after it." He slid his hands over my hips and pressed me to him. "Besides, I like fighting with you. Turns me on."

"Stop it," I said, knocking his hands away. "Be serious."

"Fine, I like fighting with you because you always press me to see another angle, another side. And it helps me strengthen my position." He grinned. "And I also think you're cute when you're angry. And that turns me on."

"I think you've got a wire crossed in your brain, *amichai*." I smiled, even though I didn't quite feel it.

He must've sensed my unease. "Look at me." He tilted my chin to meet his gaze. "If you don't want to do this, we won't. Emilie can figure out some other way to capitalize on this plane crash. Our relationship is off limits until you say otherwise."

To that, I smiled for real. "Thank you, *amichai*."

GALIAN

Although I shared some of Theo's trepidation about the interview, I also knew that it was a golden opportunity. But I wasn't going to pressure her, even if I thought it was a good idea. Her nerves were already frayed enough from the crash and Anson. That had to explain why she thought our relationship was on the rocks when I thought it was stronger than ever.

So, ignoring my own opinions, I firmly let Emilie know that we would not be participating in an interview, and used my princely powers to shut her down when she'd tried to argue about it.

That had earned me a midmorning quickie, so I was well on my way to mending fences.

Around two, Filippa stopped by to let us know Mom needed us to confirm some wedding planning details, which, I hoped, was just a cover to discuss the crash and the investigation.

"First of all, are you all right, darling?" Mom asked, taking Theo's hand once Filippa had been sent away to talk with Rhys about something trivial.

"Yeah, just a little sore," she replied, squeezing Mom's hand. "Do we have any clues about who sabotaged my plane? Was it...Anson?"

"We haven't been able to locate the perpetrator," Mom replied with a frown. "With Johar in Rave, and Kader still recovering, we don't have that many men available to do a proper investigation. But the ones who are available are working their hardest. Thanks to your description of the man."

"I shouldn't have gotten into that plane in the first place," Theo replied, before shaking her head. "Are we sure it's Anson and not Grieg? It wouldn't be the first time he tried to pass blame on someone else."

"I don't see why that would be in his best interest," Mom replied. "You two have been playing along. He has nothing to gain by your death right now. Neither does Bayard."

"Yeah, what's going on with Bayard?" I asked. "Why did he send Cannon in his place?"

Mom picked up her tea, sipping lightly. "Because we believe Anson is in Kylae now. And Bayard's not convinced Grieg will keep him safe."

Theo sucked in a breath. "Anson is here? Why?"

"My guess is that he's found the increased Kylaen presence in Rave a bit dangerous," Mom replied. "We did, however, manage to get him a message that we want to talk strategy. He's willing to send one of his contacts to the hospital to speak with us."

"That's fantastic," I said with a smile.

But Theo didn't look happy, or relieved. If anything, she looked even more worried. "That's awfully...bold of him. Is Grieg aware?"

"If he is, he considers him of little consequence," Mom replied. "Your father has focused all his energy into quelling the rebellion through brute force. He's moving fifty squadrons of planes—"

"*Fifty?*" Theo gasped. "That's... Does he need that many?"

"I don't know," Mom replied. "Even with Rave in complete turmoil, that's still overkill, especially considering that Kylaen aircraft are far superior to Raven."

"How many planes are in a squadron?" I asked.

"Twenty," Theo said. "At least, that's the size of a Raven squadron."

My jaw fell. "He sent over a *thousand* planes?"

"Is Kopec sharing any information about Grieg's plans?" Theo asked.

"That's how we know about the fifty squadrons," Mom said. "We'll keep the pressure on her and others, but going against Grieg isn't palatable to most now." She shook her head. "But I don't want you to worry about that. Right now, your job is to meet with Anson's contact and try to convince him that you're on his side. Whatever Grieg is planning in Rave, we'll find out, and we'll address it."

THEO

"What could your father need with a thousand planes in Rave?" I asked, for what felt like the millionth time. It had been fairly easy to convince Emilie that I was feeling a little lightheaded and pained after my crash, and my *amichai* wanted to run some tests at the hospital to make sure everything was fine. The reprieve had been welcome, especially when Kader arrived with the car, because it gave us a chance to discuss the latest news in confidence.

"He's already got the country, he's not going to kill everyone in it," Kader said. "And I doubt he'd send that many planes just to make a statement."

"He could be escalating the war," Galian said, watching the buildings fly by. "Or putting on a show for Jervan and Herin."

"That's an awful lot of troop movement for a show, *amichai*," I said. But so far, that seemed like the only logical explanation. "But why? He's got Rave, what could he gain by rattling his saber at Jervan and Herin?"

"Ego?" Galian said with a shrug.

I couldn't argue that point, but there was some larger plot afoot. Something akin to the surprise of our treaty, and I hated that we had no clue what it was. But my questions were soon forgotten when we saw the swarms of photographers, reporters, and general population camped out in front of the hospital, eager to see Galian and me together.

"Prepare yourselves," Kader announced from the front seat.

"Do I have to smile?" I asked Galian.

"Not unless you want to," he said, planting a kiss on my lips as the car slowed and was bombarded by photographers.

They were more eager than ever, fighting with each other for a space, their loud arguing audible even in the car. But even more, there were angry faces behind them, chanting and screaming and pressing in around us.

"Shit," Galian said, backing away from the window. "Who are all these people?"

I saw a sign, "*Go back to your country*," and it didn't take a genius to realize why they were so angry. "I don't think they like this wedding. Appears your father needs to do some work on his marketing."

"We should leave," Kader said.

"No, we need to meet with McMullen today," Galian said, tightening his hold on me. "We'll just push through it. They won't come inside the hospital."

Kader made a noise, but didn't argue. The car drove impossibly slowly, and it seemed like the crowd was climbing all over it. When we stopped, Kader turned to give me a pitying look. "Are you sure you want to do this?"

I nodded.

He opened his door and the loud roar of the crowd surrounded us for a moment, before the door slammed. Kader barked orders for the crowd to back away, but they didn't seem to listen to him.

"Just keep your head down," Galian said. "Don't say anything, don't look at anyone. I'll get us inside as quickly as possible."

Kader opened the door, and the crowd erupted around us.

"Should've died in that plane crash!"

"Raven whore!"

I kept my gaze on our interconnected hands, as Galian pushed through and dragged me with him. But, against my better judgement, I looked up and stopped short at the chaos around me. A sea of angry faces bore down on us, holding signs and pointing fingers. But I spotted more than a few dark-skinned protestors, screaming that I was a traitor.

"*The blood of Rave is on your hands!*"

I saw it before I could react; a wave of red coming at me in slow motion. I could only close my eyes and duck before the wall of water hit me.

"*Ugh!*" I screamed, but Galian yanked me inside the hospital, where we were somehow safe from the crazies outside the door.

"Are you okay?" he asked before his eyes widened. "Holy shit, Theo, *are you okay?*"

"I'm fine, I'm..." But I looked down and my breath hitched. I was covered in thick, crimson blood. I felt it dripping down my face and soaking into my clothes, "Oh my God, I'm gonna be sick..."

"Just as long as none of this is yours." He didn't flinch as he inspected my arms, my chest, my legs, and was satisfied the blood came from somewhere else. "What the actual hell was that?"

Giggling erupted from the other side of the room where two young girls hid behind a pair of magazines. One of them withdrew a small camera and took a photo.

"That's it," Galian said, charging toward them, but I stopped him before he got too far.

"Leave them. The idiots outside got enough footage to last a year," I said. "I just want a shower."

The hospital was full of people and every one of them seemed to be pleased about my current state. But Galian's hand never left mine, and he blazed a trail of daring looks and glares as we made our way to the doctor's lounge. He showed me the shower, finding me a change of clothes, soap, and a towel, before leaving to inform the custodial staff about the blood—and the security team about the protestors.

He was waiting for me by the time I finished my shower, though, in my defense, I'd cried for a few minutes under the scalding water. When I pulled on the extra scrubs he'd left for me, I saw *Helmuth* embroidered into the chest and it made me smile.

"Are you okay?" he asked when I appeared in the lounge.

"Yeah," I said, toweling off my hair again. "Thanks for the clothes..."

"Can't have you meeting with our guy covered in blood," he said with a small smile. "Though I have to say, you do look good in a pair of scrubs. Maybe you should wear them more often."

"Any scrubs, or just ones with your name on them?" I asked.

He smiled. "You don't seem as annoyed as the last time you wore clothes embroidered with my name."

I'd forgotten all about him giving me his flight suit the first day on the island and laughed. "Well, I no longer *only* associate the Helmuth name with your father. Some of you are pleasant to be around. Sometimes."

We left the doctor's lounge hand-in-hand, and Galian made a big deal about talking with me as we passed people in the hall. He introduced me to a few of his doctor colleagues, who, for the most part, didn't seem to think I was a piece of trash. They merely seemed curious, asking me how I felt after the crash and how I was liking Kylae.

"It's..." I shared a look with Galian, who shrugged.

"I'm taking her to the exam room," he said, glancing at his

watch. "We were hoping to wait until the crowd outside died down."

"Fat chance of that," said an older woman sitting at the desk. "They've tripled, from what we can tell." Her gaze landed on me, and she shook her head. "All this trouble for you."

"Rima, question for you," Galian said, pulling me toward her. "Has my patient Mr. McMullen arrived yet?"

"Yes, Doctor, he's waiting for you in twelve," she said, her gaze dancing to me as she spoke to him.

Galian thanked her with a smile, then we walked toward the other end of the hall.

"That wasn't too bad," I said quietly. "Maybe everyone doesn't hate me after all."

"See?"

"Just the swarms of protesters who think it's fun to douse me in blood." I shivered. "You don't think it was...human blood, do you?"

"Kylaens aren't *that* bad," Galian said, opening the door to room twelve.

The man inside was short and squat, with fire red hair and pale skin. How he was Anson's contact, I had no idea. He was the most Kylaen-looking Kylaen I'd ever seen.

"Gerard, how are you?" Galian said, closing the door behind him. "This is Theo, though I'm sure you know that."

"You look a bit less bloody than a few minutes ago," he said, giving me the once-over.

"Thanks," I said weakly, amazed at how quickly word had spread. "So you're the one talking with Anson?"

"Me? Hardly. I got a friend who's got a friend who's in his little web."

I balked. "So you're nobody. He's nobody—"

"He's been informing me for months," Galian said gently. "If he's got a message from Anson, it's real."

I was skeptical, but let the man speak.

He wiped his forehead with a handkerchief. "Anson ain't happy with you, I'll tell you that much. That plane crash was just the beginning."

Galian did a double take. "So it *was* Anson? How the hell did he get past security? And why target Theo?"

"It was a message for her, and for all us Kylaens. But mostly, it was for Bayard. You'll notice he sent that deputy in his place, huh? Bayard's holed up in Veres right now. He knows Anson's got it in for him, same as he has it in for you, little missy."

I swallowed, something cold in the pit of my stomach. "I'm *not* the enemy."

"You may not be, but you're working with them."

"We're trying to stop the treaty!" I said. "Surely, Anson knows I had *nothing* to do with this circus! This wedding is supposed to distract everyone—"

"Of course he knows that, everybody in Rave does. Bayard's looking to get a cushy retirement outta Grieg in exchange for handing over the country. Anson wanted to let Bayard know there wasn't a place he could run that Anson wouldn't find him."

"By making an example out of Theo?" Galian said. "He could've killed her."

"I'll say this: if he wanted you dead, you'd be dead. There's plenty of other ways to trip up a plane. And you don't survive seven years in the Raven military if you don't know how to put a plane down with broken landing gear." He snorted, and I couldn't argue that point. "But if you'd died, Anson wouldn't have cried over it. You're a turncoat in his eyes."

A weight of hopelessness hung around my neck. "All I want is for my country to have peace. I don't care how it happens, but it has to happen."

"Anson seems to think the only way to get anything done is through bloodshed," he said. "So my advice to you two is to watch yourselves. You ain't the target, but you'd make a hell of a spectacle. A double funeral might be a tad more unifying than a wedding."

I stared at him; that was the second time someone had said that to us. I was starting to believe someone might go through with it. Based on the crowd outside, I doubted anyone would mourn me.

"A... Thanks, Gerard," Galian said after a moment. "Tell Anson we're willing to negotiate, if he's willing to talk to us."

"I'll get the message to 'im but I doubt it'll do much good," McMullen said, standing and walking to the door. He nodded in my direction. "Godspeed, Theo."

The door closed, and I released a loud breath, slumping down into a nearby chair.

"Don't let him scare you," Galian said.

"I'm not scared," I said quietly. "I'm...Anson was supposed to be the good guy. What the hell are we supposed to do now?"

He chewed his lip. "We do that interview."

"What?"

"You and I go on the Kylaen media and we talk. We talk about ourselves, we talk about us. We make them fall in love with us the same way we fell in love with each other. Then, once they're on our side, we'll have the power."

"How are we supposed to do that in the span of *one* interview? It took me months to fall in love with you."

"Do you have any other options?" Galian asked, leaning against the door. "Because I don't know what other cards we've got to play."

TWENTY-THREE

Theo's blood-soaked image was splashed over the newspapers for a few days, which prompted Emilie to go ahead and set a date for the interview with Zygmont. Theo was still unconvinced about the whole thing, but didn't argue. Learning Anson *had* been responsible for sabotaging her plane had scared her more than she'd admitted to me—because it scared me too. If Anson wasn't willing to work with us, who would? But I kept my worries to myself, maintaining an optimistic outlook for Theo's sake.

Emilie was ecstatic when we told her we'd do an interview—but only with Zygmont, and only if it was live. Predictably, the live part had been dismissed by my father, but our choice of interviewer was approved and the date set for one week's time. The good news was Emilie busied herself working with Zygmont's team to come up with questions (and, of course, our prepared answers). And without her around, my mother was able to extend an invite to tea, under the auspices of planning the engagement party.

Filippa seemed to be the only person in the castle blissfully unaware (or purposefully ignoring) the ramifications of the wedding and treaty. My mother was noticeably colder toward Theo, barely asking my wife for her opinion on anything. But Theo seemed happier not being in the spotlight, so I'd squeeze her hand every few minutes to remind her that she could jump in at any time.

"We'll have to make do without Jervanian wine," Mom said with a small sigh as we nibbled on two choices of bread. "But I hear they've got a good vintage down in the Schoon province from a few years ago. Filippa, didn't Minister Bassett say something about that recently?"

"Yes, ma'am," Filippa said demurely. "Only, I believe His Highness asked Minister Bassett to assist with the rebuilding project in Rave."

If Mom had forgotten, or it was news to her, she played it off admirably. "Then would you please run down to the kitchens and see what the royal cook thinks we should order? I'd like pheasant, so I think a robust red would be an excellent pairing."

"Yes ma'am. I'll be right back."

Mom pretended to busy herself until the door clicked, then she tossed away the menu option list with a disgusted face. "Wedding planning. Such a trouble. Now, tell me about your interview. I'm very pleased you've decided to do it."

Theo made a noise and shook her head. "I'm worried. What if Zygmont decides to go off script?"

"The interview is taped, so at least we'll have some control. Remember, Grieg needs the two of you to be the positive face of the treaty, so he won't let anything get out that's unsavory." Mom sipped some of her water. "Emilie also seems to have your best interests at heart."

"My best interests as long as they make Kylae look good," Theo said with a glance at me. "We saw a draft of the questions this morning. 'How did you meet' and 'what did you think when you first saw each other' don't really lend themselves to talking about the treaty. Emilie also says we can't mention the word 'war' or anything to do with it."

"That makes it rather difficult to discuss how you met, doesn't it?" Mom replied with a small smile. "This is a negotiation, Theo. They've provided the questions—that's their initial offer, then you provide the answers—your counter. What airs is the final agreement."

"Sounds like they get the last word," Theo said with a frown.

"Not necessarily, because you two also have the advantage of being interesting," Mom said. "The people are curious, they want to know all about you."

"Last time I checked, they hated me."

"Hate, perhaps, but they're curious about you," Mom said with a wink to me. "And Galian is still very popular with his countrymen. You two can capitalize on that."

"How can we do that when they're going to tell us *exactly* what to say?" Theo asked.

"You casually add in a few extra words here and there. Slip of the mind, of course. Pardon my saying so, but Theo is known to be a bit shaky on camera, aren't you?"

Theo's hand jerked in mine, and she pursed her lips.

"Not intended as an offense, my love," Mom said with a small laugh. "But if you were to add in some commentary, it wouldn't seem too out of character for you. Such as, perhaps," she glanced at the paper, "when they ask what you love most about Galian, you could mention how he inspired you to speak from the heart in Jervan."

Theo furrowed her brow and glanced at me. "But—"

"And if memory serves, your speech was broadcast all over Rave, was it not? And the prevailing message of that speech was seeking a peaceful, independent Rave."

"You heard my speech?" Theo asked, her voice small.

"I read the transcript. Unfortunately, the video was not broadcast here," Mom replied. "But for this interview, you and Galian should be reminding the people who you are. A proud, decorated Raven major who gave seven years of her life toward Rave's independence and who was able to look past your differences to fall in love with a Kylaen prince. Anson will hear your loyalty, the Kylaens will see your love story."

"And you don't think Grieg will...have a problem with that?" I asked cautiously.

"I honestly don't know what he's thinking anymore," Mom replied, picking up her tea. "I haven't even seen the man in weeks. But the time for caution is coming to an end. We've laid the groundwork for our offense, and it's time to move on it."

I opened my mouth to reply, but the door swung open and Emilie walked through, a bright smile on her face.

"Ms. Mondra," Mom said, although there was a touch of tension in her voice, "we were having a private meeting."

"My apologies, Your Highness." She bowed slightly. "I just wanted to pass on the good news. The king has granted Zygmont's request to air the interview live."

Theo and I shared a shocked look. "L-live?" she stammered.

"Oh, don't fret, *'neechai*. We'll have your answers memorized backward and forward so you won't have to worry about a thing."

Theo did not look appeased by this news.

"That's excellent news, Emilie," Mom replied with a smile. "Could you excuse us?"

Emilie bowed at the waist, and left us in peace.

"That's awfully trusting..." Theo said after the door had shut. "Why would he have agreed to such a thing?"

Mom, too, looked concerned by this development. "I don't know, darling. But you're right, it does seem out of character for him, especially considering the circumstances."

"Can we still...I mean, this is good news for our negotiation, right?" Theo said, although she sounded as unsure as I felt.

"That remains to be seen," Mom replied, with one final, nervous look at the door.

THEO

Neither Galian nor I could figure out why Grieg would allow us to speak live. There was the chance he thought we were inconsequential, or over our rebellious streak, but I couldn't believe that. Grieg was too smart, and had too many spies. The uneasy feeling that we were again pawns in a much larger game came back with a vengeance, and I couldn't shake it.

Compounding my worry was the fear of this interview. Korina's assurances that Zygmont wanted to paint me in a positive light fell flat on me—I'd met the woman myself. After all, most of the country hated me anyway; she would lose nothing except the king's favor if she made me look like an idiot.

Emilie chalked my nervousness up to simply that—my usual fear of public speaking. But just as when we were preparing for Jervan, I stumbled over words and phrases that should've come naturally. Even Galian couldn't break through my worry, and soon enough, I found myself wide awake the night before the interview, dread, fear, and worry taking turns in the pit of my stomach.

"Go to sleep," Galian mumbled beside me as I turned on my side again.

"I'm trying," I snapped back, hating him and his ability to sleep through worry. Then again, he didn't seem too preoccupied with the interview. "I just hate it, the pressure. Thinking about what I have to say." My heart thumped in my chest. "Knowing that hundreds of thousands of people are watching me, listening to every word. What if she asks something, and I don't know how to respond?"

"Well, just talk to me then," he said, as if it were that easy. "We're just going to talk about us and the island. That's all."

I couldn't share his optimism. "Are we doing the right thing?"

"Theo, stop worrying so much."

"I can't help it."

He lifted his head, grinning in the darkness. "Then let me distract you a little bit, hm?"

Despite his best efforts, my body was not cooperating, and after an hour of unsuccessfully trying to bring me to orgasm, Galian gave up and went back to sleep.

I spent most of the day in a nervous haze, watching the clock tick closer to our interview. Galian had grown annoyed with me and left around noon to have lunch with his brother. I hoped, at least, he might find something useful to share, but when he returned, he'd said Rhys hadn't spoken with his father either.

"How are you not concerned about this interview?" I snapped, as he stretched out on the couch without a care in the world.

"Because all I'm doing is telling the world how much I love my wife," he said with his stupid, loving smile. "I could do that in my sleep."

The camera crew came in to set up around three, taking over the entire sitting room parlor. Emilie had said it would feel more homey if we were in our own space, but it just felt like a bunch of strangers were in the middle of our relationship. Which, in effect, they were.

Emilie brought in her makeup crew an hour before airtime. I tried to pepper the hairstylist with questions about the situation in Rave, but she deflected all of them and told me that if I kept talking, I'd smudge my makeup. Emilie, too, chided me about my lack of focus, and made me recite my answers back to her.

Zygmont arrived thirty minutes to air, looking flawless in a black suit and white collared shirt. She conferred with her assistants for a few minutes then settled herself in the chair across from us. The lights came on, blinding me for a moment, and I searched for Galian's hand.

"Well, this is going to be so much fun," Zygmont's voice said from somewhere in front of me. I blinked until the room came back into focus. "I have to say, I'm dying to know everything there is to know about you two."

"And we can't wait to tell you about it," came Galian's easy response.

"This is terrible. They don't look natural," Zygmont said, waving her hand at us. "Somebody fix them."

Emilie stepped in, moving Galian's hand to the back of the couch, shifting my shoulders straighter. Then, she pulled out a stick of lip gloss and tapped it against my lips with a small wink before Zygmont barked at her to move out of the way.

"Damned Ravens," Zygmont muttered.

I glared at her. "You know I am one, right?"

"Sure, sweetie." She glanced at the camera set over our shoulder. "Time?"

"Fifteen seconds."

My heart began to race, but I didn't move from where Emilie had placed me. Galian pecked me on the cheek and whispered words of encouragement in my ear, but all I saw was the light on the camera turning on and the loud sound of Zygmont starting the interview.

"Welcome, ladies and gentlemen, to a very special presentation of Zygmont Tonight. I'm broadcasting live from Kernaghan castle with two very special guests. His Royal Highness, Prince Galian Helmuth, and the woman who will be his wife."

It didn't escape my notice that she hadn't introduced me, but my nerves were too frayed to correct her.

"First, I'd like to thank you, Your Highness, for agreeing to speak with us tonight." She laughed forcefully. "You're a hard man to pin down."

"Well, the hospital keeps me busy," he replied without missing a beat. This was the princeling I'd seen growing up; the cavalier, charming man who could do no wrong. I just wished some of his confidence would rub off on me.

"We could talk all night about your great work at the Kylaen Royal Hospital, but sadly, our viewers want to know more about this..." She forced a smile onto her face. "Upcoming marriage."

I felt Galian's gaze shift to me, but I kept looking straight ahead. He moved his hand off the couch to rest against my shoulder, and my heart skipped a beat.

"We all saw the photos, the daring rescue after the plane crash the other day," she drawled. "And while we know that you, Your Highness, have such a big heart, and you're such a caring and giving person, many of us believe that this marriage may not be as...well, as arranged as we all thought at first."

Beside me, Galian laughed, but I wasn't sure I remembered how to.

"So tell us, how did this happen?"

I opened my mouth to speak, but suddenly couldn't remember what to say—Emilie's speech dancing in my head, or the truth, which had become hazy? The island part, but was I supposed to mention that we'd crashed? Or was I simply to say we'd met in Jervan. No, Jervan was another topic entirely.

"Theo and I were on the island together," Galian said, rescuing me from my inability to speak. "She was the pilot that shot me down."

"Did she?" Zygmont's curious reaction told me that Galian had already deviated from the script. But how, I couldn't tell.

Zygmont shuffled her notes for a second. "We haven't heard much about your time on the island, Your Highness."

"Well, obviously. I couldn't tell everyone that she was there with me," he said with a chuckle. "But she was. Saved my life, didn't you? Well, after I saved yours."

He looked at me, and I wished my tongue would work.

"Major Kallistrate, what did you think when you found yourself stranded on an island with His Royal Highness?"

I opened my mouth again, but no sound came out.

"Oh, Theo fell in love with me the moment she saw me, didn't you?" Galian asked, a devilish sparkle in his eye.

That snapped me right out of my reverie.

GALIAN

I watched the slow reaction with a selfish glee. First, the fear melted into confusion and then, slowly, her left brow came down over her eye and her right lip curled up as she turned to look at me with her signature "are-you-kidding-me" face.

"*What?*"

"You fell in love with me the moment you saw me," I said, knowing full well that was definitely not the case. But I'd figured poking the bear might bring her back to life. After all, the woman I'd fallen in love with was a sharp-tongued, brilliant verbal sparring partner, not this mute, terrified woman. "You were charmed by my charisma and my—"

"That's bull..." Her gaze darted to the camera. "That's bull. I *hated* you."

"Hate's a strong word, *amichai*—"

"Hated you," she said, definitively. "You were arrogant, selfish, *completely* useless except for your medical skills—"

"Which weren't so useless, if you'll recall, when you were bleeding out—"

"Be that as it may," she said, shifting against me. "I most certainly did *not* fall in love with you at first sight. In fact..." She leveled her gaze at me. "If I'd been on two legs, *you* might not have made it off the island."

"Of that, I have no doubt," I said, offering a grin to Zygmont, whose eyes had grown wide during our exchange. "Fine then, when *did* you fall in love with me?" I was actually genuinely curious. I had my recollection of the way she'd smiled at me in the mornings, and how we'd worked together to catch our food. But I'd never asked her about her feelings.

"I honestly don't know," she said after a moment, growing a little softer. "It happened very slowly, I think. The first time I felt...something was when we found the lab. And there was water and shelter and the first thing you did was find bandages for me."

I smiled until I heard Zygmont ask, "W-what lab?"

"One of my grandfather's secrets," I said. This was the first test —would they allow the interview to continue? "A laboratory that tested the effects of barethium on Raven slaves." Theo shivered beside me, and I tightened my hold on her as I was sure she remembered the photos that had told the horrific story.

"When I thought you'd fixed the radio and were going home," she said, her voice faraway and quiet, "I got really sad when I realized I'd never see you again. Even though it had only been a few days. Even though that whole place reminded me of who we were and why we were there." She sighed, shaking her head. "I knew I'd miss you."

"Miss me, sure, but when did you know you were *in love* with me?"

"When you hit your head," she said, staring at her hands. "And I thought you were dead, or you were going to be. Then I realized I could survive by myself. I didn't really *need* you around. But I wanted you."

I frowned. "That was like...two months in? We got rescued a day and a half later. You didn't love me until *then*?"

"I mean...maybe I thought you were *cute*," she said, taking my hand, "but cute and love aren't the same thing. I knew I was *in love* with you when I realized I didn't really want to live without you."

At the risk of losing my manly image on international television, I cooed at her. "That's so corny, Theo."

"Shut up, princeling." She elbowed me roughly in the stomach.

"S...so..." Zygmont said, shuffling her cards. Then, to my surprise, she put them down. "Tell me what it was like there, on the island."

I smirked; she was finally getting that truthful interview she'd wanted. And since no one had stepped in yet to stop us, I figured we could be daring.

"Cold," Theo said with a smile. "Hungry. But...peaceful, really. Especially compared to now. The only thing we had to worry about was finding dinner and making sure we had enough water."

"Now, it's...well, it's a lot more complicated," I said, running my fingers along her shoulder. "It seemed like everything could be solved so easily when we were there. Just stop the fighting."

"You talked a lot about the war, then?"

Theo shrugged, then leaned into me. "I mean, what else *was* there to talk about. Our childhoods, sure, but...everything in my life had always been about the war."

"And did you come to an agreement about things?"

Theo and I shared a glance and we began to laugh. "I don't know about agreement, but we certainly understand each other now," I said.

"In what way?"

"Empathy?" Theo said. "When we landed on the island, I thought the princeling was just that—a spoiled, out of touch playboy who cared more for his social calendar than the lives of Ravens."

"And I," I said, glaring at her, "thought you were a feral cat, biting the hand that fed you. But eventually—"

"*Eventually* we realized that we couldn't survive on our own. We needed each other—as equals. I could no more have survived without Galian's legs and medical training than he could've survived without my—"

"Survival skills," I finished for her.

"And what is your hope for your two countries?" Zygmont asked, leaning forward.

"Peace," Theo said then shook her head. "Real peace. Ravens able to leave the military and make their own decisions about their lives. Children able to go to a real school instead of military camps." She chewed her lip and shared a nervous glance with me.

"And Kylaens staying the hell out of the country," I said with a smile for her. Cutting be damned, I was going to say what I wanted to say. Mom was right. We needed to stop being cautious and start making moves. After all, if they hadn't ended the interview yet...we might as well go for it.

Theo's smile brightened. "Well, maybe one or two Kylaens can come visit."

"Rhys does want to crash on our couch sometimes," I said with a chuckle.

"So if I'm understanding you correctly," Zygmont said, a little breathlessly, "you two are opposed to the Kylaen-Raven treaty? And you do not agree that Rave should remain under Kylaen rule?"

Theo sucked in a breath, so I answered for her. "Yes, we do not agree with the treaty, we do not want our marriage associated with it, and we believe Rave should be a free and independent nation."

Zygmont touched her ear then shook her head. "Sorry, this interview has been cut short."

My heart fell. We'd been so close—how much of what we'd said had been broadcast? "What? Why?"

"Breaking news," Zygmont said, pulling the speaker out of her ear. "Apparently, there's been a large-scale attack on Rave."

TWENTY-FOUR

GALIAN

"It was an attack on the rebels," Kader said, his voice harsh. "The damage was limited to the slums. Johar and Gibbs were meeting with Odolf the baker when the first bomb hit. Gibbs got out—barely. But she said the slums were decimated—hundreds dead and probably more will be, thanks to the abysmal medical care in the city. The Raven military has been told to stand down. There's no help coming to those in the slums." He closed his eyes. "Johar didn't make it out."

There was a buzzing in my ears, and it was hard to breathe.

"There's more," Mom said quietly. "The media is reporting the attack had been perpetrated by Anson." She swallowed. "They're confirming Mansela and Bassett dead. Gren hasn't been accounted for, but...I'm sure it's only a matter of time."

I stared at my hands, wondering if this was a dream. This had to be a dream. There was no way everything could go so badly so quickly. Not when we finally had the upper hand.

"I don't understand," Rhys said, standing against the wall.

"What could he *possibly* gain by bombing Rave?"

"We believe his goal was to disrupt Anson's operations," Kader replied.

"By killing *everyone* in the slums?" Theo said. "As if the Ravens won't know that this was done by Grieg. Anson's not even *in* Rave right now. He's in Norose, isn't he?"

"And all our reports indicate his network is now limited to those who he brought with him—only a handful," Kader said. "His expansive network completely destroyed in one day."

"But Rave...Rave has to know this was Grieg. They have to."

"What would they do to retaliate?" Mom replied quietly. "Knowing that Grieg has enough firepower to level the entire island, should he choose to do so." She sighed. "There's more, I'm afraid."

"Oh, what else could go wrong?" Theo said with a whimper.

"Your father has decided to move up the treaty signing to...next week. And your wedding."

My jaw fell to the floor. "*Next week*? How is that even possible?"

"My staff has been ordered to make it happen," Mom said with a heavy sigh. "The engagement party will be the night before. Your father has asked that I..." She swallowed, obviously disgusted. "Make it perfect."

Theo sat back against the couch. "So that's it then. It's over. We're getting married. The treaty will be signed. Not that it matters because Grieg's already laid waste to my country. It's only a matter of time before the barethium miners get their hooks in. And then...then..."

"I'm sorry," Mom whispered. "I'm just... I'm sorry."

She stood and walked to the other side of her parlor, staring out the window as I'd seen her do countless times. Only this time, there was no strategy brewing, no arranging of puzzle pieces. My mother had finally been checkmated by my father.

The weight of the despair permeated the room. Mansela and Bassett were already dead, and their replacements wouldn't dare step a toe out of line. The other ministers in Kylae, the ones we'd pinned our hopes on, would probably stand firmly on his side, fearing for their lives and the lives of their families. Herin and Jervan would be our only saviors, should they decide to take up arms against my father. But I doubted they would do so willingly. I hadn't heard as much as a peep from Olivia in weeks, and I probably wouldn't now.

We'd not even discussed the broadcast the night before, or how much of it went out to the people. It didn't seem like it mattered whether the people loved us or not.

"If you'll excuse me," Kader said, breaking the tense silence of the room. I knew he was going home to Rosie, but I couldn't let him leave without offering some comfort.

"Hey, wait up," I said, jogging to him. "Are you okay?"

He snorted. "Are you?"

I couldn't honestly say that I was.

"You need to be with your wife right now."

"Theo will be fine," I said. "I want to talk to you now. Do you want to get a drink?"

His eyes flashed angrily. "No, Galian, I don't. What I want is for something to go right."

I stopped midstride. "Kader—"

"No, all this time...I've put my faith, I've put my *life* on the line believing we were doing the right thing. That what I was doing made a difference. But now the only thing that's changed is another one of my friends is dead. Rave's back under Kylaen rule, and your father remains as powerful as ever."

I'd never heard him talk so frankly, and, for once, I had no idea what to say to him.

He shook his head and clapped me on the shoulder. "I'm going home to spend time with my wife, and I hope you'll do the same. Nothing is guaranteed in this world, not anymore. Not for the two of you. Not for any of us."

He released me and walked down the hall, leaving an uneasy feeling in the pit of my stomach.

"Galian," Rhys called. "We need you."

I sighed. "Now what?"

When I returned to my mother's parlor, it was already filled with new, smiling faces. Filippa, a priest, her assistants, all looking eager and excited. My brother and Theo, however, still wore expressions of horror, although Theo's was quickly turning into one of disgust.

"What's going on?" I asked my mother.

Mom had quickly recovered from her desolation and was back to her usual, fake-chipper self. "I'm glad you're here, son. Filippa needs you to help make final decisions about the wedding. She's brought Father Mark here so we can rehearse the ceremony a few times."

"We wouldn't want any surprises at the wedding," Filippa said with a bright smile. Whether she knew about the massacre or didn't, I wanted to peel the grin right off her face. Instead, I crossed the room to sit next to my wife, throwing an arm around her in solidarity.

"The ceremony will begin at noon sharp," Filippa said. "His Majesty King Grieg will enter first, followed by you, Your Majesty," she nodded to my mother. "After the king and queen are settled, we will have the council enter and be seated."

I wanted so very much to ask if Mansela was going to be there, but I bit my tongue.

"Once they're seated, the princes will enter and stand before the king to receive his blessing," she said with a kind smile to me.

That I would even have to look at my father made me sick to my stomach.

"Finally, the bride," Filippa's gaze landed on Theo. "She will be escorted by Provincial Governor Bayard—"

"*What?*" Theo was on her feet in an instant. "No *fucking* way."

"My goodness!" Filippa said, blushing bright red and looking to the queen for guidance.

"Theo, dear—"

"No. No way," Theo said, on the verge of tears. "He sold out my country, and he destroyed my people. I don't want him in the same country as me, let alone *touching* me!"

"Theo—"

But that was her limit, and she let out a loud cry of anguish. I stood to hold her but she pushed me away. "I need...I need some air. I can't do this right now."

THEO

Everything was falling apart, and I couldn't stop it.

I was to marry Galian in front of the world next week.

Bayard would escort me as if he were my father.

Johar was dead.

My country was burning.

How utterly ridiculous my life had become.

And how utterly ridiculous that I'd let it get this far.

I'd become complacent, too gun-shy after walking into one too many traps. And now, I felt the weight of every single Raven citizen who'd lost their lives in an unnecessary airstrike—and every life I'd seen snuffed out since I'd joined the Raven military.

Galian and I had, yet again, allowed ourselves to become pawns in Grieg's game. We should've pressed harder against the live broadcast, dug a little deeper to figure out *why* he was giving us this golden opportunity. It was only to distract the country—yet again. And now, countless Ravens were dead. Johar was dead.

Their ghosts pressed in on me, accusing me of not doing more. Of letting my fear of failure overpower my will to do anything but be a puppet. And I was tired of being a puppet; I wanted to be a master. There was nothing left to lose.

When I'd first landed on the island, I'd considered my own mortality. I'd known that the Kylaens would be the ones to rescue us, and that they'd most assuredly put me to death when they did. I'd wondered if it would've been smarter to take my own life early, rather than let them do it. But I'd hesitated, holding aloft a small flame of hope that I could survive the island.

Now, those same questions were haunting me. Grieg had proven, time and again, that we were outmatched against him. Whether through his spies, or his money or his power, we were ants in his grander schemes. There was no winning against him; there never had been any chance for us, even working together.

I opened the doors of Galian's parlor, hoping to find peace, and instead I found...

"'*Neechai.*"

Perfect. The very last person I wanted to see.

"Emilie, I'm not in the mood for your lectures," I said, fearing she'd be cross with us for deviating from her carefully written script.

"Lucky for you, neither am I," she replied, a hollowness in her voice I hadn't heard before.

My anger subsided to curiosity. The papers cracked loudly as she flipped through them, her mouth pressed into a thin line. Her hair was pulled back, not the usual curled and silky texture. Her clothes were immaculate, but something about her was dulled.

"We have seven days to prepare, so..."

"Who died?"

The pen jerked in her hand. "What?"

"Did someone close to you die in the airstrike?"

I'd seen it a hundred times before, when my lieutenants had lost a good friend in battle or due to poorly-maintained aircraft and had to get up and face another day. To put aside their own devastation for the greater good of the country.

Her eyes flashed for a moment, and she returned to her binder. "There *was* no airstrike. Nothing's happening in Rave but bright smiles and happy faces."

"Emilie—"

"*Nothing* is happening."

It was the first crack I'd ever seen in her perfect veneer, shaped at the finest school in Herin and solidified at the side of the Raven president. For once, she didn't look like a perfectly coiffed version of Raven beauty; she was a real human being. Her own wishes and desires, so firmly pressed beneath several layers of political spin, were bubbling to the surface. I just needed to crack her a little more.

"One of my friends died," I said. "Her name was Sayuri Johar.

She was trying to meet with the Raven rebels."

Emilie glanced at me then shook her head. "I don't want to know what you and Korina have been doing."

"Why not? The wedding is happening. Grieg's won. All that we've been working toward is up in smoke. So what does it hurt if I tell you that Anson's in Norose, and he was responsible for that plane crash? What does it hurt if I tell you all of your machinations and spin have resulted in the deaths of thousands of our Raven brothers and sisters?"

Her eyes flashed. "I had *nothing*—"

"You've been complicit since Bayard handed over the keys to the country," I reminded her. "So any blood that's been spilled is on your hands." I sighed and looked at my own palms. "Same as mine."

Her gaze diverted for a moment, before she straightened her shoulders and opened her binder. "Back to the wedding—"

"Did you really think of me as a *'neechai*?" I asked, unwilling to give up on her yet. "Or was it just for show?"

She ran her hand down the page of the binder and then closed it. "Yes. I did. Because I'd lost mine to the rebel cause some years ago. Her name is Aline, and she's about your age. We used to be close, she was my baby sister, but...when she returned from boarding school two years ago, she'd been indoctrinated by some boy she'd met. She said Bayard was no better than Grieg, that I was just as responsible for the state of our country as they were... That was the last time we spoke." She took a shaky breath. "I don't know if she was there or not...but my gut tells me she's...she's gone."

Despite my complicated feelings for Emilie, I reached across the table and took her hand.

"I believed in what Bayard was doing, because I thought it was the best way to do things," she continued, before shaking her head. "Maybe not the best, but the most realistic. We were never going to win against Kylae, not with their current king. Not when they see us as animals. But now Aline is dead, and I just wonder..." She half-smiled. "She was going to marry that boy, you know. My mother had already commissioned a traditional Raven wedding dress. It was going to be so beautiful on her." A tear slipped out from beneath her made-up eyes and she wiped it away. "But no matter. It's your wedding I'm focused on now and—"

"I want to wear her dress," I said, the idea coming to me in a flash of light.

Emilie shook her head. "No, Theo, you know you won't be allowed to wear it."

"I don't care. I want you to get it for me."

She stared at the wall. "To what end? To protest this treaty in front of people who would rather see you dead? To let the international community know that you, a powerless girl, don't agree with what a king is doing?"

"Symbols are powerful, you taught me that," I said, taking her hand. "I want to honor your sister, and Johar, and everyone who died fighting back." I sighed. "You're right. I am powerless. The only thing I have is my own body, my willpower, and my conviction. And even if they shoot me dead wearing that dress, at least I'll go out under my own flag. The real flag." I squeezed her hand. "Our flag, *'neechai*.*"

She closed her hand around mine and squeezed it. "I'll see what I can do."

TWENTY-FIVE

GALIAN

I stood in the window, watching the sun slowly sink on the horizon. The sky was an ominous crimson and purple, a warning for what was coming. Tomorrow, the country known as Rave would formally cease to exist. Tomorrow, Theo and I would stand in front of the Kylaen media and exchange vows we hadn't written. Tonight, we had to stand in a room full of Kylaens and pretend to be okay with it.

Well, not even Filippa had asked that of us. We just had to be in the room.

I wore the traditional Kylaen military dress uniform, as requested by Grieg. The last time I'd been forced to wear this ridiculous red jacket with all the unearned medals, Kader had been breathing down my neck. Martin had been alive. I'd flirted with Olivia. I'd thought a lot about Theo, but I hadn't done anything to deserve her.

How much simpler life had been then.

I buttoned my shirt, still starchy from the wash, and stared at myself in the mirror. I reached into my pocket and pulled out my wedding band, slipping it on for a moment and realizing that, after tomorrow, I could at least wear it in public without feeling my father's wrath. One small positive amongst a sea of shit.

"Hey, *amichai*..."

I perked up at the sound of Theo's voice. She'd been strangely resolute this past week, and it had set me on edge, especially as she'd been more loving than usual. I kept her in my sights at all times, worried that this latest setback was too much for her to handle. But I knew in my gut that she wouldn't commit suicide in the privacy of our bedroom. No, Theo was planning something big, and it terrified me.

But the woman who stood in front of the mirror wasn't someone who'd been defeated. Shoulders back, smile on her face, the dress was...interesting. A long, flowing skirt detailed with intricate gold threading on a black velvet fabric, and a top that extended down to her wrists but left her stomach bare. Her hair was interlaced with diamonds and gemstones, braided and styled to sit perfectly on her shoulder.

She was, in short, the most stunning thing I'd ever seen.

She lifted her hands, which were connected to the skirt of her dress, and gave me a rather un-Theo-like bashful look. "What do you think?"

"I think...wow..." I couldn't come up with anything smarter to say. She giggled and turned slowly for me, so I could take in the sight of her. "I've never seen a dress like that in my entire life."

"It's Raven," she said, a little breathlessly. I loved the way her eyes lit up when she saw herself, how her shoulders fell backward and her chin drew higher. "A traditional Raven wedding dress. Emilie got it for me."

"E-*Emilie*? Why would she do that?"

Theo turned to the mirror. "Because she knows the power of an image. And if I'm going to be married against my will, I'm going to wear what I damned well want to the engagement party."

"Theo..."

"I'm tired of the surprise revelations, of your father using us for his own gain. I want to fight back."

"We have been fighting back—"

"No, we haven't. We've been dancing around the realities of the situation, but neither you nor I have really done *anything* in clear disobedience to your father. That ends today."

I didn't like the finality in her tone. "Theo, you're scaring me."

"What are you willing to give up?" she asked quietly. "To stop this treaty."

"Not you."

She turned in my arms, her gaze serious. "What if you had to? What if, in order to bring peace to our two nations, I had to die?"

"I don't know why we're discussing this," I said, running a hand through my hair. "You're not going to die, and neither am I."

"We could. We might. I'm willing to."

"I'm not willing to let you," I said.

She sighed and walked away from me. "Galian."

"No, Theo," I snapped. "That's not fair."

"We're way past fair," Theo said with a snort. "And life's not fair."

"I've waited a year to be with you, Theo. I'm not going to give that all up—"

She spun, and the diamonds in her hair sparkled in the light. "And how do you think Johar's family feels right now? How did Martin's family feel at his funeral?"

I had no response.

"Look," she said after a moment of silence, "we wouldn't have made it this far—"

"Just to be separated."

"I believe that in my heart, *amichai*. But your father is willing to bomb a city he now claims as his just to keep them in line. What's to say he wouldn't turn around and have us killed as well? Or disappeared to Rave like all the ministers who've opposed him? We have a choice: we can either lie down and let him kill us, or we can fight to the death. I'm choosing to fight."

She was right, of course. She was always right, my beautiful, brilliant wife. My father would never allow us to truly be together, and once the media stopped caring about us, it would only be a matter of time.

I took her hands in mine and kissed her palms. "I love you. And I'm with you, to the end."

I just prayed it didn't have to go that far.

THEO

The dress was ridiculous and impractical, but I wore it like battle armor as Galian and I strode down the corridor toward the main hall. His words hung in my ear, and I supposed I should've known he'd say them. As much as it heartened me to know that he'd lay down his life for me, I hoped I'd never have to ask him to.

"Well?" Galian said, as we arrived at the top of the staircase. "Are you ready to make a scene?"

"Let's do it," I said with a smile.

A hundred faces turned up to us, and surprise rippled across all of them. Galian smiled at me, and kissed my cheek before we made our way down the staircase. For once, I needed to say nothing to be heard. And I knew every single person in the room understood what I was trying to say.

We were halfway down the stairs when the music began again, and slowly, the conversations picked back up. Grieg was turned away from us, but I heard the boom of his voice over the conversation. He'd seen what I'd done, and he wasn't happy about it.

Good.

We reached the bottom of the staircase and Galian swiped a glass of champagne for the both of us. "Bottoms up, *amichai*. We'll need it tonight."

"My, my, that was quite an entrance."

Galian spun, raising his eyebrows. "Olivia..."

I followed his gaze and recognized the Kylaen woman who stood before us from photos. She seemed a bit more imposing in person, but the smile on her face was kind.

"What are you doing here?" Galian gasped, leaving my grasp to embrace her. "I thought you were in Jervan?"

"I was," she said with a glance at me. "Is this...your wife?"

Feeling brave, I strode forward and held out my hand. "It's nice to finally meet you."

"Same." She surveyed me for a moment, her gaze drawing to my bare navel and the jewels adorning my hair. "That's quite an outfit."

"Traditional Raven wedding dress," Galian said, standing next to me. "We're hoping to make a statement."

Olivia nodded. "Smart. Although I'm not sure how much will

get out past Kylae. The Jervanian media has been fairly quiet on the annexation. They're not interested in helping the Ravens. They've tangled with your father before, and they aren't willing to poke the bear, so to speak, anymore."

"And the Herinese?" he asked, his face growing concerned.

"Same," Olivia said, glancing around for eavesdroppers. "Although Prime Minister Bouckley is less worried about Kylae and more furious with Bayard. After all, it was their technology that went into the ocean."

"I know," I said darkly. "I was on it."

Olivia gave me a curious look, but Galian asked, "So there's no chance they'll try to intervene?"

"None. I'm sorry, Galian." She spotted another friend across the room and smiled at him. "I'm sorry, that's one of our investors. I have to talk with him, as he's thinking about pulling his money out of the company since we relocated."

"No, no," Galian said, resting his hand on the small of my back. "Go on. Thank you for your help."

"I'm sorry I couldn't do more," she said, before leaning in to speak quietly. "Say the word, and you two can join me on the plane back to Jervan."

With that, she spun on her designer heel and hurried toward her investor.

"She's different than I thought," I said, turning to Galian, but he was watching his former flame with more than a little interest.

"We could leave with Olivia."

"L-leave?" I blinked at him. "What happened to, 'I'm with you until the end?'"

"Theo, you heard her," he said. "No news is getting out of this country. I'll die for you, but right now, the only thing that would accomplish is making my mother cry."

I pushed him away angrily. "You can't be serious. Galian, if we die, that'll...that'll—"

"You can't possibly be arguing over whether or not we're going to martyr ourselves," he said with a snort. "Theo, you've got to see reason."

"I see a coward, that's what I see." His eyes widened, and I immediately regretted my words. "Galian, I didn't mean it—"

But a loud clanging interrupted our argument. Grieg stood up in front of his throne, a glass of champagne raised. I thought it was a bad omen that he was toasting when the objects of his toast were on the other side of the room.

The crowd's murmuring quieted down and Galian muttered beside me, "Where have I seen this before?"

The crowd applauded politely, but I was happy, at least, that they seemed unenthusiastic about it. Perhaps my dress had caused more conversation than I'd thought.

But Grieg was undeterred. "By accepting our Raven family back into the fold, we are entering a new chapter in Kylaen history. A brilliant chapter of newfound Kylaen resurgence in our economy, our people, and our strength as a nation."

I snorted. "Rave's not bringing any of that to the table, thanks to fifty years of bombs."

"Six months ago, the Herinese and Jervanians declared war on us," Grieg announced. "They built a weapon that could've decimated our entire country. And now, thanks to our brothers and sisters in Rave, we will finally answer their declaration."

I heard a glass shatter somewhere in the room, but other than that, there was silence. Ministers, business owners, executives...they stared at Grieg as if he were speaking a different language. And I hoped he was, because what he was saying was...

"For the past few weeks, we've been amassing planes and weapons in our bases on our new island province. I've invested heavily in rebuilding the infrastructure to support this new battlefront. Those who were once our enemy will join us in battle against those who would destroy us—"

"It was Bayard's idea!" I said, my voice echoing through the room.

Grieg's attention shifted to me, and the disdain on his face was clear. "It appears the bride has had too much to drink."

"I haven't had a drop, and you're a filthy liar." Blood pumped in my ears. "Bayard was the one who built that plane, out of desperation because *you* wouldn't stop bombing us."

"I think the bride might need to go back to her—"

"Don't touch my wife," Galian snarled next to me, grabbing my hand. "Everyone in this room knows the truth. Bayard tried to escalate the war, and we stopped it before it happened. So if you want to blame someone for making things worse, blame him. Or even better, blame yourself for not being a better king and ending this senseless war sooner."

Grieg stared at us, and then chuckled as whispered murmurings echoed through the room. "They are perfect for each other, you see! Two children who love their drink. Korina, why don't you get them to bed before the big day tomorrow?"

I saw movement out of the corner of my eye, but it wasn't Korina, or even Kader. It was Grieg's guards, and they were pushing their way through the crowd to get to us.

The warnings about a funeral instead of a wedding rang in my ear. "*Amichai*," I whispered, holding tight to his arm. "They can't separate us—"

"I'm not sure we have much of a choice," came his dry response. Could he *ever* be serious?

Grieg's men surrounded us, pushing aside the crowd of people. One guard took me and another latched on to Galian as they yanked us apart, and it felt like ripping off an arm. I tried to turn back, but the hold on my arms was too tight to do anything but move with them. They half-drug me toward the other side of the room, as I searched for Korina or Kader or even Rhys, but saw none of them. I silently begged the passive Kylaen faces to do something, to step up and stop their despot king, but they stared back, unwilling or unable to help.

"*Theo!*"

The end of the room was fast approaching, and I twisted as best I could in the grip of the guards to get one last look at my *amichai*. The only person I saw was the king, who raised his glass to me—the last thing I saw before the door closed behind me.

GALIAN

I watched them take my wife through a door, and I didn't care who saw how much I fought against them. It was no longer about appearances—Grieg would kill either of us without thinking twice. But the guards proved too powerful for me, and they wrestled me into a side room where they left me to worry and pace and feel the champagne churning unhappily in my stomach.

Hours passed, or what felt like hours, and my feet began to hurt. But I kept pacing, kept trying the door to see if I could break through it. But if I did, my father's guards would be on me in a second. There was no way out for me.

How could everything have gone so wrong in such a short time? My father had truly gone mad if he thought he could go to war with Herin and Jervan—or that they'd acquiesce as easily as Rave had. Granted, they didn't have our military might, or the resources to quickly put together a defense.

Okay, so maybe it wasn't such a mad idea. Especially since Kylae already had the military resources from fifty years of war against Rave.

Plus now, he had Raven soldiers—already trained and battle-ready—at his disposal.

I groaned and sank into a nearby chair. I hated how much sense this made to me, because I feared I was as crazy as he was.

Finally, when I thought I might tear my hair out from frustration, the door opened and my father swept into the room, rosy faced and cheery with the smell of brandy on his breath. That he could continue to wine and dine without a care in the world while keeping his own son prisoner was telling. But as soon as the door closed, his veneer dropped and there was disgust and disappointment in his snarl. How convenient that I felt the same way about him.

"Well, that was quite a scene you put on—"

"Fuck you!" I screamed. "What the *hell* is going on around here? Where is Theo?"

"Your fiancée—"

"Wife."

"Whatever you wish to call her, she's being taken care of. We wouldn't want her to be worried the night before her wedding."

"Because you're so concerned about her," I snapped. "And what, I'm not allowed to leave this room? The night before my wedding, and I'm a prisoner at gunpoint? Where's Mom? And Rhys—"

"You'll see them tomorrow," Grieg said with a wave of his hand. "I find it best to separate the three of you, as you tend to get into trouble together. I've also permanently assigned your guard, Kader, to the castle tomorrow. I'm sure he'll be receiving his retirement papers. Least I could do for all his years of service."

I wanted to punch him in the face.

"I came here to inform you myself that the wedding will go on tomorrow, as planned. You, and your mother, and brother, will hear the same thing from me: step one toe out of line, and I'll have your Raven girl killed."

My heart skipped a beat, but I couldn't believe him. "In front of all those people? In front of the international media?"

"That Anson fellow has been a good scapegoat until now. After all, with his operations decimated, it would make sense for him to become a bit...desperate. Desperate men do desperate things, like killing a woman on her wedding day."

My head swam and, again, I hated how much sense he was making.

"After all, the sight of you crying over the corpse of your fiancée—"

"*Wife.*"

"I doubt anyone would find it in their hearts to support such a merciless faction," Grieg finished.

I desperately wished for something smart to say, some brilliant repartee that would put him back in his place. But there was nothing I could say. Not when I couldn't get the image of my wife's dead body out of my mind.

TWENTY-SIX

THEO

The sun dawned on the day of my wedding, and it was all I could do not to throw up. Several armed guards had escorted me from the engagement party, careful enough not to bruise, but forceful enough to know they meant business, and put me in a car. The drive was short, and the destination horrifying—a large Kylaen church on the northern end of the city.

They'd put me in a room, alone, and locked the door. The one window was too small for me to squeeze through, and even if I could, it was covered in thick bars.

I was trapped.

I worried about my *amichai*, and what his father might do to him. I worried about Kader, and prayed he wouldn't fall to the desperation that had plagued me and do something stupid. I worried for my country. I worried for Jervan and Herin, who would be waking up to the news that they were under attack.

I worried for the Raven soldiers who'd die fighting another war they didn't want anything to do with.

But I wasn't scared for my own death. That, I was sure, was an inevitability at this point. My only question was—by whose hand would it happen?

The sun had moved higher in the sky when I finally heard voices. The door unlocked, and Emilie walked in, followed by her trusty hairstylist and Filippa, who carried a large bag. Filippa didn't stay long, although she seemed more haughty than usual.

"Emilie..." I was glad to see her, and surprised by just how glad I was.

"Sit," she said. "We have work to do."

I did as instructed and let the hairstylist curl and pin my hair, and apply makeup to my face while Emilie unzipped the dress from the bag. It was the first time I'd seen it; layers of white that cinched at the waist. Long sleeves that extended to my wrists. Very little skin would be shown; presumably, Grieg's doing.

"You looked gorgeous last night, by the way," Emilie said with a small wink. "Aline would've been proud."

"But to what end?" I said, stepping into the dress. "We failed."

Emilie said nothing as she zipped up the dress, but the zipper stuck. "Suck in, Theo. I know the Kylaens haven't been feeding you *that* well."

I did, and the dress zipped, but it seemed tight in the bust too. Emilie cocked her head at me then raised an eyebrow. "Are you pregnant?"

I barked a laugh. "There is no way I'm..."

But realization washed over me. I very well could've been. With all the stress of the wedding, Emilie watching us, the plane crash, the media pressure, I'd completely forgotten about contraception. And

Galian and I had been taking full advantage of our time together.

"Oh my God." I swooned, and Emilie steadied me. "I can't be. Not now. Not with all this going on." I shook my head. "I want to talk to my husband. I need to talk to Galian."

"Theo, right now, you know that's not an option," Emilie said. "The only way you're getting out of this room is when it's time to go."

I shook my head. I couldn't go through with this wedding, not knowing that Galian and I might've created something so precious. The danger we found ourselves in on a daily basis was far more terrifying knowing our child was involved. They would take it from us, I knew they would. Or kill me before word got out. Grieg would never allow a half-Raven child in his bloodline.

I suddenly couldn't breathe.

"P-please," I whispered. "I have to talk to him."

Emilie hesitated then helped me sit down on the chair. "Stay here. I'll see...see what I can do."

She disappeared through the door, and I pushed myself up to stand. I was so tired, but my fears kept me wide awake. I'd accepted my death as an inevitability, but now...

The dress constricted my movements, but I managed to pace a bit, pulling the tight material on my arms as far as it would go. The skirt swished as I moved, and I'd likely trip on it during my slow walk. But those were small distractions from larger fears.

The door jiggled and my heart stopped.

Was it time?

But it was Korina, not Emilie, who came into the room. She opened her mouth to speak, but I was quicker. "I think I'm pregnant and Grieg's going to kill me."

Korina stopped midstride, shock on her face. Then, she crossed the room and pulled me into an embrace. "Oh, Theo."

"I don't know what to do," I said, wrapping my arms around her. "I'm so scared."

"Ssh, it's all right, my love."

It was yet another distraction from the looming terror, but I let Korina hold me the way I'd never been held before. Like a child by her mother.

"Take a deep breath. There's a good girl," Korina said gently.

"What do I do?"

"We will get through this day," Korina whispered, holding my cheeks in her hands. "You and I will have a long conversation tonight about what this means, and how you would like this to be handled. After, of course, we celebrate." She actually smiled and chuckled. "My first grandchild. I'm so pleased."

Her joy was a little infectious, releasing some of the tension in my head. "Galian's going to be so happy."

"He's going to be a *wonderful* father," she said. "So very unlike his own. And you, my love, will make an amazing mother."

"Thank you, *'kaachai—*"

My heart stopped in my chest as I realized what I'd just said. It had just come out, the same way it had come out when I had first called Galian *amichai*. Those rare moments when all the words in the common tongue weren't enough to describe an emotion or a feeling, and all I had was the ancient Raven language.

"I'm sorry," I said, my face flaming in embarrassment.

"Why are you apologizing, my love?" Her eyes grew wetter. "Don't tell my boys, but I've always wanted a daughter. And to have someone as strong and passionate as you think of me as your mother..." She cleared her throat. "I'm honored."

"Korina, what about Grieg?" I said. "He's going to...he's going to kill me..."

"I won't let him," she said fiercely. "Nothing is going to happen to you today, Theo. You have my word."

She embraced me again, and I struggled to keep my emotions from ruining my makeup, especially as Emilie told us it was time. Everything screamed in me to dig my heels in, to refuse to go. To handcuff myself to the room and cause a scene. But knowing there was a chance—even a small one—that I could be responsible for more than myself moved my feet.

Korina held tight to me as we walked out of the room toward the main church. Everything was unfamiliar—we'd not even had a chance to rehearse. I was expected to stand there quietly and accept my fate. Perhaps Grieg had anticipated I'd be malleable. Perhaps he didn't care.

"Ah, there's the bride!" Bayard stood at the back doors, wearing a nice suit with a red tie. Red, the color of Kylae, not gold or black, like Rave. Everything about him made me sick.

"Don't talk to me," I said, standing beside him.

He chuckled and took my arm in his, much as a father would. "Smile, Theophilia. It's your wedding day."

I forced a smile onto my face as the doors opened and the congregation stood. "Fuck off."

GALIAN

Filippa stood at the entrance to the church, watching her clipboard and glancing at the time. "Where is your brother?" she muttered to no one.

If I had to guess, he'd been locked in a room much as I had. I'd spent the night pacing and hoping Theo was all right, worrying about the wedding, about the war. About what my father might do. All of my bravery had gone out the window when he'd threatened Theo. I didn't care if I had to kiss his boots in public; if it meant Theo could walk away from this wedding unharmed, I'd do it.

Finally, my brother arrived, flanked by two of my father's guards. He wore a sour expression, but nodded to me with relief in his eyes. I was sure he'd been told the same thing by my father, and I offered him a silent promise that I'd be a good boy.

"Do you know your directions?" Filippa said, with uncharacteristic authority. "Follow Father Mark out, and bow to your father as he gives you a blessing."

I nodded, as did Rhys, and he clapped me on the shoulder as we queued up behind the old priest. Filippa motioned for us to walk, and we did, entering into the cavernous space already filled with people. I scanned the room for anyone out of place, an assassin gunning for my wife. I spotted Olivia, sitting somewhere in the back of the church, and wished I'd thrown Theo over my shoulder and taken her to Jervan when she'd offered it. Kader and Rosie sat three rows away from me, both their faces grim and accepting. I caught Kader's eye and wished he could read minds.

"Kneel," Rhys muttered beside me, and I realized we'd reached my father. Against every instinct, I fell to my knee in front of my father, staring at the reflection in his black shoes and reminding myself of his threat. He was a man who had won everything. He'd played us all, keeping us in the dark while he set out to conquer the world. And for what purpose, I still had no idea. Even if he managed to take over Herin and Jervan, all the money in the world wouldn't sate him.

I looked at my mother, begging her for answers. But her gaze was on the back of the room, her expression tough and unrelenting.

"My son," Grieg began, his voice echoing through the room. "You have my blessings on this most joyous day."

I'll bet I do, you son of a bitch.

With Rhys' guidance, I stood, but refused to meet my father's gaze. Instead, I turned back to the room, looking at every face and trying to remember if I knew them or not. What I wouldn't give for Rhys' photo flash cards again...

The back doors opened and despite those in the room with their eyes on me, I sighed in relief at seeing her in one piece. She was beautiful, though she looked nothing like herself. Her brown eyes were lined, her lips a blood red. Even her skin seemed a shade lighter—no doubt Emilie's doing. Two large diamond earrings lay against her ears, and her black hair was swept up and pinned by her veil. The corset was lined with diamonds and gold, cinching at her waist then spilling out in a voluminous skirt so big Bayard could barely stand beside her. From the look on Theo's face, I could tell she'd much rather he was a continent away.

They moved slowly down the aisle, Bayard beaming as if she were his own daughter, and Theo's face pressed firmly into annoyance.

Had I been a bystander, I would've guessed she'd had no choice but to get married to me.

And of course, every fiber of my being wanted to scream at her to run away. Or to say nothing. Anything to protect her from my father.

Theo's walk was slow and measured, as if she'd practiced this a thousand times already. But as she drew closer, there was something else on her face—fear. She was afraid. My stoic, brave pilot was gone and in her place was a woman who knew her days were numbered—and was trying desperately to extend them.

She and Bayard met me at the bottom of the stairs, and I took her other arm in mine, grateful to have her close again. Theo's gaze went to Bayard, and she opened her mouth a few times, as if she wanted to tell me something, but not in front of Bayard.

"*Welcome,*" Grieg said, standing before us. "Welcome to this blessed occasion. This celebration of love, this blessed union of two souls—and two countries."

Theo's arm tensed against mine. "Galian, I think I'm—"

The crowd gasped behind us then a voice rang out, clear as day.

"*Once for Rave!*"

Bam.

My father slumped on his seat in front of me, his eyes unseeing, a trickle of blood appearing in the center of his forehead.

I spun around to see the man in the center of the aisle, his smoking gun pointed at us.

"*Twice for traitors!*"

Bam.

Bayard went down.

I had only a split second to act.

Bam.

THEO

I fell backward, landing with a grunt on the step we'd been standing on. Someone was screaming. No, hundreds of people were screaming. The back of my head hurt from where I'd fallen, pushed backward by Galian, who lay on top of me. I turned my head to the left, and my breath caught in my throat.

Grieg was dead. Slumped over on his throne with crimson trickling from a single bullet wound in his head. Nothing left of the despot but an empty shell. It seemed silly to be afraid of him now, when something so simple had felled him.

To my right, Bayard. His body had twisted in an odd way when he'd fallen. He, too, lay oddly still, his eyes open and unseeing back at me, his mouth skewed in permanent shock.

But there had been a third bullet, and although the stair pressed uncomfortably into my back, I felt no pain. Not like that, anyway. But liquid seeped down my arms, into my dress. It was warm, it was...

"N...no..."

Galian hadn't moved. Hands shaking, I pushed myself up, and he slid off me onto my lap. With a heave, I turned him over, and my whole world slowed.

He stared at the ceiling, unblinking, as he took rasping breaths. A trickle of blood dripped from the corner of his mouth, and I wiped it away with my thumb.

His gaze slid to me slowly, and a weak smile crossed his face. "Hey, beautiful."

I gasped, too shocked to form words, but terrified that if I didn't, I would regret it forever. "H-hey..." I closed my eyes and a tear fell down my face.

He pressed his thumb against my cheek to wipe it away. "None of that," he said. "You've gotta..."

"I can't," I whispered. "Not without you. Why did you do this?"

"Because," he coughed, and more blood bubbled from his lips, "I promised you I wasn't going to let you die."

He'd said that, long ago on our island. The very first day we'd met, and a few times after. But I'd always thought it an empty promise.

"N-no." This wasn't fair. This wasn't how it was supposed to happen. I needed more time, I needed to tell him. "G-Galian, *amichai*, I think...I think I'm pregnant. You can't..."

The words died on my tongue as his hand fell away from my face.

He was gone.

The world sped up, and I heard conversations, yelling, screaming, arguing. But none of it mattered. Not when half my soul was gone.

Someone was pulling me away from my husband, but I just gripped that ridiculous military outfit harder. He didn't deserve to wear it to his death—he wasn't a soldier; he was a doctor. The best doctor there was. He'd put my needs ahead of his own, he'd...

"Theo, you have to let him go."

"N-no," I snarled, furiously shaking my head. I needed this to be a dream. This had to be a dream. He wasn't gone. He couldn't be *gone...*

We were supposed to have years of breakfasts and strategy. Of arguing over little things then making up a few minutes later. Of children... Oh my God, we were going to have a child together and he'd never know. He'd never get the chance to be the wonderful father Korina thought he'd be.

"Theo, let him go." A new voice, harsher, more direct. These hands were stronger as they pried my hands open. I lunged toward the body, but something kept me away from him. Something was always keeping us apart. Our egos, our prejudices, our countries, my duty to the mission. Now, death.

"*No!*"

This couldn't be real. This couldn't be happening. It wasn't supposed to happen like this. It couldn't be happening like this.

We were supposed to win. We were supposed to figure out a way to be together, to stop the war, to end this treaty. It wasn't supposed to end like this.

Wasn't that what I'd always believed? We wouldn't have gotten this far, just to be ripped apart.

So why was I holding the lifeless body of my husband?

I'd gotten a month with him. One month of pure bliss. That *wasn't* enough. Not for all we'd sacrificed.

Bayard's unseeing gaze stared back at me, and all I could think of in that moment was revenge.

"Who did this?" I whispered.

"Theo, we need to get you out of here." Kader was pulling me to stand. "It's not safe, there could be others—"

"I don't want to leave, I want to know who did this," I said, oddly calm. "Was it Bayard? Was it Grieg?"

"Anson."

I'd known it, but needed to hear him say it. He'd wanted me dead. "And where is he now?"

"Theo, we need to get you out—"

"Don't you *dare*," I snarled, finally pushing away and seeing him clearly. The front of his shirt was covered in blood, and although his face was pale, I knew none of it was his. The sight of it just made me angrier. "I want to see him."

"Theo, it's not safe—"

I laughed, a hoarse, barking sound that didn't even sound human. "What more could they do to me? They've killed Galian. There's nothing else...there's nothing more they can take from me that wouldn't be a blessing."

But I saw him, tied up and sitting on the floor of the pew, an unabashedly smug look on his face. He thought he'd won, and he might have. There was nothing to be gained by talking with him, but I needed to. I needed to understand *why*.

I pushed my way over to the center of the circle, none of the soldiers having the heart to keep me out.

"I need to know," I said. "I need to know why you did this."

He raised his gaze to mine, and I wanted to scream that he didn't have the right to even be in the same room, let alone look at me in the face. "You betrayed the country."

"How?"

"You allied yourself with the Kylaens."

There was something so simplistic about what he said, and so wrong.

Before even I knew what I was doing, I grabbed the nearest gun I could get my hands on and pointed it at him. "I should kill you right now," I snarled. "You son of a bitch, you took him from me."

Anson lifted his head, as if he expected me to shoot him. And I could do it. As Rhys had said, I'd killed hundreds with the guns on my plane. I wasn't without blood on my hands, and I could dirty them a little more. It would be so deliciously justified. Every inch of me wanted to blow Anson's brains out, or throw away the gun and choke the life out of him, watching his life slip away the same way I'd watched Galian's.

But I lowered the gun.

"All of this...because I'd had the gall to compromise," I said. "Because I sought help from those who would help us in return."

"They would *never* help—"

"Galian did," I whispered. "He saved my life. He's...he was," I swallowed the torrent of tears, "a *good* man. He wanted Rave to thrive and flourish. He *helped* people."

"He's one of *them*."

"*He was a human being!*" I screamed. "He was human, he bled, he cried, he laughed...he loved... He loved *me*, even though everything in this world told us we couldn't be together. He saved my life after I'd tried to take his, simply because I was a fellow human. He risked his neck and closed the prison at Mael. He was Kylaen, but he was good." I let out a sob. "And you killed him. For what? Because he and I looked past the history of his country so that mine could have a brighter future? Because I had the horrible misfortune to fall in love with the enemy, and with him, tried to stop the war through words and reason, instead of violence?"

"Violence is sometimes the only way to make change."

"But when does it stop, Anson? You killed Galian, I kill you, your loved ones come for me, we take revenge. An act of war requires a response, and around and around we go. What if we just stopped? What if we said...*enough*?"

"You'd forgive Kylae for fifty years of bloodshed?"

"For the sake of my country, for the sake of our future...yes, in a heartbeat. Because I love my country more than I love my own ego. Because sometimes it's better to make space in your heart for forgiveness in order to survive together than to wither and die alone." I stared at Grieg on the throne, his eyes still unseeing, unfocused. "In the end, there's nothing we take with us. No matter how much revenge we seek, or how much power we grab, all that's left is a lifeless..."

All that was left of my *amichai*.

"So maybe I am stupid for wanting peace with words instead of bullets. Maybe my ideas of good men came from a naïve princeling who did nothing except help people and love a *kallistrate*. Or maybe I'm just a stronger person than you are—maybe Galian is stronger than..."

Galian was no longer an "is." He was gone.

Grief washed over me in a tidal wave. I felt myself falling backward, consumed by my sadness and the gaping hole of anguish growing in my chest. But where I'd expected to fall on hard ground, I was caught. Disembodied arms encircled me, lifting me against a solid chest. And as those arms carried me out of the church, I left behind a piece of my shattered heart, right where my *amichai* had fallen.

EPILOGUE

THEO

Peace is never easy.

There were ceasefire agreements, territory negotiations, commerce clauses, humanitarian support to Rave, transfer of prisoners from both sides. But for the first time, both Rave and Kylae were willing to negotiate on an even footing. My impassioned speech had been broadcast live across the four nations, and the sight of a bride covered in her husband's blood talking about forgiveness had been enough to turn the tide of public opinion.

Helped, I'm sure, by Emilie Mondra's unique brand of media relations.

And for the first time, there were leaders on both sides willing to compromise. King Rhys was coronated within days of his father's death and was quick to sign an emergency ceasefire treaty with Rave, Herin, and Jervan, though the latter two required some not-so-insignificant groveling on his part. In Rave, Mark Cannon was appointed interim president until elections could be held. It took three years before my country was able to go to the polls, years fraught with starts and stops and protest and riots. But eventually, Rave held its first internationally monitored election, where the Raven people chose a *kallistrate* to lead them.

Not me. Wilona Kallistrate, one of Anson's deputies who'd been instrumental in rebuilding trust between the Raven people and its government during Cannon's term. At my strong urging, Anson had been sentenced to life in prison by a joint Kylaen and Raven jury, but the senior members of his operation had quickly distanced themselves from him, offering their loyalties to the new Raven president. Mark had welcomed them into his cabinet, even throwing his weight behind Kallistrate during her election bid and becoming an advisor as the country figured out how to survive without the constant threat of war.

Helping matters had been heavy investment from Jervan, Herin, and, of course, Kylae. Industry was nonexistent in Rave, but there was a need to rebuild cities, so King Rhys had offered incentives for two of the three largest building companies to move operations to Rave. The third company had filed for bankruptcy, as four of the top executives were convicted for the murder of David Martin. The major Raven cities were finally beginning to see some resurgence with improved utilities and buildings. Rumor had it that the country would receive television broadcasts within the next year, but I was skeptical. Income disparity was still at an all-time high, one of the main issues I was working to address.

Both Presidents Cannon and Kallistrate had asked me to serve as an ambassador from Rave, acting as their spokesperson and liaison to Kylae. I oversaw negotiations, making sure that both Rave and Kylae got a fair shake. In the spirit of true impartiality, I'd asked the Kylaens to build a large compound on our island, where I regularly welcomed visitors of all nationalities. It had been here, three years ago, that we'd finally signed the official peace treaty between Kylae and Rave. The photo of Rhys and me standing next to the memorial to the lives lost in the barethium lab was one of my favorites in my office, right next to Lanis' medals of heroism, which he'd given me upon his official retirement from the Raven military.

The compound was private and serene, but it carried with it the memories of what Galian and I had accomplished on the island. I, of course, had my own reminder of what we'd started here.

"*Galian*!" I bellowed to the small child currently hanging by his knees from a tree branch.

A high-pitched giggle was all that came down, instead of my son. Five years old and his father incarnate, Korina assured me with a sparkle in her eyes. I'd confirmed my pregnancy soon after the wedding, and it had been every bit the light in the darkness that followed. I'd fought to keep my progress private, but both countries were eager for the joy that a new life brought, especially one born out of such tragedy. Emilie, who'd taken a job as my media relations coordinator, had respected my wishes and kept the photographers away from my son. Over the years, she'd become one of my closest friends— even though we still disagreed on many things.

I plucked the squirming child out of the tree and set him right. He had his father's eyes and smile, along with his uncanny ability to test my patience. "Please don't hang like that, *'suuchai*. You'll hurt yourself."

"Sorry, *'kaachai*," he said, although there was little sincerity in it, for as soon as I'd released him, he barreled away from me, intent on bruising every piece of his body, as little boys did. Dr. Maitland had assured me my son had a hard head, but it didn't make it less painful to see him teary-eyed.

This time, his hard head ran straight into his father.

Galian looked down at his son, confused. "Hi to you, too."

"Hi, *'saichai*," Little Galian said, and that was all the acknowledgement my *amichai* received before his son darted back inside the house.

"Please do something about your son," I said, folding my arms over my chest and glaring at my husband, who looked too innocent for his own good. "He's giving me gray hairs. You can't let him climb over whatever he wants. He's already had a concussion!"

"He's fine, he's fine. Let him be a kid," Galian said. "Olivia's pregnant anyway, so he'll be like...fifth in line or something like that."

I pursed my lips at him. "My concern for our son has nothing to do with whether or not *your* country has a king."

I had to give Olivia credit. Rhys had asked her four times to marry him, and she'd declined until he'd made what she considered a "proper effort." She and I were still learning each other, but I did admire her gumption. There was no small bit of relief, however, when she'd shared with us that she was pregnant. I hoped, for my son's sake, that there were a hundred children between him and the throne. I'd never been able to shake my old disdain for the Kylaen royal family, even though I was now a part of it.

Galian stalked toward me, a sly look on his face. "In any case, we have pressing things to discuss—"

"No, we don't. My offer is final."

My husband smiled devilishly and closed the distance between us. "We both know your offer isn't final."

"I'm not giving you five percent," I said. "Kylae doesn't need that trade agreement with Jervan. You've plenty of money and plenty of wheat. Eat your own."

Galian scowled at me. "There is no way Rhys is going to go for a one percent share of Jervan's wheat supply."

"You have your own fields. Rave doesn't have the soil for it."

He reached for his shirt, and I was already half to rolling my eyes. "But *amichai*..." He pointed to the gruesome scar still visible on his left chest. "I lost a lung for you."

I'd truly thought my *amichai* had died, but thanks to Dr. Maitland's quick actions, and no shortage of prayer on my part, he'd pulled through. After Little Galian arrived, and Cannon had asked me to step in as ambassador, Rhys had convinced his brother to sit on the opposite side of the table from me—although most days, I thought Rhys should probably consider appointing a better negotiator. Sad eyes and whining about an injury only went so far with me.

"You lost a third of one, and that stopped counting after I gave birth to your son."

"But my scar..." he tried again, before releasing his shirt and frowning. "Fine. Two percent. But that's as far as Rhys will budge, I promise you."

I considered his offer. I would've accepted three, but I wasn't going to tell him that. Instead I said, "One and a half."

"Done." He grinned at me. "As long as you give me something in return."

"I already gave you one and a half percent of Jervan's wheat. What more do you want?"

"Oh, lots of things," he said, threading his arm through mine. "Duck for dinner tonight. A glass of good wine. Another kid..."

I stopped midstride. "You can't be serious."

"Why not?" he said with a frown. "Little G is almost five."

But that wasn't the reason for my disbelief. Rather, it was that I'd found out a few days ago, the last time I'd been in Kylae. I'd been feeling a bit off and stopped in to see Maitland, who confirmed that I was a few weeks along. I cleared my throat and wore a smile I'd hoped would be enigmatic and daring.

But damned if my *amichai* didn't already know, as he placed a hand over my stomach where the product of our love lay. "I hope it's a girl."

"Maitland told you, didn't he?"

"What? No. I just know you so well that—"

"You're such a terrible liar. But can we *please* wait a few months this time?" I asked, remembering my horror when Galian had used his first post-hospital news conference to announce proudly that I was pregnant. I hadn't even told his mother that I'd confirmed it. He claimed he'd been delirious on pain medicine, but I'd never believed him.

"Whatever you say, *amichai*. Now, how about we chat a little bit more about that wheat treaty, hm? Maybe you're feeling maternal, want to give us two percent?"

"One and a half, and a little girl. And *that* is my final offer."

THE END

As always, thank you, dear reader, for going with me on this adventure. As an indie author, I rely on my awesome folks like yourselves to help share the word about my work. Please consider leaving a review on your favorite book retailer. I am so excited to hear what you think—even if it's a short review.

ALSO BY S. USHER EVANS

DEMON SPRING TRILOGY

Three years ago, Jack Grenard's wife was brutally murdered by demons. Now, along with his partner Cam Macarro, he's trying to rebuild his life in Atlanta. But on a routine investigation, they find a demon who saves instead of kills. They must discover who she is before Demon Spring, the quadrennial breach between the human world and demon realm, when all hell—literally—breaks loose.

The Demon Spring Trilogy is the first urban fantasy from S. Usher Evans and will be released in 2018 in eBook, Paperback, and Hardcover.

The Razia Series

Lyssa Peate is living a double life as a planet discovering scientist and a space pirate bounty hunter. Unfortunately, neither life is going very well. She's the least wanted pirate in the universe and her brand new scientist intern is spying on her. Things get worse when her intern is mistaken for her hostage by the Universal Police.

The Razia Series is a four-book space opera series and is available now for eBook, Audiobook. Paperback, and Hardcover.

ALSO BY S. USHER EVANS

The Lexie Carrigan Chronicles

Lexie Carrigan thought she was weird enough until her family drops a bomb on her—she's magical. Now the girl who's never made waves is blowing up her nightstand and no one seems to want to help her. That is, until a kindle gentleman shows up with all the answers. But Lexie finds out being magical is the least weird thing about her.

Spells and Sorcery is the first book in the Lexie Carrigan Chronicles, and is available now in eBook, Paperback, Audiobook, and Hardcover.

empath

Lauren Dailey is in break-up hell, but if you ask her she's doing just great. She hears a mysterious voice promising an easy escape from her problems and finds herself in a brand new world where she has the power to feel what others are feeling. Just one problem—there's a dragon in the mountains that happens to eat Empaths. And it might be the source of the mysterious voice tempting her deeper into her own darkness.

Empath is a stand-alone fantasy that is available now in eBook, Paperback, and Hardcover.

Acknowledgements

Thank you to my beta readers—Brett, Julia, Kristin, Em L., Amanda P., Emily G., and Melissa. I really could not have done this without you. Thanks for going on this journey with me and helping me make the final book as awesome as it could possibly be.

Thank you Dani, for being wonderful as always. I am so lucky to have found someone so wonderful to help bring my books to the next level.

Thank you to my typo checkers, who are fast becoming my favorite humans in the world: Lisa, Em L., MC, and my Mom.

About the Author

S. Usher Evans was born and raised in Pensacola, Florida. After a decade of fighting bureaucratic battles as an IT consultant in Washington, DC, she suffered a massive quarter-life-crisis. She decided fighting dragons was more fun than writing policy, so she moved back to Pensacola to write books full-time. She currently resides with her two dogs, Zoe and Mr. Biscuit, and frequently can be found plotting on the beach.

Visit S. Usher Evans online at:
http://www.susherevans.com/

Twitter: www.twitter.com/susherevans
Facebook: www.facebook.com/susherevans
Instagram: www.instagram.com/susherevans